FORSAKEN BY LOVE

HIS HEART'S LONG JOURNEY, BOOK 1

JEANNE HARDT

James —
I hope you
enjoy this new
adventure !

Jeanne
Hardt

This book is dedicated to my dear friend, Ann Wood, who blessed me with the wonderful story of her grandfather, the *real* Vern Harpole. Thank you, Ann, for allowing me to tell his tale in my own unique way.

CHAPTER 1

"**B**oy."

Boy?

A light poke in the ribs opened Vern's eyes. He gasped, finding a stranger peering down at him.

The man held up a hand and stepped back. "Why are you out here?" He spoke calmly, with concern—like his mama often did.

Vern slowly sat up, pushing against a hard surface. Though disoriented from being brought out of a deep sleep, his head felt lighter than usual. The world seemed to be spinning.

He managed to look around and didn't see *anything* familiar.

His heart raced. He often had bad dreams, so maybe he was in the middle of one. Panicked, he rubbed his tired eyes, trying to clear it away. Nothing changed.

The last he remembered, he'd fallen asleep in the bed at the hotel, so how did he get into the open air and onto this wood-slatted porch?

"Where am I?" he fearfully squeaked out.

The man pointed behind him. "My bakery. Few folks are up before sunrise, so you gave me quite a start when I found you here. I came out for a smoke and there you were."

His heart beat harder. "Where's my mama?"

The man scratched the back of his partially bald head. "No one else was here, Son. Only you." His forehead creased as he leaned over and studied Vern more closely. "Are you all right?"

"No." Vern got to his feet, wavered, and grabbed one of the porch's support posts. He looked up and down the dark dirt road. Everything was eerily quiet. "Mama!" Tears filled his eyes, but he quickly wiped them away. His mama had told him he'd gotten too old to cry.

He craned his neck in the other direction. "Mama!"

"Son." The baker lightly grabbed onto his shoulder. "Come inside with me, and we'll sort this out."

Vern panted heavy breaths. "I'm not *your* son. I want my mama." Scared and unable to control himself, he sobbed.

The stranger drew him against his rounded belly and patted his back. "We'll sort this out," he said again, and with firm gentleness led him inside.

Vern stumbled across the threshold, not only blinded by tears, but his head still felt *fuzzy*.

The man kept him upright and guided him to a chair, then pulled up another one beside it and sat. "Tell me your name, boy."

"V-Vern." He sucked in gasps of air. "I gotta go find my mama."

"Dietrich?"

Vern turned in the direction of the woman's voice, but found her to be a stranger, too. Unlike the man, she wasn't properly dressed. She was wearing her nightclothes, covered by a robe that touched the floor, and her long brown hair draped over her shoulders. He guessed her to be his mama's age.

She had a kind face, but frowned as she approached. "Who is this boy?"

"He said his name's Vern. He was sleeping on the porch."

"Give him your handkerchief, sweetheart. He needs it." No doubt, she was the baker's wife. She hovered close, studying Vern all the while, just as her husband had. Also like him—even with a frown—she didn't look mad. He was pretty sure she felt sorry for him.

Her husband dug into his pocket and brought out a white handkerchief, then passed it to him. "We're Mr. and Mrs. Hinze. We've run this bakery for a long time, but I'm guessing you've never been here before. We came here a few years after the end of the war. By the looks of you, you're not old enough to know much about the war between the states. How old *are* you?"

"Eight. Nearly nine." Vern wiped his eyes with the hankie, then loudly blew his nose. "All I know about the war was my daddy died in it. That is, Mama *thinks* he did. She said he didn't come home after it ended."

The pity in Mrs. Hinze's eyes grew. "You poor boy." She knelt beside him. "Where's your mother now?"

The question stung, and he could only shrug. His chin started to quiver, so he held the hankie to his face to hide it. "I was with Mama and my sister in a hotel. Don't know how I got on your porch." He sniffled. "Am I still in Kansas?"

"Yes. Kansas City."

"Then, my mama's close. I gotta go find her." He tried to stand, but once again wavered.

Mr. Hinze grabbed hold of his arm. "The sun won't be up for several hours. You can't go off in the dark." He looked him in the eyes. "What hotel were you staying at?"

"I don't know the name, but it was by the river."

The man slowly nodded, then gestured to the chair. "You should sit. You seem out of sorts, and we can't do much of anything till daylight." He wrung his hands. "I need to speak with my wife."

Vern reluctantly sat. He wanted to run out their door and find his mama, but the man made sense. He needed more rest to clear his head, and even if he felt fine, it was too dark to hunt for *anyone*.

Mrs. Hinze smiled at him, then ran her hand over his hair the way his mama sometimes did. She followed her husband to the other side of the room, and they stood behind a long counter.

They spoke so low Vern couldn't make out their words. Every once in a while, they'd glance his way, then mumble some more to each other.

After several long minutes, Mrs. Hinze left her husband and returned to him. "You look tired. Why don't you come with me, and I can make you a bed in the back room behind the kitchen?" Again, she stroked his hair. "It would do you well to sleep. Tomorrow, we'll help find your mother."

She lifted a lantern from one of several small round tables in the room, then extended her free hand. He hesitated, but took it. Not only was he truly tired, Mrs. Hinze seemed nice and he decided to trust her.

She led him through a door and into a large kitchen. They continued into a small pantry, where shelves filled with canned goods lined the walls. No one would go hungry here.

She gathered several old flour sacks and stacked them in the corner. "This isn't much, but it's better than the porch. And you'll be warm."

"It's fine, ma'am. After all, it's only for one night." He eased onto the floor and rolled one of the sacks into a ball to make a pillow.

She cast a worried-looking half-smile, then turned in the opposite direction. "I'll get a blanket to cover you, in case you're not warm enough." As she moved farther away with the lamp, the room darkened.

He swallowed hard. "After you bring the blanket, are you going back to bed?"

"Yes."

"With your husband?"

"No. Dietrich is working the dough. A baker's day starts early."

"Oh." Vern cautiously laid down. Though this small room was better than the open air, he'd never felt so out of place and utterly *lost*. A whimper escaped him.

Mrs. Hinze completely stopped and faced him. "You're safe here, Vern. And in the morning, I'll give you one of the finest pastries you've ever tasted. My husband is the best baker in all the states."

"Thank you, ma'am." He curled up and hugged himself, then shut his eyes.

In almost no time at all, she came back and draped a soft blanket over him. "Good night, Vern."

"Good night." The words made little sense. Nothing about this night was good, but he'd been taught it was the proper thing to say.

She walked off, and a trace of light came in from the kitchen. As before, he heard her voice mingled with her husband's, then soon after, nothing except the sound of light thuds. He assumed the baker was kneading the dough. Vern had watched his mama bake bread many times, but he'd never thought much about the sound of it before. Aside from where she was, everything about her seemed clearer.

His tears returned.

He pulled the blanket tighter around himself, and holding onto thoughts of his mama, he drifted into sleep.

* * *

The most wonderful aroma woke Vern, but his aching head instantly overshadowed the pleasantness of it.

As he sat upright, truth set in. The strangeness of everything around him proved he'd not dreamed what had happened last night. Panic struck harder than ever, and he jumped to his feet. And though his head hurt, his thoughts were less muddy.

He hurried from the pantry into the kitchen, where Mr. and Mrs. Hinze were bustling about.

Mrs. Hinze smiled at him. "I see you're awake. Are you hungry?"

"Kinda, but my head hurts." He crossed his legs, sensing something more urgent. "You got an outhouse?"

Mr. Hinze wiped his flour-covered hands on a towel and gestured to a back door. "I'll show you." He removed his white apron and hung it on a peg, then pointed at one of three brick ovens. "Those loaves are about done."

"I'll watch them," his wife said. "You go on."

They acted more uneasy this morning, but since Vern didn't know much about them, he couldn't really judge their behavior. His mama had always warned him about strangers. Still, he thought the Hinzes were truly nice and wouldn't try to hurt him.

He eagerly followed the man to the outhouse.

When Vern reemerged—after doing his business—he found Mr. Hinze waiting.

"You said your head hurts?" The man peered closely at Vern's face.

"Yes, sir."

"Your eyes are quite red." He firmly folded his arms. "Did you *drink* something last night before bed?"

"Drink? You mean like *booze*?"

The man solemnly nodded.

"I'm a boy. Why would I do that?"

"You acted inebriated when I found you. Not just tired. In addition, your breath smelled of alcohol. So, tell me—and even if you did, I won't get angry—did you drink?"

Vern shut his eyes, trying to recall all he could about the previous evening. "Before Mama put me to bed, she gave me some warm cider. She gives it to me sometimes to help me sleep. That musta been what you smelled on my breath. The cider I drank last night tasted kinda strong. I thought maybe the apples had went bad, but I drank it anyways. Mama said I had to drink every drop."

Mr. Hinze dimly smiled. "Let's get some food in your belly. It'll help."

They went back inside.

"Wash your hands in the basin over there," Mrs. Hinze said, "then you can sit in this chair, Vern." She set a plate in front of the spot on a small table that was butted against the wall, then moved to an icebox in the corner of the room and pulled out a bottle of milk.

A cake of soap sat by the basin, so he grabbed it and washed up as he'd been taught.

His capable action brought out a large smile from the woman, and she gave him a towel to dry his hands.

He eased into the chair that faced the food. His stomach rumbled. Two fried eggs, a strip of bacon, and some sort of brown roll lay on his plate. The roll smelled like cinnamon, and when he poked a finger into it, he found it sticky and warm.

"That's a *schnecken*," Mrs. Hinze said as she set a glass of milk in front of him. "It's a German sweet roll."

"Schnecken?" He stared up at her. Different from last night, she'd braided her hair into a ring that spun around the top of her head, and instead of nightclothes, she wore a blue day dress, covered by a white apron. She looked pretty. "Schnecken's a funny word."

"It means snail."

He grimaced. "There's snails in there?"

"No." She let out a nice laugh. "The name comes from the shape. Dietrich's family immigrated from Germany and brought this recipe with them. He makes the schnecken to carry on his family's traditions."

Vern glanced behind him. Mr. Hinze was using a huge, long wooden paddle to remove loaves of bread from the oven. The white cap he wore covered the bald spot on his head and made him look younger.

When he met Vern's gaze, he grinned. "Try the food, Vern. You need to eat."

"Yes, sir." He decided to try the bacon and eggs first, and they sure went down easy. He was hungrier than he'd realized.

When he finally bit into the sweet roll, he swore it had come straight from heaven. Never before had anything so good passed his lips. Filled with plenty of sugar, cinnamon, butter, and nuts, he'd discovered his new favorite food. Considering Mr. Hinze's size, Vern assumed he liked schnecken, too.

"Can I take one of these to my mama and sister?"

Mrs. Hinze smiled, but it looked as if she had a hard time doing it. "Of course," she finally said. "Dietrich will take you to find her once he's done with those loaves."

"Are you coming with us?"

"No. I need to stay here and mind the bakery. We open soon, and I'll need to tend our customers."

"You must sell *lots* of these." He stuffed more schnecken into his mouth.

She smiled again. A *real* big one.

* * *

Vern sat high on the seat of the buggy, watching everything and everyone as they drove along the road to the river. Mrs. Hinze had given him a plate with two sweet rolls on it. She'd covered it with a light cloth to keep off the dust from the road. Excited to give the schnecken to his mama and sister, he held the plate securely on his lap. They'd be so surprised to get the sweet rolls, and he knew they'd love them as much as he did.

Mr. Hinze had seemed nervous about leaving the bakery. He'd gone in and out the door more than once, always claiming he'd forgotten to tell his wife something. Vern doubted the man had ever left the shop in her care, which made the help he'd offered even kinder. At least they wouldn't have to fuss over him much longer. As soon as Vern found his mama, everyone would be put back in their proper place. Especially *him*.

The city bustled with activity. His mama had told him it was one of the fastest growing cities in the state. The riverfront was the busiest place of all.

"I like them steamboats," Vern said. "Ever been on one?"

"Yes. A long time ago. There used to be a lot more on the river, but folks prefer traveling by train now."

"Someday, I wanna hop a train and go all the way to the Pacific Ocean." Vern scanned the area for the hotel. "Mama says there's money to be had out west. That's why we left North Carolina."

"There's money to be made most anywhere, Vern. You just have to be willing to work for it." Mr. Hinze kept the horse moving at a slow pace. "Do you see the hotel?"

No sooner had he finished asking, and Vern spotted it. "There!" He pointed at the three-story brick building not far ahead.

Mr. Hinze clicked to the horse and got it moving a little faster. He pulled the buggy up in front of the hotel, then took the plate from Vern and put it on the seat. He then passed over the reins. "I want you to wait here with Betsy, while I go and talk to the desk clerk. What's your mother's name, Vern?"

"Mrs. Harpole. My sister's Virginia." Vern stared at the reins laced in his fingers. "Why can't I go in with you? I can show you where our room is."

The man rubbed his jaw. "I'm trusting you with Betsy. She gets lonely if left by herself."

Vern turned and looked at the brown mare. She tossed her head as if knowing they were talking about her. "All right. Mama let me drive our wagon a time or two. I can take care of Betsy."

Mr. Hinze stepped to the ground. "Just keep her *here*." He shook a finger. "Don't go off driving around town."

Vern sat tall. "I won't leave this spot till you come back here with my mama and she says I gotta go." He jerked his head toward the sweet rolls. "They're gonna love them rolls."

Mr. Hinze's mouth sort of twitched into a smile, but he didn't say a word. As he headed to the front door of the hotel, he glanced over his shoulder. His smile had become a frown. He acted a lot sadder than when he'd been in the bakery making bread. Maybe it bothered him to leave his wife there by herself.

Vern kept a tight grip on the reins, but Betsy acted content staying put.

As folks passed by, he politely nodded to them, proud to be sitting in such a fine buggy. It was nicer than his mama's old wagon, and he assumed Mr. Hinze made good money selling bread and such. As delicious as his sweet rolls were, Vern assumed everything in the bakery was just as tasty. If *he* had money, he'd gladly pay for schnecken every day.

"Schnecken . . ." He laughed saying the funny word—the only thing foreign about his new friends.

Mr. Hinze sounded like most every other man Vern had known and had no hint of a German accent. His family had probably lived in America long enough to have lost it.

Many minutes passed. It made no sense for him to be taking so long. Thankfully, they'd left the bakery in the cool of the morning. If he had to sit on this hot road in the heat of the summer day, he'd be miserable.

Betsy pawed the ground.

"You thirsty, girl?"

Vern was about to pop the reins and guide the horse to the drinking trough, when Mr. Hinze appeared, coming out the door of the hotel.

Alone.

The man frowned as he approached the buggy.

"Did Mama tell you to send me in?"

"No, Son." Mr. Hinze stepped up and grabbed the plate from the seat. He took his place beside him, then returned the rolls to Vern's lap and reached for the reins. But he didn't get the horse moving. The man shut his eyes, lowered his head, and let out the longest breath.

Vern's insides twisted.

Mr. Hinze swallowed hard, then faced him. "Your mother's gone, Vern, along with your sister. They checked out late last night."

"Where'd they go?"

"I don't know. By now, they could be anywhere."

Vern jumped from the buggy, sending the plate through the air. It smashed against the road and broke into pieces. "I gotta find her!"

Mr. Hinze sprung out beside him and grabbed his shoulders. "You can't. The clerk said she offered to sell him some of her belongings. She was trying to sell *everything*. Likely the covered wagon you came in as well. If she kept it, we don't know which direction she went. And if she did sell it, she could've booked passage on any one of those steamboats, or left by train. There's no way to know where to find her."

"No. Mama wouldn't leave me." Tears bubbled up, but he couldn't stop them.

Mr. Hinze didn't ease his hold. "She did, Son. Last night, when she made you drink that cider, I believe she put liquor in it to make you sleep more deeply. That's how she was able to put you on my porch without waking you up."

"No." He sniffled and shook his head. "That's a lie." He sobbed harder and pinched his eyes together so he wouldn't have to look at the man.

Mr. Hinze grabbed hold of him and lifted him from the ground, then hastened with him into the hotel.

The minute he set him on the floor, Vern raced down the hallway to number sixteen. He beat on the door.

No one opened it.

"I'll show you," a man said over his shoulder and jiggled a key into the lock. The door swung open.

The beds were neatly made, and there was no sign that Vern's mother and sister had ever been there.

"Mama!" Vern dropped to the floor and covered his face with his hands. He didn't want anyone to see him crying.

The strong arms of Mr. Hinze scooped him up. He cradled Vern close and carried him back outside. When they reached the buggy, the man held him tighter and didn't let go.

CHAPTER 2

Vern sat in the corner of the pantry with his back to the wall and his head rested against his knees. Once he and Mr. Hinze had returned to the bakery, it was the only place Vern felt he belonged—even after sleeping only one night in this spot. Mrs. Hinze had left the flour sacks on the floor, so Vern figured she meant him to be there, too. Then again, more likely, she hadn't had the chance to pick them up—too busy waiting on customers.

Several hours had passed. He'd cried so much, his head hurt worse than it had that morning, and his heart felt as if someone had crushed it—stomped on it with the heaviest boot imaginable.

Since he'd gotten back, both Mr. and Mrs. Hinze had hardly said anything to him. For a while, he heard nothing at all coming from the kitchen. Now he could hear them talking to each other. Sometimes they got really loud, but their words had lowered to a mumble. No matter the volume of their conversation, he shut it out, lost in his own troubles.

Without his mama, he had no home. He had nothing except the clothes he was wearing. If his mama had been selling everything, that meant she must've sold the wood train engine Mr. Campbell had carved for him in North Carolina. The only toy Vern owned. And maybe some other boy his age would be wearing his winter coat this year. If his mama purposefully put him on the

Hinze's porch, she could have at least left his clothes in a bag beside him.

He sniffled.

"I thought you loved me, Mama . . ." Saying it aloud brought out more tears.

"Vern?" Mrs. Hinze crept into the pantry as if she feared bothering him. She extended a glass of water. "Drink this. It might help."

Because he'd nearly cried himself dry, he took it, then stared into the cup. "Is it just water?" He'd never again let someone give him something to make him sleepy.

"Yes. Straight from the pump." There was more pity in her eyes than before, then he noticed something else.

"Have *you* been crying, Mrs. Hinze?" Her eyes were red and puffy.

She withdrew a hankie from the pocket of her apron and dabbed at them. Her handkerchief was prettier than the one Mr. Hinze had used. Hers had embroidered flowers on it. "I'm afraid so. When Dietrich told me what happened . . ." She turned her head, then took a deep breath and faced him again. "We want to talk with you. Will you come and sit with us?"

"Don't you gotta work?"

"Our busiest time has passed. Right now, you're most important." She held out a hand.

He looked away and sniffed the glass of water. Since it smelled like *nothing*, he drank down every bit, then got to his feet. He didn't take her hand, but followed her from the pantry.

Before entering the kitchen, he glanced back at his spot on the floor. Surely, he'd be given over to the authorities and would never see this place again. And though his mama wasn't dead, maybe he'd be sent to one of those awful orphanages he'd heard about. After all, any mama who'd leave her little boy with nothing, was as good as dead. He should hate her for being so cruel and couldn't understand why he didn't. His broken heart ached, but it hadn't stopped loving her.

They passed the long kitchen counters that were covered with assorted baked goods, some cooling on racks. He eyed a pan of schnecken, then remembered Mrs. Hinze's plate.

"Ma'am," he whispered. "I'm sorry I broke your plate. It was an accident."

"I know, Vern. Don't trouble yourself with that. Plates are replaceable." Again, she pressed the hankie to her eyes.

They went through the door leading into the bakery itself. Now that he had time to take it in, he decided their shop was nice enough. It had a long counter, and in front of that, shelves filled with bread, rolls, pies, and cakes. There was even a small wooden barrel holding paper-wrapped candy. He thought it was taffy— something he'd only had once, two Christmases ago. He rarely got sweets.

The whole place smelled delicious, but as miserable as he felt, it was hard to appreciate.

Mr. Hinze gave a bag to a woman at the counter. "Thank you, Mrs. Trumbull." A long loaf stuck out from one end of the paper sack.

Mrs. Trumbull looked older than Mrs. Hinze and not nearly as pretty. Even so, she had a friendly face and was wearing a nice yellow dress—fancy with a lot of lace, like the sort his mama sometimes wore.

"Thank *you*." Mrs. Trumbull's voice rumbled low like a man's. "I'll return tomorrow for another. My husband's nephew is arriving for a brief visit, and when he previously stayed with us, he had a hefty appetite." She bent down and eyed the schnecken. "I may need some of that as well."

"I'll be sure to have some hot and ready." Mr. Hinze gave her a large smile that lifted the corners of his mustache.

The woman stood fully upright, then faced Vern. "Hello, young man." Her eyes shifted to Mrs. Hinze. "I see *you* have a visitor as well."

"Yes." She pushed out her own smile, but Vern wondered if Mrs. Trumbull could tell Mrs. Hinze had been crying. "We hope he'll be with us for a long while."

Huh? Did they want him to stay?

Mrs. Trumbull put her gaze back on Vern. "You're a fortunate young man to be surrounded by all these treats."

He roughly cleared his throat. "Yes'm."

The woman headed for the door. "Thank you again, Mr. Hinze." As she went out, a little bell above the exit jingled. Vern vaguely recalled hearing it the first time he'd entered the shop. At least it let them know when they had customers.

Mr. Hinze came out from behind the counter and gestured to one of the three round tables in the shop. His smile had been replaced by a more serious expression. He exchanged glances with his wife, and they both sat.

Vern slowly took his own seat. "Mrs. Hinze, why did you say you hoped I'd be with you for a long while?"

She folded her hands on the table and stared at them. "We understand there's the possibility your mother may come back for you, however . . ." Her eyes lifted, and she looked right at Vern. "The way she left you makes us believe she has no intention to." She reached out and took his hand. "Because you were left on our porch, we feel she purposefully chose us to watch over you."

"But . . ." All of this was so confusing. "You didn't know my mama. Why would she choose you?"

"Many people in this city *do* know us. She may have learned Dietrich and I are childless—unable to have our own children."

"Yes," Mr. Hinze said, "childless and stable. Our business is steady and successful. But whether or not your mother chose us, we believe you're meant to be here." He lifted the base of his apron and wiped sweat from his brow. "There's a great deal of work to be done, and if you can prove yourself capable, we'll take you in. We can provide a place for you to sleep, and food to fill your stomach. As for education—can you read?"

"Yes, sir. My mama schooled me *some*."

"Good. That'll be helpful as you grow." He readjusted in the chair. "When I spoke to the hotel clerk this morning and asked his advice, he reminded me of a home for orphaned children on the other side of the river that might take you in. However, I don't see it as an option. That place is wretched and overcrowded. And while you were in the back room, I left briefly to speak with the town marshal. I explained the situation, and he said if we're willing to care for you, it would be best for everyone."

"Is he going to look for my mama?"

"In a city this large, and with the many ways she could have left it, he's not able to seek her out. But he made note of her name and will put a post in the newspaper asking for information. If anyone knows of her, surely, they'll report to him."

"So, she could come for me?"

Mr. and Mrs. Hinze glanced at each other again.

"It's possible," Mrs. Hinze said. "In the meanwhile, are you agreeable to helping here? Earning your keep?"

He shrugged. "I don't know nothing about baking."

"You can learn." She gave his hand a squeeze, then released it. "To begin with, you can help Dietrich by sweeping the floors and greasing the pans. He'll show you what to do." Her eyes searched his face. "Most importantly, you must always be kind to our patrons. Without customers, we'd have nothing."

"Is that back room where I'll keep sleeping at night?"

"For now," Mr. Hinze sternly said. "My wife and I live in the quarters above the bakery. It's our home. Once we're certain this arrangement will suit all of us, we may move you in there with us."

"In a real bed?"

"Yes."

Mrs. Hinze frowned and turned her head. "Dietrich," she softly said. "Can't we allow him there now? It's a shame to have him sleep on the floor."

Mr. Hinze stood. "A word, Annie?" He gestured to the other side of the room.

Annie?

Vern liked the name. It fit her.

They went off behind the counter and talked in whispers. After several minutes, Mrs. Hinze let out a long sad sigh and returned to Vern. "For now, you'll sleep in the pantry. Please understand, you're essentially a stranger."

"It's all right. I don't know you neither, so I'm better off down here by myself." He drew invisible patterns on the table. "I promise not to be a bother. I don't eat much, and I figure I could live just fine off schnecken." He stood and crossed to Mr. Hinze. "You've been nice to me. I'll do whatever you need to earn my keep." Gulping, he looked over his shoulder out the window, then back to the baker. "But, if I mess up, like I did with the plate, please don't send me out there alone."

Mr. Hinze dropped down on one knee and gripped Vern's shoulder. "Son, if this doesn't work out, we'll find someone else to take you. We will *never* leave you to fend for yourself."

Vern lowered his head. He felt more tears coming. "I'm scared, Mr. Hinze."

The man pulled him into his arms and firmly held him. "I know. I am, too. I haven't been responsible for a child before." He lightly patted Vern's back. "We'll all learn together."

The soft hand of Mrs. Hinze rested on Vern's head. When he looked up at her, she had more tears falling, just like his. Seemed they were both big babies.

The bell jingled and Mr. Hinze stood. All three of them turned toward the front door, and Mrs. Hinze quickly wiped her eyes.

A young woman with long brown ringlets and a dress fancier than Mrs. Trumbull's walked toward the counter. "Good afternoon, Mr. Hinze."

"Miss Clara. What can I get for you today?"

She pursed her lips. "Three dozen rolls. Our baker is out of sorts, and we have a dinner party booked at the restaurant at five o'clock." She peered at the items in front of her. "Please, tell me you have them."

"I have more in the kitchen, but only two dozen in total. However, I can easily bake additional rolls before that time."

Miss Clara let out a relieved breath. "Thank goodness." She opened a small satchel that hung from her wrist. "I'll pay you now and send my driver to pick up the rolls at four o'clock. Will it give you enough time?" She laid a number of coins on the countertop. "Thirty-five cents a dozen, isn't that right?"

"Yes. I'll get to baking, and we'll have your order ready when your driver arrives." He glanced at Vern and grinned.

"Yes, ma'am, we will," Vern hastily said.

She laughed. "You have a new helper?"

"That I do. He just arrived from North Carolina, and he says he's ready to work."

Miss Clara tipped her head and smiled at Vern. "I started working when I was quite young as well. My father owns the restaurant, and now that I'm nearly a full-grown woman, he relies on my help even more. He says I'm *invaluable*." She proudly lifted her chin, then went to the door. Before leaving, she gave a little wave. "Thank you, Mr. Hinze, and you, too, young man."

And as fast as she'd entered, she left.

Mr. Hinze put her money into a drawer. "I believe you impressed Miss Clara, Vern."

"How? I didn't say much."

"Perhaps not, but you did just as my wife instructed. You treated our customer politely."

Vern ground the tip of his shoe into the floor. "My mama taught me how to act right. That's why I don't understand why she did something so mean. She was always nice to everyone we met. I'd think folks would treat their own family better than anyone else." His throat tightened. "Will I ever know why she left me?"

"I don't know, Son."

Vern rubbed across his aching chest. "Will it ever stop hurtin'?"

Mrs. Hinze put an arm around him. "Probably not, but it'll get easier with time." She turned to her husband. "I'll mind the front. You go on with Vern and show him how you make rolls."

Mr. Hinze moved from behind the counter and approached his wife. Vern's eyes nearly popped from their sockets, when he kissed her cheek right there with him watching. "Thank you, Annie."

Her face became as red as her eyes. "Heavens, Dietrich. You should mind yourself in front of the child."

"It's all right," Vern said. "It's nice to know you love each other." He dimly smiled at them, then headed for the kitchen door.

If only *he* was so loved . . .

CHAPTER 3

"Vern."

A light poke in the ribs opened Vern's eyes, and the light from the lantern Mr. Hinze had lit pierced them. He pinched them shut again.

"*Vern*," the man earnestly repeated. "You need to get up."

"Already?" He pulled a pillow over his face and moaned. "I just got in bed."

Mr. Hinze laughed. "Seven hours ago. The bread won't wait." He took the pillow and tossed it aside. "C'mon, Son. We can have a smoke and a cup of coffee before we get started."

Vern yawned, then sat up and stretched. "I'll meet you on the porch."

"I thought that might entice you." He patted Vern's shoulder. "I'll be waiting."

Vern yawned even broader, nodding all the while, as the man walked from his room. After nine long years, all of this had become routine, but waking up so early never got easier.

He pushed aside his blankets and swung his legs over the side of the bed.

The older he'd gotten, the tinier his bedroom felt. It held the simple bed, a wardrobe, and a small table where the lantern was kept. The room had originally been used for storage, then became his after he'd proven his worth.

This wasn't the life he'd expected, but they'd all benefited from the arrangement. They'd grown to genuinely care for each other. Yet, Mr. and Mrs. Hinze weren't his real family. He was cheap labor for them, and they'd become the steady foundation he'd needed after his mama left. If only, after all these years, he wouldn't wake up every day wondering where she and his sister were. It would be easier to believe they were dead, but his heart said otherwise.

As always, he cast aside those dismal thoughts and quickly dressed, then grabbed the lantern and trudged to the small wash-room where Mrs. Hinze kept fresh water and a cake of soap. A round metal tub sat empty in the corner, where they took their weekly baths. Vern preferred dousing himself in the river. Not only was it bothersome to haul buckets of hot water up the stairs to fill the tub, with his long legs, the vessel was cramped and uncomfortable.

The cool water from the basin felt good on his skin and perked him right up. He studied himself in a mirror that hung above the wash basin and examined his chin. No need to shave today. Because of his work in the bakery and the risk of shed hair, Mr. Hinze insisted he not grow a beard, but that suited him. He didn't want one. And unlike the older man, he chose not to wear a mustache either. Vern kept his face completely clean-shaven, which was relatively easy at present. His facial hair grew sluggishly, and he saw it as a good thing. Whenever it did emerge, it was light in color with bits of red, just like his hair. Luckily, he had a headful of it. Over the years, Mr. Hinze had lost almost all of his.

At seventeen, Vern had passed the man in height, yet not in size. He was by no means small-framed, but he wasn't portly like the baker, and intended to keep himself that way. For the past year, he'd begun to notice the pretty girls that came into the bakery. For them to notice *him*, he needed to look his best. At least he'd gotten his fill of schnecken long ago, as well as most every other item in the bakery. He'd learned to taste his wares with a simple bite and leave it at that. If he forced himself to eat all of what he tasted, he'd need bigger clothes.

Now fully awake, he crept past the Hinze's bedroom. Mrs. Hinze would probably sleep for another hour or more, and he always tried not to wake her. He eased down the steep narrow stairs that led to the back of the kitchen, then made his way outside. Before that promised smoke, he had to make a stop at the outhouse.

Once done, he returned inside, washed his hands, and headed through the bakery to the front porch.

The scent of the baker's lit cigarette greeted him. He extended another to Vern. "It's a fine morning."

"Yes, it is." Vern set down the lantern and took the cigarette. "Thank you for rolling this for me. Someday, I want to try the machine-rolled kind." He used the flame from the lamp to light it, then took a long drag. "I wonder if they taste any different."

"One thing's for certain." Mr. Hinze sat down on the long bench butted to the wall of the bakery. "You'll need plenty of money to smoke them. That man, Bonsack, made a fortune inventing the machine, but the product is a luxury most folks can't afford."

Vern sat beside him. "Once the newness wears off, they'll probably get cheaper." He leaned against the wall. "I hope I can eventually buy whatever I want and not have to fret about money."

Mr. Hinze handed him a steaming cup of coffee. "I know you, Vern. You're thinking about going west again, aren't you? All that talk of men striking it rich in gold has you itching. Am I right?"

"Maybe it's in my blood. The thing I remember most about my mother is that she said there was money to be made out there. I suppose I *am* itching."

"But Kansas City keeps growing, and we've got a successful business here. I thought by now you'd realize what a good living you can make as a baker." Mr. Hinze blew rings of smoke into the air. "Why not take over for me someday? After all, I don't intend to do this forever."

"Baking's fine, still . . ." He shifted to face the man straight on. "I want more. I can bake anywhere, but if I go to one of those mining towns, I'm sure the men get plenty hungry digging for gold. I could probably charge more for bread there than here, and they'd gladly pay it."

"Maybe so, but it's never wise to take advantage of men, hungry or not. Give them a fair deal, and they'll respect you for it." He huffed. "Can you try to be content here at least till you're eighteen?"

"That's not too far away, since my birthday's in January."

"True. But if I can get you to stay till then, I doubt you'll want to travel in the middle of winter, and therefore, you'll remain a little longer."

Vern laughed. "Worried you won't be able to find help as *affordable* as me?"

The man ruffled his hair. "No one can replace you, Son. I selfishly don't want you to leave. It's hard for me to imagine life here without you. And Annie . . ." He frowned and shook his head. "For now, don't say anything to her about this. All right? She loves you, and I know it's going to break her heart when you go."

"I love her, too." It felt strange saying it, yet he knew Mr. Hinze understood. Vern had grown to love her like a mother. The only one he really had.

He gazed up at the dark sky, where the stars and partial moon could still be seen, then looked again at Mr. Hinze. "We can keep this between us for now. I'm just glad you understand. Something keeps pulling at my heart, and I know I can't stay here forever."

"You're becoming a man, and as such, you need to go where your heart leads. Even so, *will* you stay another year?"

Vern comfortably reclined against the wall. He took a sip of coffee, then a drag from his cigarette. He leisurely blew out the smoke. "All right. A year will give me the time I need to save up money to ride a train and get settled somewhere. I don't want to go by wagon. The journey would be miserably slow."

"Some things are best done gradually." The man chuckled. "But, as I said, I know you. Once you set your mind to something, you want to accomplish it quickly. It took me forever to teach you patience with the dough. You used to think you could just snap your fingers and it would rise."

"I know better. And heaven help me if I forget to set the sponge."

They both laughed, even though a baker's sponge was no laughing matter. If forgotten, they'd have no dough ready for the following day's baking.

Mr. Hinze sobered and shook his head. "In all seriousness, how do you plan to save for a train ticket, much less setting up a home elsewhere? You spend every penny of the allowance you're given."

"Oscar and I have come up with an idea to make money." He grinned. "We plan to try it out real soon to see if it'll work."

Mr. Hinze shook a finger. "Please tell me it's not unlawful."

"You know me better than that."

"It's not *you* who concerns me." He stood, then snuffed out his cigarette. "That friend of yours is a mischief-maker."

"Oscar's harmless." Vern also stood, though not quite ready to give up his smoke. "Yes, he likes to pull pranks, but he's never broken the law."

"And it had better stay that way, or you'll need to find a new best friend." Mr. Hinze grabbed the handle of the door. "I'm going inside. I need to get busy."

"I'll be right there."

The man gave a single nod and went in.

Vern moved to the edge of the porch and gazed down the quiet road. Soon, the sun would rise and the city would come to life. With every passing year, additional businesses had arrived, along with hundreds of people. Maybe that had something to do with his reason for wanting to leave. The more crowded Kansas City became, the more he longed for open land.

As for the gold . . .

Mrs. Hinze always said that other things were more important than money, and Vern agreed. Love and honesty were her top priorities, just as they were for him. He vowed never to hurt anyone the way his mama had hurt him.

As for money, it might not be as important as those other things, but it sure made life easier. If he had it, he could do anything he wanted. Besides, panning for gold sounded exciting. More so than panning dough.

* * *

Oscar took Vern's arm and led him to the far side of the back room at Fields' Tavern. Oscar's father owned the place, and the sometimes-questionable business was part of the reason Mr. Hinze worried when the two of them were together. Excessive drinking often led to trouble, even if Vern wasn't the one partaking.

Oscar grinned and nodded at the pool table. "You can do this, dough head. Just keep calm and stick to the plan."

"Don't call me *dough head*." He elbowed his friend and released a nervous breath.

"I'm only trying to help you relax, Harp."

"I'm fine."

The instant the words left his mouth, two men dressed in fancy suits strutted over. One puffed on a cigar. He blew a cloud of smoke into the air, then pointed at Vern. "What kind of a name is Harp?"

Vern faced him directly. "My last name's Harpole. Most all my friends call me Harp."

"Are you the one who thinks he can beat me?"

The man beside him chuckled. "He's a kid. He probably doesn't even have money to bet."

Oscar laid five dollars on the pool table, then stood taller and yanked his shoulders back.

Although Vern hadn't felt nervous going into this, seeing the money laid out put knots in his gut. If he failed his friend, it would take a long time to make it up to him.

"Fine." The man with the cigar looked around the room, found an ashtray and set the lit cigar on it. With a confident smirk, he took off his jacket and handed it to the other man. He then dug into his pants' pocket and produced a fancy leather wallet. He opened it, pulled out his own five-dollar bill, and slapped it beside Oscar's. "It's a bet."

Vern's heart raced at the blessed words. If this worked, it would be a fine start to the money he needed to go west.

Oscar eyed the money. "Who should hold the bills while you play?"

The man let out a little whistle. "Hey, sweetheart." He motioned to a blonde woman serving drinks. "We need you over here."

She crossed to a table, set down two mugs of beer in front of the men sitting there, then sauntered over. The pretty barmaid took all of them in with her eyes, and Vern stood a bit taller, drinking *her* in like water. Her dress hugged her upper body to the point of pushing some of the best part of it up and out.

He gulped and averted his eyes. Whenever he'd come here with Oscar to practice pool, he'd purposefully kept himself from looking at the female help. Women definitely had an effect on him and were too much of a distraction. Maybe that was why the man called her over. He *wanted* him befuddled.

"What do you need?" she sweetly asked. "Beer? Whiskey?" She moved closer to Vern. "Lemonade?" Grinning, she lightly tapped his arm. "I've seen you in here before, and I know you don't drink liquor."

"Don't tease him, Minnie," Oscar said. "We don't need drinks. Mr. . . . ?" He gestured at the man.

"Thompson," the man said and lifted a coin in front of Minnie's face. "There's more of these to be had if you help us." He jiggled his brows and grinned in a disgusting way.

"Mr. Thompson wants you to hold our wagers," Oscar quickly said, "while he and Harp play pool."

She glanced nervously behind her. "I can't stop working."

Mr. Thompson took the money from the tabletop. "There's no need. Tuck this somewhere safe and we'll retrieve it when we're done." He waved the bills in the air, all the while eyeing the cleft of her bosom. "And this coin is for your trouble." He had it pinched between his fingers and as he moved closer to her, Vern swore he intended to drop the coin into the front of her dress.

Her cheeks reddened. "I'll keep it safe." She nabbed the coin, then grabbed the bills and put them into the pocket of her skirt.

Mr. Thompson grumbled something and walked away from her.

"Thank you, Minnie," Oscar said. "We'll call you over when we need it."

She smiled anxiously and hurried off.

The way Mr. Thompson had acted fueled Vern's fire. He most definitely wanted to beat the pompous man. True, Minnie was showing more of herself than she probably should, but it didn't seem right for anyone to assume she was easy pickings. After all, this wasn't a house of ill repute. Those were down by the river, and Vern swore he'd never go there. He wanted a woman for something long-term, not a thirty-minute romp.

"Let's get down to business," Mr. Thompson said, grabbing a pool cue.

Oscar racked the balls, while Vern hugged onto his own cue stick.

"You nervous?" Mr. Thompson chortled.

"No, sir." Vern let out an intentional shaky breath. "I'm just putting my mind right."

"Ready to lose your money?" The man cast an even bolder smirk than before, grabbed his cigar, and took a drag. "Tell you what. I'll be generous and let you break."

Vern had hoped for that very thing. "Thank you, sir." He briefly eyed Oscar, then bent over, lined up his shot and let it fly. As he'd planned, the ball flew off the table and onto the floor.

Mr. Thompson's friend spewed a mouthful of beer. "He's the genius player you bragged about?" he said to Oscar, laughing between words.

Vern covered his face to feign embarrassment, then put his back to them to amplify his mock shame. After several moments passed, he snuck a look behind him and found Mr. Thompson chuckling along with his friend.

"Harp!" the man barked.

Appropriately frowning, Vern slowly turned toward the table.

"Watch and learn." Mr. Thompson leaned down, lined up his cue stick, and made his own break shot. "That's how it's done, boy."

It was a clean break with no fouls. The man had skill, and Vern hoped to high heaven he could beat him.

Just not yet . . .

It was important to show he had a trace amount of ability, so he capably landed the next shots. The one and two easily went down, then he purposefully missed the three.

From then on, he made certain Mr. Thompson would win the frame.

As much as he didn't like losing, it was necessary to reap the most benefits.

"It's all right, boy." Mr. Thompson smacked him on the back. "You'll grow into yourself one day." He turned and reached for his jacket. "Time to call over that sweet little gal to get my money."

"Wait," Oscar said. "You only played one frame. Can't we go best two out of three?"

"Why? Your boy doesn't measure up, and I don't care to waste my time."

Oscar dug into his pants pocket. "Double or nothing?"

Mr. Thompson roared with laughter. "You must like losing money."

"Please?" Oscar extended the five. "I know he can do better. He just got off to a bad start."

Vern waved his hands in the air. "No, Oscar. I don't want you to put your money on me again. It's not right."

Scowling, Oscar stalked over to him. "You losing that first frame wasn't right." He sounded genuinely angry and poked a finger into Vern's chest. "You told me you could win. I want my money back, and you're going to get it for me. Hear?" He gave Vern a little shove. Oscar's capable acting could put him on the stage one day.

Vern sluggishly nodded. "But Mr. Thompson said he doesn't want to play anymore." He shamefully lowered his head.

"I'll play," the man huffed. "You two boys can battle it out later." He whistled for Minnie. "Come over here sweetheart!" He grabbed Oscar's five and produced another of his own, and when Minnie came near him, he pressed both bills into her palm, then whispered something in her ear.

Her eyes widened as he spoke. She glanced at Vern, frowned, pocketed the money, and wandered off, anything but happy.

Vern leaned close to Oscar. "Don't let him near her when we're through here." He spoke low enough so no one else could hear.

"I'll take care of her," Oscar whispered back. "Now let's give him the squeeze."

"Gladly."

Vern approached the table. "Let's do a lag shot to see who breaks this time."

"This should be amusing," the man mumbled, then set up his shot. After banking off the far end and returning, the ball came within inches of the edge.

Vern wanted to best him, but if he appeared instantly skilled, it would raise suspicion. So, he faltered enough to let Mr. Thompson win the break.

Once the game got fully underway, Vern gave it his full effort. "I think I've finally got my mind in the right place," he said after taking the lead.

"We'll see how long that lasts," Mr. Thompson grumbled.

Other men wandered over and gathered around the table. Smoke from their cigars and cigarettes circled their heads, and the scent of alcohol grew stronger. But even with the added distractions, Vern kept calm.

When he won the second frame, the men cheered.

"The kid's got talent," some man said.

"Rack 'em again!" Mr. Thompson yelled to his friend. "Best two out of three!"

This time, when they lagged for the break, Vern won it.

He looked at Mr. Thompson and shrugged. "I don't know how I did it." He went on to knock in four straight shots.

When Mr. Thompson took his turn, he missed his ball, and Vern once again took over the table. He landed shot after shot, sinking the appropriate ball into a pocket. With every one that fell, the cheering around them grew.

Vern kept his focus on the balls and shut out the sounds. Even when Minnie came close, he managed to ignore her.

As he lined up the final shot, his mouth brutally dried. A lemonade would sure be good about now, but he had no time for it. He examined the table and every angle, and positioned his cue stick. As he let it slide through his fingers toward the cue ball, his heart pounded. The clack of the ball hitting its mark intensified the rapid beat.

The final ball fell perfectly into the pocket and the shouts around him were almost deafening.

It felt amazing.

Broadly grinning, Minnie drew the money from her pocket and handed it to Oscar, who passed over half of it to Vern. Ten whole dollars for a simple game of pool. Almost three week's wages—or *allowance* as Mr. Hinze called it.

To Minnie's good fortune, Mr. Thompson scowled, grabbed his jacket, and stomped from the room. Vern doubted he'd want a rematch.

After getting numerous pats on the back, Vern watched the men slowly disburse into the main part of the tavern. Now that they'd seen his capability, he knew none of them would want to challenge him. But Oscar had told him there were many other pool tables in back rooms of taverns—some even in the homes of wealthy men. They might have to travel some distance to accomplish it, but they could play this game over and over and reap the rewards.

"Here." He put one of the fives in Oscar's palm. "You fronted the money. You should get half the earnings."

Oscar pushed it away. "Not this time. And when I *do* let you pay me, I want no more than twenty percent. You do all the hard work."

"True." Vern laughed, then swiped across his forehead. He'd been sweating more than he'd realized. "That was incredible. Someday, when I'm rich and living out west, I'll buy you whatever you want. After all, your plan made this work."

"You talk as if you're going there without me." He took Vern's pool cue and put it in the rack. "If you go west, you're taking me with you."

Vern studied his face, and sure enough, his friend wasn't joking. "Fine. But it's not *if* I go, it's *when*. I promised Mr. Hinze I'd wait till I'm eighteen, then as soon as the weather warms up, I'm buying that train ticket out of here."

"*Two* train tickets." Oscar held up two fingers. "I'm *already* eighteen, but I can wait." He crossed his arms and smirked. "Besides, I don't want to go anywhere without you. Call me selfish. I like using your talent for my gain."

Minnie tapped Vern's shoulder. "Want some of that lemonade now?" Her long lashes fluttered as she spoke.

Vern gulped. "Yes, ma'am."

She walked away, then coyly looked over her shoulder.

"She likes you," Oscar said.

"Maybe so. But I want another kind of girl."

Oscar's head drew back. "What other kind is there?"

"One like Mrs. Hinze. Someone with a big heart, who'll never leave me."

Oscar looked at him as if he'd lost his mind. Vern didn't care. Minnie was probably a nice enough girl, but any woman who felt comfortable dressed that way probably wasn't the marrying type—regardless of whether or not she sold herself to men.

What troubled him more than anything were memories of his mama dressed similarly. He'd been too young then to understand. Thinking back on it now, he assumed she wore such dresses to attract male attention. And since she was a pretty woman, she likely got it. He'd been put to bed too often with doctored cider. Only God knew what she did while he slept.

No. He didn't want a woman anything like his mother. He wanted someone decent, and he wouldn't settle for anything less.

CHAPTER 4

It had taken Vern a long time to fall asleep. The excitement over winning so much money had kept his mind tumbling for hours. Unfortunately, he was suffering from the lack of rest. His eyes felt as if filled with sand, and he could barely keep them open.

He punched his fist into a ball of dough, then slapped it onto the flour-dusted wood countertop. As tired as he felt, even kneading was a greater chore than it should be.

Mr. Hinze grunted. "Are you ready to tell me what you and Oscar were doing last night? You came home later than usual."

Although Vern felt proud of his accomplishment, he feared Mr. Hinze wouldn't approve. Still, he couldn't lie to the man. "Well . . ." He put greater effort into working the dough. It helped to have his eyes on it rather than Mr. Hinze. "Remember when I told you Oscar and I had a plan to make some money?"

"Y—es . . ."

"Well . . . it worked."

"I see." Mr. Hinze crossed the room and stood in front of him. "*How*?"

Vern lifted his head. If he truly believed he'd done nothing wrong, he shouldn't act at all ashamed. "I won a game of pool."

"You gambled?" The man's brows drew together tighter than they'd ever been.

"I wouldn't exactly call it *gambling*. It was more of a skilled match." He flashed a grin, then resumed kneading.

Mr. Hinze laid a hand over his and stopped him. "I knew you'd been playing the game with Oscar at his father's tavern. However, I assumed it was only for enjoyment. Are you that good?"

Relief flooded over him. Mr. Hinze didn't seem angry. "Yes, sir, I am." He shrugged. "I don't really understand why, but it comes naturally to me. It's as if I can see the invisible lines on the table, showing me exactly what angle to shoot the ball. It just . . . I don't know . . . makes sense."

"Hmm . . ." He rubbed his jaw. "How much did you win?"

"Ten dollars."

"Ten dollars?" The man's eyes popped wide. "For how many games?"

"One match. Best two out of three frames. I beat a man named Thompson, and it sure felt good. He thought he was something special, but I put him in his place."

Mr. Hinze shook a finger. "Winning is admirable. Putting on airs isn't." He folded his arms and jutted his chin. "Did you win fairly?"

"Yes, sir." He had no intention of telling him how he and Oscar had initially set up the game.

"Then you can be proud of your accomplishment. Regardless, never gloat. Humility will gain you more respect." He eyed the oven, then returned his gaze to Vern. "I don't mind you playing, but from now on, I want you home by nine. You need your rest. You've committed to another year here, and I expect your best work."

"Yes, sir." It helped having Fields' Tavern within walking distance.

The sweet sound of humming filtered into the kitchen. Mrs. Hinze was awake.

"We shouldn't tell Annie right now," Mr. Hinze whispered. "You know how she worries."

Vern chuckled. "You make it hard for me to know what I *can* say to her," he whispered back. "Whenever you and I discuss something, you say, *don't tell Annie.*"

"Women are delicate. I merely want to protect her feelings."

Vern nodded and grabbed a rolling pin. While this current ball of dough rose, another was ready to be rolled out and cut.

"Good morning," Mrs. Hinze cheerfully said, while grabbing an apron. "Who's hungry?"

"I am," Vern and Mr. Hinze said in unison.

She laughed and moved to the stove. Within minutes, she was cooking bacon and eggs. Her presence alone uplifted the feelings in the room. Vern cared a great deal for *Mr.* Hinze, but his wife made the place feel like home.

That was the kind of woman Vern wanted.

* * *

Vern brought the horse and buggy to a stop in front of the bakery's porch. He'd been sent to the livery to get it, having been asked to make a delivery across town.

It was a true disadvantage at times to have their residence above their place of business. They had nowhere to keep a horse or any other livestock, so they were forced to rely on others. Betsy had been boarded at the livery longer than any other horse, and in ordinary circumstances, the cost wouldn't be worth owning her at all. But Mr. Hinze had worked a deal with Mr. Simpson, the livery owner, and he paid the majority of the fee in baked goods. Mr. Simpson liked pastry.

Ol' Betsy seemed happy to be out of her stall. All the way, she'd kept her head high and had trotted along as if carefree. The mare was Vern's oldest friend, and strangely, they were almost the same age. She was a year younger. Of course, in horse years, she was much older, but Mr. Hinze assured him she had several good years left in her.

Vern gave her a pat. "Wait right here."

Betsy tossed her head, and he hurried up the steps and into the bakery.

Mrs. Hinze handed him several stacked boxes. "Go straight to the restaurant and don't forget to collect our pay. Dietrich wrote up an invoice." She passed over the small sheet of paper. "You know where to go, don't you?"

"Yes,'m. Linderman's restaurant. It's by the river, next to that hotel I hate."

She gave him a sideways look he knew well. "You know what I've told you about hate. It festers inside you." Her head tipped to one side, and she smiled. "Let it go, Vern."

"Yes'm." He sighed. "I don't actually hate it. I figured by saying that, you'd understand I know where to go."

"Why not use the name of the hotel? Wouldn't that be easier?"

"I suppose." He headed for the door.

She rushed past him and opened it, then held it wide. "Be sure to tell Miss Clara thank you."

"I thought she was Mrs. Archer now?" It had taken many years, but her driver had managed to win her heart and married her.

"She is. Yet I've known her so long as Miss Clara, it's difficult to wrap my mind around her new name."

He readjusted the boxes and went out the door, then carefully minded his footing as he descended the steps to the road and the waiting buggy.

After securing the boxes on the floorboards, he stepped up and took the reins. When he clicked to Betsy, she eagerly got moving.

He enjoyed times like this in the open air and away from the heat of the bakery. Signs of fall were everywhere. Being late September, many of the trees were changing color and dropping leaves. The weather was still fairly warm, but the air had lost its heaviness and summery scent, replaced by a crisp freshness. The winter always brought additional challenges to everyday life, yet he looked forward to the snowfalls.

As he neared Linderman's, he couldn't help but stare at the old hotel beside it.

Number sixteen.

Odd, the things he remembered. He'd not stepped a foot in that building since that horrible day, but the image of the number on that room's door hadn't faded from his memory.

Why did it never stop hurting?

He huffed a breath, then shifted his thoughts and steered the buggy toward the back entrance to the restaurant.

The older he got, many perspectives about life changed. As a boy, he couldn't understand why the restaurant baker was frequently *out of sorts*, and therefore, Miss Clara would come to Mr. Hinze for baked goods. It wasn't until he'd turned fourteen and Mr. Hinze sat down and explained some of life's most crucial facts, that he finally understood. Their baker was another Linderman—Edwin, the brother of the restaurant's owner—and the man had a fondness for whiskey.

When he wasn't drinking, his work was exceptional. Vern had tried the man's bread and pastries on more than one occasion. Sadly, when Edwin drank, he wasn't much good for anything. If he hadn't been part of the family, his brother probably would've dismissed him long ago and replaced him with another baker.

Along with warnings against excessive drinking, Mr. Hinze had also bravely explained the *intimate* facts of life. Vern had already come to many of his own conclusions about how men and women came together, but he appreciated Mr. Hinze validating his assumptions—as uncomfortable as it had been for the man.

Vern chuckled as he stepped down from the buggy, recalling their conversation. Why it had come to mind now, he wasn't certain, though it could have something to do with the dream he'd had about Minnie last night.

He lifted the boxes from the floorboards. "Gee whiz, what a dream," he mumbled, then crossed to the back door and knocked.

Miss Clara opened it. "Hello, Mrs. Archer," he said, smiling. "I brought the pastries you ordered." She no longer wore ringlets, but kept her hair in a tight bun. A style more suitable for her age, marital status, and current condition. She was due to have a baby in another month.

"Thank you." Beaming, she waved him in, then pointed across the room. "You can put them on that counter."

Their head cook stood at one of the stoves, stirring the contents of a pot. He was about the size of Mr. Hinze and dressed in solid white. Yet, unlike the flour that constantly dotted Mr. Hinze's attire, there were splatters of food in assorted colors on this man's apron.

The kitchen smelled like roasted chicken, or some other sort of savory meat. Vern's mouth watered. "I love coming in here. I never know what might be cooking, but it always smells delicious." He carefully set the boxes where she'd indicated.

"Like your bakery," Mrs. Archer said.

"Yes. But in a different way. A man can't live on bread and sweets alone."

She opened one of the boxes and peered inside. "They look perfect, and I have no doubt they're just as tasty." She spun to face him. "They'll be a wonderful conclusion to an exceptional meal. Are you hungry, Vern?"

"I . . ." Since she asked . . . "I'm always hungry."

She laughed. "Then after I settle your bill, I'll show my gratitude for your delivery by allowing you to sample some of tonight's dinner. How would that be?"

"Wonderful. Thank you." Mrs. Hinze had told him to go straight to the restaurant and be certain to get paid, but she didn't say he had to come right back.

"Excellent. All I ask is that you tell me how the food tasted to you—whether or not you enjoyed it."

"I will." He extended the invoice.

She briefly examined it, then motioned for him to follow her. They went through a swinging door that led into the restaurant. Being mid-afternoon, few patrons sat at the numerous tables. However, by five o'clock, the place was sure to be full. It was the most popular eating establishment at the riverfront, patronized by plenty of hungry men who worked at the docks.

She wound around several tables and took him to the front station positioned not far from the main entrance.

"Miss Jordan," Mrs. Archer said. "Please pay this young man from the money in the drawer." She set the invoice down.

Vern craned his neck. He saw no one else and wondered who she was talking to.

"Certainly, ma'am." The woman's heavy Irish brogue intrigued him, and when she slowly arose from behind the counter, his heart constricted.

He froze, staring.

He'd never seen a more beautiful woman. Her abundant hair was twisted and rolled perfectly onto her head, and it was redder than his. Her pretty eyes were as green as the grassy fields in spring, and when she glanced his way, his breath caught.

Mrs. Archer cleared her throat. "Your money, Vern."

"Oh. Yes." He gulped and took it from Miss Jordan's outstretched hand. When he lightly brushed her skin, he tingled everywhere. "Well, that is . . . it's not really my money. It belongs to the bakery." He stuffed it into his pocket. "I'm Vern by the way. Vern Harpole."

Miss Jordan lowered her eyes. "Margaret Jordan."

Margaret. A lovely, fitting name.

"It's a pleasure to meet you."

She said nothing in return and kept her gaze focused downward.

"Vern will be having a meal before he departs," Mrs. Archer said. "Free of charge."

"Yes, ma'am," Margaret said. "I understand."

Mrs. Archer gestured across the room. "You can sit at the table by the window, Vern."

He reluctantly left Margaret and sat where he'd been told, with one small change. He adjusted the position of the chair at the table and faced it in Margaret's direction. The view out the window wasn't nearly as nice.

When the food was brought out and he ate his first bite, he still felt partially frozen. Even after all the pretty girls he'd waited on at the bakery, he'd never been affected by a woman this way. Maybe the difference was the very fact that Margaret wasn't a *girl*, but a full-fledged woman in every sense of the word. Somehow, he had to find a way to learn more about her.

One thing he *did* notice—aside from her beauty—was her bare hands. He felt confident she wasn't married, but surely, someone so pretty would have a beau.

As much as the food had enticed him when he'd entered the kitchen, he cared little about the bites he swallowed. He could be eating paper and he wouldn't know the difference. Miss Margaret Jordan had mesmerized him.

Several people filtered in while he ate, and she greeted them at the door and took them to their tables. The brown dress she wore was by no means fancy, but it looked fine and *proper* for her position. She carried herself well, yet her shoulders appeared weighed down. Vern knew folks well enough to believe something troubled her.

Maybe it's me.

A ridiculous thought. Margaret hadn't paid him any mind at all. In a good *or* bad way. She probably didn't even realize he was still sitting there.

How long *had* he been in the restaurant?

"Betsy!" He slapped a hand to his mouth, realizing he'd loudly uttered his thoughts, then jumped to his feet and raced out the door, passing Margaret as he went. She gave him an odd look, but he couldn't worry about her any longer. He'd neglected his horse, and he feared she might be gone, along with his way home.

To his relief, the loyal mare was exactly where he'd left her.

He stroked her mane. "I'm sorry, girl." Without climbing into the buggy, he took the reins and led her to the front of the restaurant where they kept a trough of water. Betsy blissfully drank.

Vern had lost track of time, too caught up watching Margaret.

Once Betsy got her fill, he climbed into the buggy and headed home. The Hinzes were sure to be worried. He prayed they'd understand.

CHAPTER 5

Vern's stomach had been in knots for days. He'd been so unlike himself he'd not even gone to Fields for a game of a pool as he'd done most every afternoon for months. Surely, Oscar would come by soon to find out why, but Vern wasn't ready to tell him. It would only prompt teasing and add to his frustration.

At least baking helped keep Vern's mind off Margaret. *Somewhat.*

Mrs. Hinze stood near, mixing a bowl of glaze. "You need to go and talk to her, Vern."

"What?" He wiped his floury hands on his apron. How did she know what he was thinking?

"You've not been yourself since you made that delivery to Linderman's. Given your behavior as of late, I can only assume you're thinking about that girl." She dipped her fingers into the sugary glaze, then drizzled it across a sheet of pastries. It fell in perfect lines from her fingertips.

"You're right, but I don't understand it. She didn't talk to me and seemed completely disinterested. I have no reason to be thinking about her."

Mrs. Hinze finished with the glaze, then wandered to the sink to rewash her hands. She returned to Vern, drying them with a towel. "Attraction doesn't always make sense." She let out a light laugh. "The first time I saw Dietrich, I thought he was foolish, but handsome. I loved the way his mustache wiggled when he talked."

Vern looked beyond her to where Mr. Hinze was busily cleaning the ovens and apparently oblivious to their discussion. "Why did you think he was foolish?"

Another laugh. "He stumbled over his words, as if my presence made him forget how to speak."

"I understand that feeling. When I saw Margaret, I froze, then bumbled out some sort of nonsense. She hardly even looked at me." He blew out a frustrated breath. "I suppose she thinks I'm a fool, too. And I'm sure she doesn't think I'm handsome."

Mrs. Hinze cast the kindest of her smiles and cupped his cheek. "You're *very* handsome. I've seen the way girls admire you. Don't doubt yourself, Vern. You have a lot to offer a woman."

A rush of heat filled his cheeks. "You see me through a mother's eyes, so of course, you'd say that."

"It's always warmed my heart to know you think of me as such. Yes, you are my boy, but I can also step out of that motherly role and view you as a woman would. Since, I *am* a woman."

Maybe his embarrassment stemmed from his endless comparison between every woman he met to her. He assumed his youthful infatuation toward her had come from her being the first female who'd shown him genuine affection. Utterly different from his mother, Mrs. Hinze truly cared. He understood *she* couldn't be his, but he wanted someone similar.

He braced his hands on the counter. "So, what do I do? I can't stop thinking about Margaret, and I feel like I might bust."

She pointed to the pastry. "Take one of these to her. Something sweet will usually open the door to conversation."

"That's impossible. I don't know where she lives, or when she works." He shook his head. "It's hopeless."

"You truly are smitten." Mrs. Hinze patted the top of his hand. "Finish what you're doing, then go by the livery and get the buggy, so you can take a pastry to Linderman's. If Margaret isn't there, leave it for her. Just jot a note so she knows who left it."

"What if she doesn't care for pastry?"

"Then I will consider her *unusual*." She giggled, then instantly sobered. "Forgive me. I'm certain she's perfectly lovely and by no means strange. Even if she doesn't care for it, it will make an impression. Knowing you took the time and effort to bring it across town will mean a great deal. In addition, your action will make her aware you're thinking about her."

"That could be a bad thing."

"Why? I'm sure she'll be flattered."

"Unless she finds me repulsive." He clutched his stomach. "Why does the thought of seeing her again make me feel sick?"

"It's your nerves. You're growing up, Vern—becoming a man. Finding the right woman to share your life is part of it."

He held up his hands. "Please, don't rush this. I can't think that far ahead. First, I just want her to like me."

"She'd be foolish not to." She jerked her head to the flour-dusted counter. "Get that cleaned up, then go. And when you see her, just be yourself. You're very likable."

Simply hearing her encouragement to leave fluttered his insides, but he chose not to argue. "All right. I'll do it."

With a large smile, Mrs. Hinze gave a single firm nod.

Since *he* hadn't come up with a plan to get to know Margaret, he hoped Mrs. Hinze's idea would work. And though it twisted his gut merely thinking about Miss Jordan, he *wanted* to see her. More than anything he'd ever wanted before.

* * *

Before leaving the bakery, Vern penned more than one note to Margaret, in the event she wasn't at Linderman's when he arrived. He scribbled out senseless words, trying to sound important, caring, and gracious. But every one of them seemed unsatisfactory. And signing the note posed an even greater problem.

He tried: *Sincerely, Vern Harpole, With affection, Vern Harpole,* and *Yours Truly, Vern Harpole.*

None of them looked right. So, he opted for complete straight-forwardness. The note merely said:

I hope you like pastry. Vern Harpole

Several times on the road to Linderman's, he considered turning the buggy around. His mouth had dried out, and he feared he might vomit.

Just be yourself.

Mrs. Hinze's words kept running through his mind. Since he didn't know how to be anyone else, this shouldn't be difficult. And if Miss Margaret Jordan didn't care for him as he was, they weren't meant to be together, and he could dismiss all thoughts of her.

Besides, once he got to know her, he might decide he didn't care for her either. No matter how beautiful she was, she might be ugly on the inside and a dreary conversationalist.

There was only one way to know for certain, so he kept Betsy moving.

He stopped the buggy at the front of the restaurant and hopped down. Without thinking, he headed for the door, then spun around to get the pastry. Mrs. Hinze had put it in a small box and secured it with a red ribbon. That alone said a lot.

He checked to make sure the note was still in his pocket, then blew out a breath and walked toward the entrance. Like the other day, it was mid-afternoon, so he didn't expect to see a lot of diners. He grabbed the door handle and went in.

If only he could dislodge the lump that had taken residence in his throat. Worse yet, with every step he took, his legs wobbled as if made from putty. He'd never impress the girl if he fell to his knees in front of her and sputtered out indiscernible words.

He contemplated turning around once again, but kept his feet moving forward, only to find the front station empty. No one greeted him.

The beat of his heart slowed. Seemed he wouldn't be seeing her after all.

He withdrew the note and tucked it under the ribbon, then realized he'd not written her name on it. Anyone at all could pick up the box.

"Welcome to Linderman's."

The voice came from across the room, yet he'd know it anywhere. No one had a brogue like Margaret's.

He carefully pivoted to face her and gulped. She looked prettier than ever, dressed in deep burgundy. The color was more elegant than the brown dress she'd worn before.

She stopped within several feet of him. "Aren't you the lad who was here a few days ago?"

"Lad," he absentmindedly repeated, then felt the familiar rush of heat in his cheeks. He liked how she'd said it. It was so *Irish.* "That is. Yes. I was here. I brought pastries to Mrs. Archer."

"You're the baker." She eyed the box in his hands. "Is that for Mrs. Archer as well?"

"Um . . ." He stared at the thing as if he'd forgotten it was there. "Yes. I mean . . . no." He gulped. "It's for you." He shoved it toward her, and she jerked back.

"For me?" Her eyes darted around the room as if she feared being discovered. "Why did you bring something for me?"

"Because . . ." Sweat formed on his brow.

What should he say?

She hadn't taken the box, and he stood there foolishly holding it out to her. If he really wanted to *be himself*, he might as well speak his mind and be done with it.

He pulled the pastry close and straightened his posture. "Do you have a beau, Miss Jordan?"

Every bit of color drained from her face. "You're quite forth-right."

"You didn't answer my question."

She crossed her arms and scowled. "I have no beau and I don't care to acquire one." Hatefulness came through every word.

She definitely showed indications of ugliness inside, but her behavior didn't hurt his pride, it made him sad. "I don't know why you're so angry. I thought women felt flattered when a man showed interest." He set the box on the closest table and moved toward the door.

"I see no man," she defiantly said. "You're a mere lad."

No longer nervous, he faced her. "Years ago, I learned the importance of showing kindness to others. If I'd come here as a patron and you spoke so rudely to me, I wouldn't return. Mrs. Archer is a good woman with a successful business. Since she chose to employ you, you should try to be better-natured and treat every-one who walks in with respect."

Her features remained hard as stone. "Are you saying I should have willingly allowed you to make advances?"

He marched over to her. "Advances? I brought you a pastry." He sadly shook his head. "You know nothing about *me*, but I can surmise something about *you*. The first time I saw you, I noticed how you walked with your shoulders weighted down. And now— the way you snapped at me—affirmed my suspicions. I think you've been hurt and that's why you're so guarded."

He stared straight into her eyes. "If I'm correct, I'm truly sorry for whatever happened to you, and maybe I could've been some-one to listen to your troubles. However, you think I'm a mere *lad* and unworthy of your attention, so I won't bother you again." Every word spilled easily from his mouth, yet he didn't know why he'd said so much.

He spun on his heels, headed out the door, and didn't look back.

* * *

"Foolish lad."

Margaret kept her eyes affixed to the direction he'd gone.

Honestly, he wasn't so foolish. He'd read her behavior better than anyone she'd met since she'd arrived in America.

She picked up the box he'd left on the table and found a note tucked under the ribbon that tied it closed. Her mum had taught her to read, and fortunately, the young man had excellent penmanship.

I hope you like pastry. Vern Harpole

The simplicity of it shamed her further. He'd attempted an act of kindness and nothing more.

"God forgive me, I shouldn't have been so hateful," she muttered to herself.

Mrs. Archer lightly tapped her shoulder. "What have you got there?"

She slightly turned her head. "A pastry from Vern Harpole."

Her employer craned her neck toward the door. "Was that Vern who just left?"

"Yes'm." Margaret shifted completely around to face her. "I wasn't polite to him."

"Why? Did he do something inappropriate?"

"No, ma'am. He merely caught me by surprise, giving me this." She held up the little box. "I accused him of making advances."

Mrs. Archer gestured to a table. "Let's sit, so we can comfortably talk."

Since no customers required her attention, Margaret complied. Besides, Mrs. Archer was in charge and shouldn't be challenged, regardless. In addition, the woman was heavy with child and spent too many hours on her feet. Sitting would benefit her.

Margaret silently sat, then fiddled with the ribbon on the box. She never dealt well with confrontation and kept her eyes on the package.

"When you came to us," Mrs. Archer began, "we chose to give you the opportunity to work, because we understood your need, *and* we saw your potential." She tapped the table. "Please, look at me when I'm speaking to you, Miss Jordan."

She slowly lifted her head. "Yes'm."

"I'm not angry with you, I've grown concerned. From the first day you began your employment, I noticed how you distance yourself—especially from men. A woman your age should be married by now, and finding a husband would greatly improve your circumstances. A man could offer security, and you wouldn't have to spend your days toiling here."

Mrs. Archer folded her hands. "I was reared in this restaurant and know nothing else. I happen to enjoy the work, but most women are meant to be wives and mothers alone. Although I don't know your history or your expectations in coming to this country, if there's something deeper troubling you, I hope you'll feel comfortable enough with me to discuss it."

"M' personal life shouldn't concern you, Mrs. Archer, which includes m' reason for being here. As long as I carry out the tasks you give me—to the best of my ability—I hope you'll be satisfied. I'll try harder to be kind, yet where men are concerned, I'll always be leery."

The woman set her hand atop Margaret's and studied her face. "Was your father abusive?"

"Mercy, no. M' da treated me well." *Until he asked me to leave Ireland.*

"Did someone else—"

"Please." Margaret pulled away. "I don't care to speak of it."

Mrs. Archer frowned, then looked at her with sympathy. Margaret didn't want it or feel she deserved it.

"Very well," the woman said. "I won't press you. But if you change your mind and want to talk, come to me." She pointed at the pastry box. "As for Vern Harpole, I've known him since he was a boy. As a very young child, he was abandoned by his mother and raised by Mr. and Mrs. Hinze. He has an enormous heart and has somehow found a way to overcome what happened to him. Surprisingly, I believe he's one of the most joyful people I know. Of all the young men in Kansas City, he's the least of your worries."

"He was abandoned?"

"Yes. His mother deposited him on the front porch of the bakery in the middle of the night and left town. No one ever discovered where she went." She rubbed her swollen belly. "I can't imagine showing a child such cruelty."

Margaret turned her head, unable to continue watching the woman. "She left no note? No reason?"

"Nothing."

Margaret fingered the pastry box. "Vern said he won't be back. If I'd known . . ." Guilt flooded over her, and she wished she hadn't been so harsh. How could she assume only she carried heavy burdens?

Mrs. Archer gradually stood, pushing herself up with some difficulty.

"I should've helped you," Margaret said, also rising.

"I'm fine. But I'll be glad when this baby comes." She lightly grasped Margaret's shoulder. "I'm going to say this now as a friend, and not as your employer."

"Yes'm?"

"Go to the bakery and thank Vern for the pastry."

Margaret lowered her head. "Because you're not demanding it as m' employer, then isn't it up to me whether or not I comply?"

"Yes. And since the bakery is on the other side of town, if you choose to go, it will require some orchestrating. However, my uncle is well today, and if you should ask him to take you there, I'm certain he'd be agreeable."

"And if I choose to go at another time—or not at all?"

"That's your decision alone." Mrs. Archer blew out a lengthy breath and circled her hand around her stomach. "I need to lie down before we get busy." She headed off.

"Mrs. Archer!" Margaret stopped her.

"Yes?"

"Thank you for not pressuring me. And as I said before, I'll make greater effort showing kindness."

The woman smiled, nodded, and went on her way.

Margaret picked up the pastry box and returned to the front station. Ever so slowly, she untied the ribbon and opened the container. Though not hungry, she lifted the pastry and took a bite for good measure. Its flaky sweetness was unsurpassed. Truly a delicious treat.

She wiped some crumbs from the corner of her mouth and put the rest of it back into the box. She'd take it with her to the boarding house and enjoy it before retiring for the night.

She needed to apologize to Vern, but not today. Maybe not even tomorrow. Seeing him again would mean putting herself near a man. True, she had called him a mere lad—another cutting remark that shouldn't have passed her lips. After all, he'd behaved more mature than she. Unfortunately, no matter how kind a man acted, maturity brought on greater troubles.

She'd crossed a vast ocean and distanced herself from the physical reminders of her pain, but the memories of her ordeal remained. She doubted her internal scars would ever heal.

CHAPTER 6

The air whistling through the slats of the stock car got colder by the minute. At least it helped overcome the stench.

Vern hugged himself and put his nose to one of the long, narrow openings. "I wish we'd known what had been in this car before we climbed in."

Oscar shrugged. "The pigs were transported in *half* the car." His friend gestured to a large mound of stacked crates. "The rest of it was used for *that*."

"Unfortunately, the part for the hogs is the only area we have room to stand in. They may be long gone, but their smell isn't. It soaked through the straw and into the floorboards." The section had been partitioned off, and they had no choice but to stay in the livestock stall.

Vern kept his face to the open air and breathed deeply, hoping to ease his churning stomach.

This trip had been an *interesting* way to spend a Sunday—the only day of the week the bakery was closed. He'd told Mr. Hinze he'd be with Oscar all day, yet omitted the part about *where*. The ride *to* Topeka had been in a regular boxcar, not this *combination* sort made to accommodate freight and livestock together. All they'd learned about this particular train was that it was going to Kansas City, and they'd had to quickly select a car.

The sun had started to set. Fortunately, the trip had taken scarcely more than two hours and they'd soon be home. If he had to be exposed to the nasty odor any longer, he might upchuck everything he'd eaten.

He wished he felt as unbothered as Oscar appeared to be. "Why doesn't the smell make *you* sick?"

Oscar eased up beside him, all the while briskly rubbing his arms. "Because I'm happy about what we accomplished. You should be, too. If you put your mind on the money we made, that'll help you feel better. Topeka was good to us, and with that girl finally out of your head, we can get down to business and continue what we started. You *do* want to stick to our plan, don't you?"

Vern nodded and faced him. "Now more than ever, going west seems like a good idea." Aside from the smell, he enjoyed riding on the train. He'd grown accustomed to the movement and found it soothing. Something he needed. "And when we do, I plan to be inside a passenger car—maybe even one of those fancy sleeping cars. For that, we'll need plenty of money." He leaned against the slatted wall. "I still can't believe I let you talk me into hopping a train at all." Laughing, he clutched his stomach. "I admit, I was nervous when we got into that boxcar, but the ride to Topeka ended up being exhilarating and *fun*. This would be, too, if not for the stink."

Oscar dug into his coat pocket and withdrew a wad of bills. He fanned them in front of Vern's nose. "Smell that?"

"Yep. Much better than pig pee." He huffed. "I'm glad it all turned out as we'd hoped. I was worried I'd let you down that first game. As hard as I've tried to forget about Margaret, she keeps creeping into my thoughts, and it was difficult to focus on pool."

Oscar's eyes narrowed. "Playing pool is the *only* thing you should be thinking about right now."

"Maybe so. But since you're always reminding me how you're older and worldlier than I am, I'd like to know what you really think about what happened—why Margaret acted so cold to me."

"You told me you don't care about her anymore." Oscar folded his arms. "If that's true, why even wonder about her? Whatever happened to her shouldn't matter."

"But . . . she's hurting. I hate seeing a woman suffer that way."

"You're hopeless." Oscar frowned and dramatically shook his head. It appeared his mind was going in a million different directions and he had a lot more to say. "You saw the girl *twice*. She spurned you when you'd barely said hello. If you really need a woman, unlike Margaret, Minnie *wants* to be with you. I know you were attracted to her, and she told me she *adores* your red hair. I flirted with her myself, and I got nowhere. I guess my *golden locks* don't interest her." Grinning, he ruffled both of his hands through his headful of curly blond hair. He caused it to stick up on end, every which way, and he looked half-crazed.

He'd definitely had plenty else to say, but it wasn't a good time to horse around. Vern needed him to be serious. This situation mangled his mind, and if he couldn't put it in the proper place, they'd risk losing everything they'd accomplished. More specifically, they could lose the money.

He pivoted toward the open air once more. "I don't want Minnie." He said it as sternly as he could, hoping Oscar wouldn't press the issue.

Oscar soundly cleared his throat. "Not even for a little while?"

Vern grunted at the implication, then startled when Oscar tapped his shoulder.

"You haven't been much fun lately," Oscar said. "You used to laugh whenever I got a bit crazy."

"Sorry. I've had my mind on too many things."

"No, you've been preoccupied with *one* thing. That pretty Irish *lassie*. Don't you understand? Now and then it's good to get with girls who aren't interested in a lifetime commitment. I wager Minnie could make you forget about *Miss Margaret Jordan*." He said her name with the worst Irish brogue imaginable.

Vern chose to ignore his jesting. "I can't do that, Oscar. I want someone *good*."

Oscar chuckled. "Men at the tavern say Minnie is *very* good."

Why did he have to say that?

Vern had been feeling guilty enough over the dream he'd had about her and shouldn't even be *considering* that line of thought.

He faced his obnoxious friend. "It's sad you say that about Minnie, because it only reinforces my feelings. I feel as bad for her as I do Margaret. But in a different way. Minnie chooses to work at the tavern, and because of that and the way she dresses, she draws attention to herself. I don't care what she does with men, as long as she's not being forced to do something she doesn't want to do. Regardless, I think deep down she's a nice girl who wants more for her life, so that's why I feel bad for her.

"As for Margaret, she made the choice to work in a *fine* establishment." He shook a single finger in the air. "And don't take that as an offense to your father and his tavern." After studying Oscar briefly for a reaction and getting none, he continued. "In addition, Margaret dresses respectfully and doesn't flaunt herself. But from what I can tell, someone has hurt her, and I doubt she brought it on herself."

"So . . ." Oscar tapped his chin. "You think Minnie is miserable, yet it's her own fault because she works around drunk men and wears provocative clothing, and Margaret is even more miserable because she wants to be upstanding, but someone has stripped that from her?"

"Exactly." He firmly nodded.

"You don't understand women at all." Again, Oscar folded his arms. "All they really want is a man to take care of them. Minnie is willing to give you that chance, and obviously Margaret isn't. She thinks you're too young for her, but Minnie is ready and able *now*. All you have to do is say *yes*."

"*No*." He stared straight into Oscar's eyes to drive his point.

The train screeched to a stop, jarring them both.

Oscar grabbed the door handle. "If you change your mind, let me know, and I'll pass on the good word to Minnie. Otherwise, we'll concentrate solely on pool. I wanted to help you make your way fully into manhood." He huffed. "I suppose that'll have to wait. I'm sure there are plenty of able-bodied women out west." He slowly slid the door open and craned his neck, peering out. "Let's go."

Without waiting for a reply, Oscar jumped to the ground.

Vern quickly followed. They wound in and out of the line of cars until they were free of the train yard.

Hopping trains had been almost too easy. Far easier than his dilemma over Margaret.

As much as he hated to admit, Oscar was right about one thing. She shouldn't matter to him in the slightest. But every morning—alongside those of his mother—were thoughts of Miss Margaret Jordan.

The only woman in his life who hadn't caused him inner turmoil was Mrs. Hinze. Maybe he needed to go to her again and seek advice. Oscar might be his best friend and worldly by his own declaration, but Mrs. Hinze understood him better than anyone, and she would never suggest he do something against his nature.

* * *

A full week had passed since Margaret's encounter with Vern Harpole, and it still troubled her. After Sunday Mass, she'd spent additional hours at St. Patrick's praying for divine guidance, and it hit her hard. Prayer had most definitely opened her mind.

She'd been raised to believe that the Lord intended for people to treat each other with goodness, so therefore, she knew full well what she had to do, as difficult as it might be.

Life shouldn't be this hard, and it certainly wasn't what she'd hoped for. She'd spent her youth in Ireland joyful and carefree. Her da had called her his *happy wee lass*. If only she had stayed young.

Because she was required to work at the restaurant all weekend long, including Sunday evenings, Mrs. Archer allowed her to have every Monday free. She usually spent the day reading, or if the weather was agreeable, she'd take long walks. Today's would be the longest yet.

Mrs. Archer had claimed the bakery was too far away to consider walking to it, but Margaret had nothing else to do, so she took on the endeavor. Of course, she risked Vern not being there when she arrived, and if that happened, she intended to turn around and go back home. The only good that would come from her effort would be a slight ease to her troubled heart. After all, her intentions were honorable.

She donned a conservative pale blue day dress and her most comfortable shoes and set out. She'd been told October could be quite brisk, yet the autumn sun shed enough warmth to keep her comfortable, but not so much heat that would cause her to excessively perspire. The last thing she wanted was to offend the young baker by her offensive odor. She'd insulted him enough with her poor disposition.

Mrs. Archer had given her good directions, along with a simple chiding for not enlisting the aid of her uncle. True, had Edwin Linderman taken her to the bakery, she would've already gotten this over and done with, but she didn't care for the idea of sitting beside the man on the buggy seat. Although he'd never acted unkind to her, she had difficulty trusting him.

The exact problem she faced with every male she encountered.

As she passed strangers on the road, she kept her eyes focused downward, feeling it wise not to acknowledge anyone—man *or* woman.

The lengthy walk gave her plenty of time to think, and more importantly, decide what to say to Vern Harpole.

Honestly, if she hadn't taken the position at Linderman's, this wouldn't be an issue at all. Yet, working in such a busy establishment had exposed her to the general public. She'd pushed herself to take the job, believing it would help her overcome her fears. Perhaps it had been a foolish mistake and she should've resorted to working from her room at the boarding house. She could've set herself up as a seamstress, but finding customers posed another problem. Besides, if she'd done that, she'd spend her days alone.

Life lived in utter solitude didn't appeal to her, and yet, she'd put herself in that position by blatantly shutting people out.

"I'm a mess," she mumbled and kept walking.

Mrs. Archer had told her about several landmark buildings that would assure her she was going in the correct direction. Margaret passed a tavern with a sign posted above it that read, *Fields*, so she knew she was indeed heading the right way. A short distance later, the wonderful aroma of baking bread greeted her.

She stopped cold in the middle of the road and simply stared at the Hinze Bakery sign. A pit formed in her stomach.

"For mercy sakes, Margaret," she muttered. "You're a grown woman, so stop behaving as a child."

Chiding herself helped. She marched up the steps of the porch and kept going.

As she opened the door, the jingling of a bell startled her, and she let out a nervous giggle.

A pretty woman with a kind smile entered from what she assumed was the kitchen, and stood behind a long counter filled with bread and other baked goods. "May I help you?" The woman took Margaret in from head to toe in a questioning fashion, eyeing her up and down.

"Could I trouble you for a glass of water?" Margaret swiped at her damp brow. The long walk had taken its toll.

The woman's smile broadened. "It's no trouble at all. Wait here and I'll bring it." She hastened from the room.

As soon as the door shut, excited chatter came from the other side, but Margaret couldn't understand a single word. However, it would seem her arrival had created a stir.

The woman reappeared with a surprisingly larger smile, along with the water. She extended it to her. "Would you like a pastry as well, or perhaps a loaf of bread?"

"Just the water at present." Margaret took the glass and eagerly drank. Whether from exertion or nervousness, her throat had become parched. She finished every last drop.

"More?" the woman politely asked.

"No, thank you." She handed over the empty glass. "Are you Mrs. Hinze? The baker's wife?"

"Yes, I am. And you are . . . ?"

She swallowed hard. "Margaret Jordan. I work at Linderman's restaurant."

Mrs. Hinze tipped her head to one side. "You didn't *walk* all the way from there, did you?"

"Yes'm. I did indeed."

"It's no wonder you're thirsty." She held the empty glass aloft. "Are you certain I can't offer you more?"

"I'm fine. That is . . ." She blew out a lengthy breath. "Is your son here?"

The woman's head drew back. "My son?"

"Yes. Vern. Vern Harpole." Heat rushed into her cheeks. "Forgive me. I was told you raised him, so I assumed . . ." Nothing she said was coming out properly.

Mrs. Hinze moved from behind the counter and came to her side. "There's no need to apologize. He may not be my blood, but I consider him a son. Still, I confess, I'm not used to him being referred to as such, so your remark took me by surprise." She pointed over her shoulder. "He's here, currently helping my husband scrub pans. A daily afternoon chore."

Margaret almost wished he wasn't, and she found herself staring in the direction Mrs. Hinze had indicated.

Mrs. Hinze stepped into her line of sight. "Shall I get him for you?"

"I don't want to interrupt his work. If you care to, you can tell him I came by."

"Came by?" The woman slapped a hand to her mouth, and it looked as if she'd stifled a laugh. "Miss Jordan, you walked several miles to get here. If you came for the purpose of seeing Vern, I'd best get him. The pots and pans can wait."

"But . . ."

She left before Margaret could come up with an excuse to keep her there.

Margaret put her back to the kitchen and crossed to the window, facing the road. As usual, when preparing to converse with a male, her heart beat hard as if in warning. She hated feeling this way, yet hadn't been able to control it since . . .

She hurriedly pushed the horrid memories aside.

The kitchen door reopened, but she couldn't move. She kept her eyes on the window and stared vacantly through it, sensing someone's presence behind her.

"You asked for me?"

Though their encounter had been brief, she knew Vern's voice.

"Yes," she managed to say.

His footsteps neared. "Then why are you talking to the window?"

She breathed deeply to steady her heart, then slowly faced him. A tiny laugh escaped her.

His head snapped back and he frowned. "Are you laughing at me?"

"Forgive me." She wiggled a finger at his face. "There's a large smudge of flour on your nose."

"What?" As he swiped at it, his cheeks grew as red as his hair. "Mrs. Hinze should've told me." He rubbed across it again. "Is it gone?"

"Yes." Every word she'd intended to say vanished from her mind, and she found herself at a loss.

"I don't understand why you're here." Vern widened his stance and fisted his hands on his hips. "I know you didn't come for bread or pastry. Mrs. Hinze said she offered it and you declined, wanting only to speak to me. That makes no sense. Last week, you made it plain you weren't interested in talking to me—*young lad* that I am."

Her remark had stuck with him, further proving she'd offended him. "I was wrong to say it." Shamefully, she lowered her gaze. "You showed kindness bringing the pastry, and I foolishly made assumptions in regard to your purpose for doing so." She pushed herself to look at him directly. "Most men give gifts and expect something in return."

His expression hardened. "I *did* expect something."

She took a step back. "I was right about you." Her chest tightened and caution ignited through every part of her, and she hastened toward the door. "I shouldn't have come."

"Miss Jordan." He quickly crossed the floor and put himself between her and the exit. "You misunderstood. All I wanted was a *thank you,* but I confess, I had hoped for more."

"As all men do." She eyed the door handle, begging with her eyes for him to let her pass.

"No. That's not what I meant." He stood firmly. "Will you sit down and let me explain myself? Please?" He pointed at a nearby table and chairs. "After all, you came all this way, which tells me you must've been inclined to have a conversation with me."

"Fine." She moved to the table and sat in the chair closest to the door.

Vern took the seat across from her. "Can we start over?"

"How?"

"Tell me why you walked all this way to see me."

She stared at the table. "To thank you for the pastry."

"Aha!" He laughed and shook a finger. "Exactly what I wanted."

She gaped at him. His outburst seemed odd, then again, he was young, so she shouldn't expect maturity, regardless of how prudently he'd spoken to her before.

He leaned across the table. "Was that so hard, Miss Margaret Jordan?" He jiggled his brows.

"You're a strange lad, Vern Harpole. How old *are* you?"

"Seventeen." He sat back and crossed his arms. "Old enough."

She narrowed her eyes. "For what purpose?"

"To be your friend. Because I think you need one. How old are *you*?"

"'Tis unwise to ask a woman her age." She jutted her chin. "But I'll tell you. I'm twenty-three and proud of it." *Why did I say that?* It was never good to be prideful about anything.

He laughed, and as hard as she tried to refrain from it, she laughed with him. It had been a very long while since anything had struck her as humorous.

His laughter softened into a smile. Though young, she couldn't deny Vern was handsome and would grow into a fine-looking man. Mrs. Archer had claimed him to be the most harmless of young men in the city, so perhaps she should make an attempt to trust him. "Do you truly want to be m' friend and nothing more?"

"Can I be honest with you?"

"Of course. I want nothing less than truthfulness."

He sat higher in his chair and puffed out his chest. "You're the most beautiful woman I've ever seen, and I'd be lying if I told you friendship is the only thing that crossed my mind where you're concerned. But I learned long ago, that looks might be the first thing people notice about each other, yet appearance doesn't matter a lick if a person's heart is ugly."

He studied her face, then took a big breath. "The first time I saw you at the restaurant, I watched you for over an hour—maybe *two*, because I completely lost track of time. I thought you were polite, but *sad*. I couldn't stop thinking about you, and that's why I brought the pastry. I know how it feels to be hurt, so I thought maybe I could help you feel better—be your friend."

"And I slapped you with m' rudeness." She briefly shut her eyes, then opened them again and forced herself to look at him.

"You may be merely seventeen, yet you talk like an older man. Someone who's experienced life and understands it." She folded her hands on top of the table. "I do indeed need a friend, but please, expect no more."

He cast the nicest smile ever. "If I'm allowed to call you my friend, I'll consider myself lucky." His smile grew. "I enjoy listening to you talk. Your accent intrigues me."

"As you know, m' tongue can be sharp." She averted her eyes from his unending grin, feeling undeserving of such kindness. It was easier to stare at the table. "I promised Mrs. Archer I would try and be more pleasant. The dear woman has been exceedingly patient with me."

"From what I saw, you're nice enough. Just a little standoffish."

She lifted her head. "Standoffish?"

He gazed upward as if in deep thought, then looked right at her. "Aloof?"

"Oh. Yes. I know *that* word."

Again, he leaned forward. "If I'm to be your friend, can I give you my first piece of *friendly* advice?"

She nodded.

"Mr. and Mrs. Hinze taught me the importance of being polite to everyone who comes into the bakery. They said without patrons, we'd have nothing. It's the same for the restaurant, so it's good that you told Mrs. Archer you'd try to be more pleasant. If you act suspicious of everyone who comes through the door, you might chase away business. Because you're pretty, men can't help but notice you. Still, don't assume the worst in them. Speak kindly and leave it at that, *but* . . ." He'd never looked more serious.

"Go on . . ."

His stern eyes pierced hers. "If they *ever* get out of line, slap them with that sharp tongue."

She lifted her head high. "Or m' capable hand?"

"Yes." Seemingly satisfied, he sat tall. "If a man says or does anything inappropriate, he'll deserve it."

"First, I must be certain he's not merely offering a pastry out of the goodness of his heart." She easily smiled, and it felt wonderful. "I'm glad I didn't strike *you*. If I had, I doubt you'd be acting so nice to me now."

"From the moment I met you, I had a good feeling about you, Miss Jordan, and I'm glad to learn your beauty goes deep."

"Please, stop flattering me. I don't deserve your praise." She stood. As much as she liked him, she was ready to be on her way. "Could I trouble you for another glass of water before I go? It's a long walk back."

He got to his feet and held up a hand. "I can't let you walk all that way again. Wait here, and I'll get our buggy. Mrs. Hinze suggested I should drive you home."

"Did she now?"

"Yes. She felt badly that you'd walked so far."

"Then perhaps *she* should take me home."

"What?" His face fell. "But—"

"I'm teasing you, Vern." She wasn't sure what had come over her. "And please, call me Margaret. If we're to be friends, we should use our given names."

"If you want, you can call me Harp. All my other friends do."

"Harp?" She shook her head. "I prefer Vern. Besides, I doubt I'm anything like your other friends."

"Not at all." His smile returned. "Wait here." He pointed at the spot she now stood, then rushed into the kitchen. Within mere moments, he reemerged and flew out the front door.

Mrs. Hinze came out from the kitchen, drying her hands on a towel. "How about a pastry while you wait?" The woman beamed as if someone had just given her a fine gift.

Before Margaret could answer, the door swung wide again, and a man—presumably her husband—appeared and walked up behind her. He, too, beamed, and his wide smile lifted the corners of his mustache. "I'm Mr. Hinze, the baker. You must be Miss Margaret Jordan."

"I am, sir." She shyly looked away. Their enthusiasm over her seemed unwarranted.

He crossed to the rack of pastries, put one in a box, and gave it to her. "You can take this home with you and eat it later."

"Thank you."

A flood of discomfort washed over her, and once again, she found herself at a loss for words. Surely, they perceived her to be interested in their son in a more-than-friendly way. What else could she expect them to think, after she walked miles to see him?

She fidgeted with the box. "Are you perhaps *Catholic*?" The question came out of nowhere and spilled from her mouth.

"No," the couple answered simultaneously.

"Oh." She stared at the floor. "*I* am."

"That's good," Mrs. Hinze said.

Silence followed and hung heavy, and many long, uncomfortable moments passed. Maybe they had no faith at all, but Margaret certainly wasn't going to ask.

"Well," Mr. Hinze finally said. "It was fine meeting you. Now, if you'll excuse me, there's plenty of work to be done."

"Of course." Margaret pushed out a smile.

The man shuffled off, apparently relieved to have an excuse to go.

Mrs. Hinze pointed over her shoulder. "There's always so much to do." She eased across the floor and lessened the space between them. "I'm glad you came, Miss Jordan. I know it means a great deal to Vern."

Margaret clutched the pastry box close, feeling some security from the simple object. "Please, don't misunderstand my intent. I merely came to apologize for not thanking him immediately for his kindness."

"I understand." The woman's expression softened into a calmer —less enthusiastic—smile. At least it didn't feel quite so threatening. "The effort you put into doing so is commendable."

Numerous thoughts flooded Margaret's mind, but she chose not to voice them. If she hadn't blurted out about being Catholic, Mrs. Hinze would know next-to-nothing about her.

Maybe it was best to keep it that way.

* * *

Vern whistled as he steered the buggy toward the bakery. Oscar had told him on more than one occasion that he whistled off tune. Vern didn't care. Whistling meant he was happy, and he saw that as a step in the right direction. He hadn't felt like doing it for quite a while, but Margaret had sparked something in him. He'd come close to *singing* her praises.

Since he didn't want to scare her away, by the time he reached the porch, he chose to be quiet.

He brought Betsy to a stop, leapt from the seat, and skipped up the steps.

When the shop bell jingled, Margaret spun to face the door, clinging to a pastry box. "Are you ready to go?"

"Yes. If you are." He glanced beyond her to Mrs. Hinze, who stood a short distance away. He didn't know what they'd talked about while he was gone, but he hoped nothing bad had been said. Mrs. Hinze seemed slightly unsure of the situation.

"I am." Margaret turned to Mrs. Hinze. "Thank you for the pastry . . . and the water. You've been exceedingly gracious."

"You're quite welcome." Mrs. Hinze cast her *motherly* smile, then went behind the counter and acted as though trying to busy herself.

Odd . . .

Vern opened the door wide and motioned Margaret outside. She wasted no time exiting, and he followed.

"I won't be gone long!" he called out to Mrs. Hinze as he left.

She gave a little wave, and he shut the door.

He had every intention of helping Margaret into the buggy, but she rushed to it so fast, she got into the seat before he could blink. He climbed in beside her and took the reins. When he cut his eyes sideways to see her, he found her sitting rigidly faced forward while wringing her hands together over her lap. Uncomfortable, to say the least.

He almost popped the reins, then thought better of it and shifted his knees toward her. "Did something happen while I was gone?"

"No. Why?"

"You're acting strange."

She sharply snapped her head toward him. "How can you judge m' behavior? You scarcely know me."

"I'm trying to change that." He scratched his head. "What did you and Mrs. Hinze talk about?"

"I told her I'm Catholic." Her face was hard as stone. "After that, the conversation ended." She briskly nodded.

"Oh." He clicked to Betsy and gave the reins a light snap. "So, you're Catholic . . ."

"That I am. And what are you?"

He chuckled. "A man."

Her eyes narrowed. "Religion isn't to be taken lightly. If we're to be friends, I expect you to respect m' beliefs. They mean everything to me."

The buggy hit a hole in the road, jarring them. Her arms flailed, then she grabbed the sideboard with one hand and his leg with the other.

When he looked down and grinned, she jerked away, releasing a tiny whimper. "That was unplanned."

"It's all right, Margaret. If you'd like, I can steer toward another rut and make it happen again."

"Shame on you, Vern!" She inched farther from him. "I may reconsider your offer."

"Should I stop the buggy and let you walk?"

"'Tis not the offer I'm referring to. You know full well I was speaking of your friendship."

He smiled. "Friends can jest with each other—the way you did with me earlier." He rolled his eyes and shook his head. "I like you, Margaret, and one day—if given the chance—I think you'll like me, too."

He sat more erect and began to whistle.

For now, no more needed to be said, and maybe she'd appreciate the lack of conversation.

Besides, he had a lot to think about. Not only did he enjoy driving through town with such a pretty woman by his side, he had the first inkling of what made her tick. She was Catholic, and though he knew next-to-nothing about the faith—or any religion for that matter—he knew churchgoers tended to be good people, and he was willing to find out more about it.

From what he *did* know about religion, he thought it had to do with forgiveness and people being kind to each other. Maybe that's why she walked all the way across the city to see him. Her beliefs had compelled her to make amends.

"Hmm . . ." He hoped it was more than that.

After giving her a quick glance, he put his sights back on the road and returned to whistling.

Oscar wouldn't be happy about this change of affairs. Not when he learned that Vern's mind would have to accommodate both pool *and* Margaret Jordan.

CHAPTER 7

Vern had assumed that once he set things right with Margaret, his mind could occasionally rest. He'd never been more wrong. Now that she'd agreed to forming a friendship, thoughts of her exploded. They ran rampant through his head day and night.

True to their morning ritual, he sat beside Mr. Hinze on the bakery porch bench, while they enjoyed a cup of coffee and a smoke. Once the sun rose, the wispy white puffs they exhaled would scarcely be noticed, but against the dark sky, they boldly stood out.

As each wisp dissipated, Vern followed it with his eyes. "Was it difficult to get to know your wife—before she became *Mrs*. Hinze?"

The man chuckled. "You're thinking about Miss Jordan, aren't you?"

"I can't stop." He scooted to the edge of the bench and rocked back and forth. "I need to see her again. *Soon*."

"Be careful, Vern." Mr. Hinze gave him that cautionary single finger in the air that he'd grown accustomed to seeing whenever the man wanted to drive a point. "I understand why you're taken with her. She's a lovely woman. But . . ."

Vern leaned against the wall, yet wasn't at all comfortable. "But what?"

"She's much older than you, and in my experience, when a woman her age is unmarried, there's a good reason."

"So, I shouldn't pursue her, because she's *not* married?" He grunted. "You think there's something wrong with her, don't you?"

Mr. Hinze nodded. "When Annie and I were alone with her, she acted odd and extremely uneasy. We talk to people every day, and we've never found it so difficult to converse." His eyes pinched into slits. "I think she's hiding something." He shook his stiff finger. "And we don't want you to be hurt by her."

Vern took a quick drag and blew it out just as fast. "I know how it feels to be hurt, and I won't let that happen with Margaret. She agreed to be my friend and nothing more, so I'm going into this expecting very little."

"If that's true, why do you look so defensive right now?"

"Because I think she's a good person, and you've misread her. She had a decent reason to be uncomfortable when she came here. She walked miles to see me, and you and Mrs. Hinze both made assumptions about her purpose." He stood, walked to the side of the porch, then turned to face the man. "It's been almost a week. If you'll allow it, I'd like to use the buggy Monday afternoon. Once I get my work done, I want to go see Margaret."

"If you call on her, people will assume you're courting. However, if you insist on seeing her, it would be better to visit with her in a public setting. Or take Oscar with you. Someone who can chaperone."

"Chaperone?" Vern dropped his cigarette on the ground and smushed it with his foot. "That may have been necessary when you and Mrs. Hinze were courting, but this is the 1880s. From what I've seen, interaction between men and women isn't as guarded as it used to be. Besides, I'm *not* courting her."

"The interactions you've witnessed happened in taverns. That's not the sort of place to gauge what is and isn't appropriate. Outside those establishments, things haven't changed as much as you think, and regardless of the decade, proper appearances have to be maintained." He stood and crossed to Vern. "What people perceive matters. If you genuinely care about her, don't be alone with her. It could soil her reputation."

"I *do* care." His mind spun. "If I sit with her on the porch of her boarding house in full view of anyone who cares to watch, is that acceptable?"

"As long as you don't sit too close to each other." Mr. Hinze rubbed his jaw. "So, you know where she lives."

"Of course, I do. I took her home, remember?"

"I thought you took her to Linderman's." The man's brows wove. "A boarding house, hmm? Does she have other family in the city?"

"No. From my understanding, she came to America by herself."

"Knowing that adds to her oddity. Why would a young woman travel across the ocean alone? It makes little sense."

Vern shrugged. "I have the same questions, but I don't think she's *odd*. I like her, Mr. Hinze, and I want to get to know her better. Not long ago, you told me that as I get older, I should follow where my heart leads. Right now, it's telling me Margaret needs my help. Maybe she was abandoned like me, and that's why I'm drawn to her."

"As a *friend*?"

"I told your wife I didn't want to rush this, and that I wanted to start by getting Margaret to like me. I made her laugh, and I think it's a good beginning. Where it goes from here, only God knows." He gazed upward, then back at Mr. Hinze. "And since I mentioned God . . . Margaret said her religion means everything to her. I've seen Mrs. Hinze pray now and then, but neither of you have ever said much about God. Do you believe?"

He sluggishly nodded. "I was raised Lutheran, yet when I settled here, I couldn't find a place of worship that suited me, so I stopped going to formal services. I admit, I enjoy sleeping late on Sunday mornings. It's the only day of the week we're closed, so it would be wrong not to take advantage of it. I'd like to believe God understands."

"*I* understand. I appreciate my Sunday mornings, too." Vern laughed, then immediately sobered. "Maybe I could start going to church as a way to get to know Margaret better. No place is more *chaperoned*."

"No, Son. That's not the purpose of worship. You go in order to give your reverence to God, not to another person." He wrapped an arm over Vern's shoulder. "The front porch of the boarding house should suit your purpose. After that—"

"So, you think there'll be an *after that*?"

"Time will tell." He jerked his head toward the bakery door. "And it managed to creep up on us. The bread won't bake itself."

"Actually, it does—once we get it in the oven." Vern headed inside with Mr. Hinze at his heels.

He'd gotten the feeling that both Mr. and Mrs. Hinze were uncertain about Margaret, but having her referred to as *odd* troubled him. He wanted them to like her as much as he did. Then again, why should they? They had each other and didn't need someone else to concern themselves with.

Vern, on the other hand, wanted more in his life than the two adults he saw day in and day out. And as much as he enjoyed spending time with Oscar, he didn't come close to satisfying the emptiness in his life.

Vern was ready for something greater, in the form of a special someone. And all the unanswered questions about Margaret Jordan made her more interesting. She filled his thoughts and tugged on his heart. She even overshadowed the memories of his mama.

He needed answers, and Monday couldn't come fast enough.

* * *

Margaret tried as hard as she could to quietly shut the front door. However, it squeaked so loudly, it was impossible.

"Is that you, Margaret?" Mrs. Williams called out from her bedroom.

"Yes, ma'am." She approached the old woman's room, then stood in the doorway and peered into the dark interior. "I hope I didn't wake you."

"You *always* wake me. But now, I can sleep." Her bed creaked and she let out an enormous breath. "Good night, Margaret."

"Good night, Mrs. Williams." Margaret pivoted on her heels and headed for the staircase. She tiptoed to the second floor, then continued to her own room. Hopefully, she wouldn't disturb anyone else in the boarding house.

She hated coming in so late on Sunday nights, but by the time the dinner crowd disbursed and she helped clean the restaurant, it was dark when she arrived home. And honestly, it wasn't *that* late by most people's standards. Mrs. Williams, however, was *nothing* like them and believed in going to bed as soon as the sun set.

Margaret removed her coat and hung it on a peg next to her door, then lit the lamp on her nightstand. Her room was small, yet comfortable. More importantly, it was affordable and close to her place of employment. Fortunately, it was several blocks from the river and away from the many raucous activities that took place there in the evenings.

She liked the feel of the old house, and although Mrs. Williams could be cranky, she reminded her of one her aunts in Ireland. They were both aged and crotchety, but for the most part kept their noses out of her business. Therefore, Margaret could go about her daily life and called this temporary house a home.

If only Mrs. Williams didn't intend to turn her business over to her daughter. Whenever Patsy arrived, she inquired about *everything*. Margaret told her as little as possible, yet she knew the young woman wasn't satisfied with simple details. Surely, if Patsy got her way and took over, she'd pry deeper. If that happened, Margaret would have to find another place to live. No one needed to know her most sacred secrets.

She slipped out of her day dress and into a warm flannel nightgown, then carefully folded back her quilt and climbed into bed.

Not the least bit tired, she lifted *Little Women* from its place on the nightstand and opened it to chapter three. Right where she'd left off.

Perhaps reading about families who truly cared about each other wasn't wise. It could make her more miserable by reminding her what she no longer had. Then again, in some ways, it gave her hope and helped her forget her own troubles, if only for a short time.

She'd had her eyes glued to the same paragraph for a long while and hadn't read it. Thoughts of Vern Harpole's freckled face kept her from concentrating.

"Admit it, Margaret," she mumbled. "You're upset he hasn't come calling."

She tried reading again, then slammed the book shut and set it down. "This is foolishness!"

Why was she even contemplating the *boy*?

Possibly because he was the first person who'd held her interest since she'd arrived in Kansas City. But why hadn't he made an effort to see her? She'd told him he was welcome to come by for conversation. Nearly a week had passed, and he'd not even bothered to stop by the restaurant.

Maybe it was for the best. Her life was complicated enough.

Still . . . he'd been right about her. She needed a friend.

She had acquaintances at St. Patrick's, but couldn't find someone she wanted to befriend outside of services. Most assuredly, no one seemed to be interested in learning anything at all about her. Yet, there again, she blamed herself for that. Just as she avoided Patsy's prying questions, she refused to share her private details with anyone and therefore acted *aloof*.

"Standoffish," she whispered.

Feeling too frustrated to attempt doing much of anything, she dimmed her lantern, then nestled under the covers and blinked into the darkness.

"Lord, what am I to do with m'self?"

As she shut her eyes, a sense of calm covered her. Perhaps God had brought Vern into her life for a greater purpose, and therefore, she couldn't dismiss him from her thoughts. Not only had the young baker been forthright about setting her straight, he'd made her laugh—something she'd forgotten she was capable of.

She *wanted* to see him again and prayed he'd been truthful about his desire for friendship.

* * *

Light rain pattered against the top of the buggy. On days like today, Vern was grateful Mr. Hinze had such a fine means of transportation. A roofless wagon would be a miserable way to travel in such conditions.

He hoped Margaret wouldn't object to his arrival, and although it wasn't the nicest weather for porch-sitting, he intended to suggest it. Especially since he had no idea what else to do with her. Even if the boarding house had a parlor for entertaining visitors, as Mr. Hinze had said, folks might misinterpret the situation if they stumbled in on them. Being out in the open was the wisest idea, no matter how cold it was.

"Sorry about the rain, Betsy," he called to the mare.

The faithful horse kept on walking, apparently unbothered by the drizzle. Maybe it felt good.

He steered her toward the two-story boarding house. He'd heard Miss Polly's was a decent place to live, and it eased him slightly knowing Margaret had other residents who could look out for her.

He laughed. Likely, if anyone even *tried* to look out for her, she'd use her sharp tongue to chase them away.

"I shouldn't have laughed, Betsy. It's sad that Margaret is so distant." It might be foolish to talk to the horse, yet saner than having a conversation with himself.

A large oak grew near the road at the edge of Miss Polly's property. The tree still retained most of its leaves and looked to be a good place to park the buggy and shield Betsy from the rain. He guided her there and brought her to a stop.

Vern set the brake, then jumped to the ground. After giving Betsy a reassuring pat, he headed up the pathway to the house.

He'd expected to feel nervous, but instead, happy excitement pumped through his body. Even the raindrops that dotted his skin didn't dampen his enthusiasm. He whistled as he climbed the six steps to the covered porch and approached the front door.

The stone house was one of the finest, most pristine homes in the vicinity. It was well kept and the kind of dwelling Vern wanted to own someday. The perfect place to raise a large family. From what he could tell by all the windows, it had abundant rooms. And of course, being a boarding house, that was necessary.

He eagerly knocked.

The door squeaked open, and the mere sound ignited Vern's nerves and made his stomach flip. Seemed he was right about his earlier presumptions. If a simple squeak made him jumpy, he was *definitely* nervous.

The old white-haired woman who answered the door eyed him up and down. "All my rooms are full." She pointed at the road. "You might try Morgan's. Two streets over. Near the water."

She started to shut the door again, but Vern held up a hand and stopped her. "I don't need a room, ma'am. I've come to see Miss Jordan."

She squinted, then took him in for a second time, intensely studying him. "You've come calling?"

"Not exactly. I'm her friend, and I'd like to speak with her."

"Friend, hmm?" She puckered her lips, deepening the wrinkles in her face. "You got mud on my porch."

He looked down, and sure enough, his muddy feet had made tracks up the steps and all the way to the door. "I'm sorry, ma'am."

"You should be. It's not easy for a woman my age to clean up this sort of mess."

"If you'll bring me an old rag, *I* can do it."

Her upper lip curled, then she grunted. "Men can't clean."

"But—"

"Margaret Jordan, hmm?"

"Yes, ma'am."

"Wait here."

He spotted a rocking chair and gestured to it. "Is it all right if I sit there?"

She craned her neck and looked where he'd indicated. "Take them filthy boots off first, then you can sit." Scowling, she shut the door.

Not the friendliest woman he'd ever met.

At least her abrupt behavior had defused his nerves. He took off his shoes and set them close to the steps so they'd be ready when he needed to leave. Good thing he'd worn clean, hole-free socks.

Feeling slightly foolish, he went to the chair and sat, then slowly started to rock.

When the door creaked and reopened, he shot to his feet. And when Margaret emerged, his heart pounded. She was wearing the brown dress she'd had on the first time he'd seen her, but unlike then, she wore her hair utterly different. She had it down and loose around her shoulders, and it fell nearly to her waist in beautiful waves of red.

He gulped, finding it difficult to breathe. How could any woman look so fine?

She tightened a white shawl around herself and took several steps nearer. At first, she seemed as cautious of him as the old woman had been, then her expression changed and she softly smiled. "You came."

"You say that as if you didn't think I would."

"It's been a week. I'd begun to wonder."

Vern opened his mouth to respond, when the old woman popped her head out the door. "How long do you plan to be here?"

He turned to Margaret for help.

"Mrs. Williams," Margaret calmly said, "this young man is Vern Harpole. He works at Hinze Bakery, and he's m' friend." She cut her eyes toward him. "You've come to talk with me. Isn't that right?"

"Yes. *Talk*." He stood as tall as possible.

"How long?" the woman persisted.

The rain came down harder as if her ill-tempered nature had fueled it.

"Considering the weather," Vern said, "I suppose not long, bearing in mind ol' Betsy out there."

"Animals are used to being in the rain," the woman grumbled, then jerked her head toward Margaret. "He got my porch muddy. You'd best tend it and don't be too loud."

The door slammed shut.

Margaret snapped her head around, then faced Vern wide-eyed. "I'm sorry about that."

"It's all right. She must not be used to visitors." Grinning, he wiggled his sock-covered toes and motioned to another chair. "Tiptoe over here and have a seat."

"Tiptoe?"

"She said we can't be loud." He flashed another grin and Margaret released a soft laugh. It sounded like music. "Just be glad *your* feet aren't muddy."

The rain pelted against the roof of the porch and thunder rumbled in the distance. Though surrounded by a multitude of noises, Vern focused fully on her laughter—something he'd be glad to hear for a lifetime.

Nope. He needed to put his mind right.

Friends . . .

He returned to the rocker and Margaret sat in a chair not too far away. Even so, it wasn't so close as to raise eyebrows.

Shivering, she readjusted her shawl.

"This wasn't such a good idea," Vern said. "If you catch a chill, I'll never forgive myself."

"I'm fine. I grew up with a fair share of cold rain in Ireland." She dropped her gaze and stared at her hands, which were folded on her lap. "I don't mind the weather."

"I'm happy to hear it." He scooted to the edge of the rocker and bent forward. "Did you really think I wouldn't come?"

"A full week has passed. I suppose you've been too busy working to bother with me."

"Bother?" He shuffled the chair closer to her. "You aren't a bother. Yes, I do work a lot, but you're important, too. I just struggled coming up with a way to spend time with you, so as not to make folks think we're courting."

"Courting?" She lifted her head, then waved a hand in dismissal. "Surely, no one would think that."

"Why?" He leaned back and crossed his arms. "Because I'm so young, or because you're so *old*?"

Her mouth opened, but not a word came out.

"I'm sorry," he quickly said. "Mr. Hinze tells me I occasionally act defensive."

"You have every right to behave that way. Not only do you have to put up with m' poor ability to communicate, from what I was told, your life began with tremendous difficulties."

What?

Immediate worry sickened him, and his insides twisted. "What do you know about my life?"

Her face paled. "Please, don't be upset. Mrs. Archer spoke to me about you—in a *good* way. She assured me you were harmless and kind, and she mentioned how you'd been abandoned by your mum." Her eyes searched his. "Because of Mrs. Archer's encouragement, I sought you out."

"To thank me for the pastry, or out of pity for the poor lad whose own mother didn't love him enough to keep him?" The instant the words left his mouth, his heart constricted. He didn't need this brutal reminder of his loss.

"A wee bit of both, I suppose."

"I don't want to be pitied. Mr. and Mrs. Hinze have been good to me, and they've given me a fine upbringing. And next year, I aim to go west. I plan to make something of my life and plenty of money to boot."

She frowned. "You'll leave Kansas City?"

"Yep." He puffed up with pride, then thought better of it and deflated. She seemed genuinely bothered by the idea. "Why would it matter to you if I go?"

"I've come to appreciate the thought of having a friend. And not only that, I don't understand why you'd leave your livelihood and go off by yourself to somewhere unknown."

He gaped at her, then snapped his mouth shut. "Didn't *you* do that very thing?"

She looked away and her breathing grew more rapid. "I had good reason for leaving Ireland."

"Which was . . . ?" He circled his hand for her to continue.

"None of your concern!"

He'd definitely struck a tender chord and leaned back again to distance himself from her. "So, *you* can know about *me*," he whispered, "but *I* can't know about *you*."

It wasn't a question, rather a sad statement he knew to be true. Trouble was, he believed wholeheartedly, she needed to talk about whatever had happened. Maybe if he could get her to trust him, she'd eventually tell him.

She said nothing in response, but he didn't expect her to. Still, *he* needed to say more. "Margaret?"

Ever so slowly, she looked at him and questioned with her eyes.

"It's fine if you don't want to tell me." As hard as it was to say it, he meant it. He'd never push her. "Is there anything you *would* like to talk about? Maybe you can tell me about that old woman who answered the door. I assume she owns the place?"

"Yes. Mrs. Williams."

"Is she *Miss Polly*?" He pointed at the sign hanging above the door.

Margaret nodded. "Though she's a missus. Her husband died in the war. I imagine that's why she's grown bitter."

"Do you like living here?"

"For now, it suits me." She rubbed up and down her arms. "It's getting quite cold."

He glanced over his shoulder at his waiting buggy, where Betsy stood, unmoving. "My horse would probably be happier at the livery." He got up from the rocker, feeling as if he'd accomplished nothing at all. "Margaret?" He stared down at her.

Her head tipped back and she blinked several times. "Yes?"

"I'd like to see you again. I just don't know where or how, or whether or not you even want me to."

"We tend to oftentimes say the wrong things to each other, but . . . I like you. And since you're m' only friend at present, I'd appreciate seeing you again. As for where, perhaps somewhere warmer?"

He grunted a laugh, then moved to the edge of the porch, grasped the railing that circled it, and stared off into the rain. "I hope it's not pity making you say that."

"I've seen the way you look at me, Vern Harpole, and there's pity in your eyes as well. We're a fine pair, we two." She stood and moved beside him. "We see the pain in each other. From what I know of friendship, we're meant to help one another through it."

He turned to face her and propped himself against the rail. "If you'll let me, I want to be that kind of friend."

Even with their difference in height and the many inches separating them in that regard, they were likely closer than they should be by Mr. Hinze's standards. But Vern had no intention of moving away. Truth be told, he felt inclined to kiss her.

That's too *friendly.*

Regardless, he wanted to capture her mouth with his. And tonight, he'd probably dream about that very thing. It was all he could do to keep from reaching out and threading his fingers through her pretty hair.

She moistened her lips and twirled a long red lock around her finger as if she'd read his thoughts. "Someplace warmer, Vern?" Then again, her actions seemed more like a reflection of nervousness—discomfort over their close proximity.

He took a small step to the side, farther down the porch rail. "I know it's more than a month away, but will you come to our house for Thanksgiving dinner?" He searched her eyes, praying for a *yes*. "Mrs. Hinze cooks up a delicious turkey." Maybe the declaration would help her decision.

"I'd like that very much. But are you certain they want me there? They appeared to be uncomfortable with me."

He grinned. "They thought *you* were uneasy."

"I was. 'Tis not every day a woman walks for miles to see a man. I fear I gave them the wrong impression."

He smiled even broader. "You called me a *man*. If you no longer consider me a *mere lad*, I'd say we made some progress today, Miss Jordan."

"*Margaret*." She folded her arms and cocked her head. "So, I won't see you for an entire month?"

"I can't swear to that. If I can figure out a way to talk to you without risking the spread of hateful gossip, you'll see me before then."

"You're concerned about m' reputation, are ye?"

He cast his most serious expression and nodded. "I may not know what hurt you in the past, but God help me if I cause you any further pain."

"'Tis God alone who has helped me thus far." She cautiously reached out and touched his shoulder. "You're a good soul." With a slight gasp, she jerked away as if deciding she'd made an error in judgment. "You'd best get your horse to the livery."

"All right. I'll go." He moved toward the steps, then put on his boots. "Tell Mrs. Williams I'm sorry about the mud."

"Once I clean it up, I doubt she'll say another word about it."

"Thank you."

He hurried into the downpour and didn't stop until he got onto the driver's seat of the buggy. It wasn't easy leaving with none of his questions answered, yet he'd still made progress. She'd admitted she wanted to see him again, and although she'd snapped at him when he'd asked about her past, at least she hadn't told him to stay away. Quite the opposite.

He'd have been wiser to ask Mr. and Mrs. Hinze first before inviting Margaret to their Thanksgiving meal, but surely, they wouldn't object. Besides, he doubted Margaret ate much.

CHAPTER 8

Margaret sat frozen to the buggy seat. Her inability to move had nothing to do with the crisp November air. She'd worn her heavy wool coat over her usual layers of clothing and undergarments and was plenty warm, but her nerves had immobilized her. She simply stared at the bakery door.

Ever since Mrs. Archer's baby had come, Margaret had willingly helped her do whatever she requested. Because of the woman's additional responsibilities with the child, she'd asked Margaret to assist with the restaurant's business in a greater capacity. If only that hadn't included this particular venture.

She shifted slightly toward Mr. Archer, who had driven her here at his wife's request. "Perhaps *you* should go in for the bread."

His lip curled, and he looked at her as if she were crazed. "Me? Wasn't the sole reason for bringing you, so *you* could purchase it?" He pointed at the satchel dangling from her wrist. "Didn't my wife give you the money for that very purpose?"

"Yes." She fingered the satchel, then readjusted her gloves and again eyed the bakery.

Perhaps Vern had gone out of town and that was why he'd not contacted her in any manner. At the very least, she'd expected a confirmation of their upcoming dinner plans. Thanksgiving was only nine days away.

Mr. Archer loudly cleared his throat. "May I help you down from the buggy?"

"No. I'm quite capable." She inched to the edge, then carefully stepped to the ground. The road was completely hard from the frigid day and thankfully not muddy or slick with ice. That would come soon enough.

She slightly lifted her skirt to ascend the steps and with as much confidence as she could muster, she opened the door. This time, the tingling bell didn't startle her, but when Mrs. Hinze recognized her, *her* alarm showed in her widened eyes.

"Miss Jordan?" Had the woman seen a phantom, Margaret doubted she'd look so surprised.

"Good day, Mrs. Hinze. I fear our baker is indisposed, and you may have heard that Mrs. Archer recently gave birth, so she sent me to purchase three dozen rolls." She pushed out her best smile. "Do you have that many?"

The flustered woman glanced nervously behind her, then braced her hands on the counter and bent forward. "I hadn't heard about Mrs. Archer's baby. Did she have a boy or a girl?"

"A boy. Matthew Thomas." She swallowed hard, dreading Vern might emerge at any moment. "Do you have the rolls?"

"I believe so. Give me a moment, and I'll look in the kitchen."

"Thank you." Margaret folded her hands casually in front of herself. Now in the warmth of the bakery, they'd begun to perspire, but she chose not to remove her gloves. After all, she wouldn't be here long.

As soon as Mrs. Hinze disappeared from view, muffled chatter seeped from the kitchen into the shop.

Margaret inched nearer the door that separated the spaces and instantly caught a trace of Vern's voice, followed by a much louder Mrs. Hinze stating plainly, *you need to.*

Need to what?

Tell her he'd changed his mind about her? Likely, since she could be so difficult. Of course, she tended to approach everything with negativity, so perhaps she was utterly wrong and what he needed to do was tell her when he'd arrive to take her to dinner on Thanksgiving Day. Or, was she supposed to find her own way here?

She apprehensively tapped her foot, then stopped when the door swung wide.

Mrs. Hinze reemerged, carrying a large box. "We had plenty of rolls. Do you need anything else?"

"Yes." A burst of gumption swept over her. "'Tis nearly Thanksgiving. Were you aware your son invited me to eat with you?"

"I . . ." Her face flushed red. "Yes. I've been planning the meal for four." She set the box on the counter, then came around and stood beside her. "Vern feels badly for not coming by to see you. He just needed more time."

"More time? I don't understand." She gestured to the kitchen door. "Why doesn't he come out now and speak to me? I know he's here. I heard him."

"I told him he needs to, but he's *embarrassed*."

"Embarrassed?"

Mrs. Hinze leaned close. "He had a little incident," she whispered. "He fell and cut his face. So severely, it required stitches."

"Oh, my." Margaret clutched over her heart. "'Tis no reason to be ashamed. I want to see him. Please tell him so."

"I tried." She glanced back, then leaned even closer. "He doesn't want you to see him looking so *poorly*." Somehow, she'd managed to lower her voice further.

Again, Margaret pointed at the closed door. "May I?"

Though the dear woman's brows creased in worry, she fanned her arm toward it in approval, and Margaret wasted no time. She marched through the door, carrying her gumption with her, and stopped abruptly on the other side of it.

"Margaret?" Vern spun around and put his back to her so fast she scarcely knew it was him. "Why'd you come in here?"

"Because you wouldn't come out."

Mr. Hinze wiped his hands on his apron and moved nearer. "Hello, Miss Jordan. It's good to see you again."

"You as well. Now, please tell your son how foolish he's behaving. I've seen cuts and bruises before. 'Tis no reason to hide—especially from a friend."

The man smiled. "Honestly, I don't believe you need *me* to say anything at all. And since I'm not required at present, I'll let you two talk privately. But, before I go, I hope you know how much my wife and I are looking forward to having you join us for the holiday."

"Thank you, sir."

He politely dipped his head, then went out the door and into the shop.

She found it odd for him to leave the kitchen, yet from what she could tell, nothing was presently baking. They seemed to be doing more cleaning than creating.

Vern stood rigidly, facing the other direction.

"As I said," she persisted, "I've seen wounds. Are you so vain you're ashamed of a simple cut? Mrs. Hinze said you fell."

His head slowly shook back and forth. "That's what I told her."

"Is it not true?" She eased nearer to him.

"Not exactly. Mr. Hinze knows what *really* happened, and he didn't want to worry her, so I made up a story."

She crept even closer. "I thought honesty was important to you."

"It is. So is protecting Mrs. Hinze's feelings." His shoulders drooped. "I'd planned to come by Linderman's to see you and bring a pastry, but after this happened, I couldn't do it. I didn't want to be forced to explain how I got hurt, and I knew if I saw you, I couldn't lie."

Her chest painfully tightened. "Face me, Vern. It can't be that bad." Even after saying it, she didn't fully believe it. Everything about this situation felt dreadful. She'd wanted to trust him, yet putting her faith in a man who'd lied to the woman who'd raised him wouldn't be easy.

He huffed, sounding terribly sad. "It's worse than bad."

She held her breath, fearing what she might see, and as he turned toward her, she gasped. "Heaven's mercy."

He lifted his hand to cover the wound, but she pulled it away. "Don't. You could bump it accidentally, and I won't have you hurting yourself further."

The cut over his left eye was twice the length of his eyebrow and bore tiny stitch marks. She could tell it had been there a while, but the area around it was still bruised, though greenish-yellow in color, with patches of light purple. It had surely faded from something much darker.

He shamefully lowered his head. "I wanted to wait till it healed before I saw you. Then, I wouldn't have to tell you how it happened. You'd be none-the-wiser."

"So, you leave me to wonder about Thanksgiving?" She folded her arms and stared at him, expressionless. "'Twill be Christmas before that fully heals. Even then, you may have a scar. If we're to be friends, you shouldn't hide from me. No matter what you did." She yanked her shoulders back. "Will you tell me how it happened?"

He looked away, then took off his apron and hung it on a peg. "I doubt you have time to hear it. I assume someone's waiting to take you back to Linderman's?"

She loudly tapped her foot. "Someone is indeed, and he's probably freezing out there in the cold. But he can wait. Are you in some sort of trouble?"

His mouth dropped wide, then he shook his head. "Not exactly."

She narrowed her eyes, feeling like his mother rather than his friend. "What did you do?"

He kept his gaze on the floor. "I made someone mad."

"Did you get in a fist fight?"

"*I* didn't throw any punches, but I took a few."

This made no sense. "If you didn't fight back, you're not to blame for this. Regardless of whether or not you said something to drive a man to anger, he had no right to assault you."

"It wasn't what I *said*, but what I *did*. Men don't take kindly to losing money." His head gradually lifted. "Especially when they think they've been cheated out of it."

She stepped away. "Did you *gamble*, Vern?"

"Not exactly."

She threw up her hands. "How many times will you use those words? Whatever happened to being forthright?"

"Shh!" He frantically waved, motioning her down. "I don't want Mrs. Hinze to hear what we're saying," he forcefully whispered.

Although she may have spoken a bit louder than normal, at present she didn't care. "That poor woman should know what you've been doing." She leaned in and pointed a stern finger. "If you're up to no good, you deserve whatever you get. Including that cut over your eye."

"I wasn't doing anything wrong. I happen to be skilled at pool." He puffed up tall. "Men wager against me, assuming I'm a *mere* incapable *lad*, and I beat them fairly."

He chided her with her own words. "Fairly?" She cocked her head. "No scheming on your part? Can you honestly say you've never led them into *believing* you're incapable when you're actually skilled—as you just claimed to be?"

"I . . ." Again, he opened his mouth wide, similar to a gaping fish. The truth screamed from his silence.

She poked him in the chest. "Shame on you, Vern Harpole." Disgusted and sad, she headed for the door.

"Margaret." He hurried after her. "It wasn't my fault."

"If you're engaged in gambling, 'twas indeed."

She marched out the door and grabbed the box of rolls from the counter. "Good day, Mr. and Mrs. Hinze."

Without waiting for a reply, she kept going until she reached the waiting buggy.

Mr. Archer held the box while she climbed in, then passed it over and got the horses moving. They were some distance down the road, when a horrible thought struck hard. She'd neglected to pay for the baked goods.

Regardless, she couldn't go back.

Her temper often got the best of her, and this instance was no exception.

It would seem her Thanksgiving plans had most assuredly changed.

* * *

Vern stood dumbfounded, rethinking all that had been said between him and Margaret, then rushed from the kitchen to plead his case with her.

Adding to his mounting frustration, she was nowhere to be seen.

"She's gone, Vern," Mrs. Hinze said. "She went out the door faster than I could blink."

He raced outside, only to watch the back of Margaret's head vanish from view.

No, he couldn't let this lie. Somehow, he had to explain *everything,* if only she'd listen.

He swung the bakery door wide and rushed to the counter. "Mr. Hinze? Can I use the buggy?"

The man held up a hand. "Slow down and take a breath, Vern. I don't know what the two of you said to each other, but from what I could tell, Miss Jordan needs time to calm herself. She looked fit to be tied."

"That she did." Mrs. Hinze came from behind the counter and took hold of Vern's arm. "I admit, I don't know her well enough to properly judge her character, but she was rather impolite. I thought she'd be more understanding with your reluctance to see her, considering your unfortunate accident." She released a disgusted sigh. "She also neglected to pay for the rolls."

Her anger toward Margaret wasn't right. *She* wasn't at fault, *he* was.

"Vern?" Mrs. Hinze released him, then lightly patted his hand. "I think it would be best to forget her. There are many fine young women who'd be more sympathetic. Mrs. Pennington was here the other day, telling me about her niece. I could arrange a meeting—"

"No!" He shut his eyes, heavily exhaled, then reopened them. "I'm sorry. I didn't mean to yell. I'm just so frustrated . . ."

She rubbed up and down his arm, looking at him with pity. "I understand. That woman could enrage the calmest of souls."

He gazed beyond her to Mr. Hinze, who appeared to be wishing he was anywhere but here at the moment. He fidgeted with the empty pastry boxes and bags on the countertop.

When he lifted his head and met Vern's gaze, the man's eyes widened, then he shrugged. "Go on and tell her, Vern."

He wished Mr. Hinze had encouraged him to do so from the very beginning, instead of insisting he keep the truth from her to protect her *delicate feelings*.

Mrs. Hinze shifted her eyes back and forth between her husband and him. "Tell me what?"

Vern huffed. "The reason why Margaret is so angry."

Her brows dipped low. "How would Dietrich know? Neither of us could hear what the two of you were saying to each other."

"Because he knows the truth about this." Vern pointed at his stitches. "I didn't fall, I got hit by a man who accused me of cheating at pool."

"You were in a fight?" Her troubled gaze once again moved to her husband. "You knew about this?"

He inched from behind the counter, skulked across the room, and stood beside them. The man had never looked more sheepish. "I didn't want you to worry, Annie. Besides, Vern didn't throw a single punch."

"And that makes it acceptable?" She put her back to Mr. Hinze and faced Vern straight on. "Is that what you and Oscar have been doing most every afternoon? Gambling on pool games?"

"Please don't call it gambling. It's a challenge of skill."

"Poppycock!"

Vern stepped back. In all the years he'd known her, she hadn't raised her voice this way. "I'm sorry," he said again, but doubted it would help. He'd angered the one person he cared about the most.

She leaned in. "You *should* be sorry. It's no wonder Miss Jordan was upset. I led her to believe you'd had a fall, and I suppose in some ways, you did. You fell from her good graces. She's Catholic, and if I'm not mistaken, they don't approve of gambling. Or drinking, for that matter. And if you were playing pool with Oscar, you had to have been at his father's tavern. Did she know you were there?"

"I . . . um . . ." He shook his head. "I don't think I mentioned the location. Even if I did, what difference would it make? I don't drink."

"But everyone around you does. Isn't that right?"

"Yes'm." He moved to the nearest chair, dropped into it, then put his head in his hands, only to hurt himself by touching his wounded eye. He winced and grunted. "I suppose I deserved that."

Mr. and Mrs. Hinze joined him at the table, but silence hovered between them.

How would he ever fix this?

"Do you know what hurts worse than my eye, Mrs. Hinze?"

She frowned. "What?"

He rubbed across his heart. "I ache inside knowing you're disappointed in me. I really am sorry. Would it help to know we meant well, keeping it from you?"

She laid her hands on the table, folded them together, and stared at them. "I'm afraid not. And I'm just as displeased with you, Dietrich, as I am Vern. Is there anything else you've neglected to tell me?"

Mr. Hinze gazed upward as if unsure, but Vern knew full well what needed to be said. "The reason I've been playing pool . . ." The instant he said it, Mr. Hinze shook his head, stopping Vern in mid-sentence. Since he couldn't hide this any longer, he pressed on. "I'm playing to make money, so I can save enough to go west next year."

Mr. Hinze deflated.

His wife, however, sat taller in her chair. "You're planning to leave us?"

Vern reached over and took her hand. "Once I'm eighteen and spring comes."

He thought he couldn't feel worse than he already did, but when her eyes teared up, he wanted to shrivel. "Please, don't cry. You've been a wonderful mother—better than I deserved—but I know I'm not meant to live here forever. Something deep inside me is pushing me to move on. I want to go west to the mining towns and see what I can make of my life."

"I thought . . ." She sniffled. "That is, I *assumed* you'd be a baker like Dietrich."

"I will be. Only, not in Kansas City."

Mr. Hinze laid his large hand atop theirs. "I'm sorry, too. I knew you'd be upset by this, Annie, and I hate to see you cry."

She turned her head slightly toward him. "I have every right to cry about this, but it doesn't mean I'm weak. From now on, trust me, and include me in everything. Even difficult things."

He caressed her cheek. "I will, starting now. What do you think about sending Vern to collect the money for our rolls?"

She wiped away her tears and actually smiled. "That's a fine idea."

"So," Vern said, "you'll let me use the buggy?"

Both Mr. and Mrs. Hinze nodded.

"If Miss Jordan is going to join us for Thanksgiving," Mrs. Hinze said, "she'll need to know the time. She's overdue for a formal invitation."

Vern leaned back in his chair. "I doubt she'll want to come. If you'd seen the disappointment in her eyes, you'd understand why. She told me I deserved getting punched."

Mrs. Hinze's head tipped to one side. "Did you cheat the man, Vern?"

"No, ma'am. It was a fair game. I swear it."

"Then explain that to Miss Jordan and perhaps you can mend fences."

He doubted it would be that easy. "She has a temper, that's for certain, but for some odd reason, I like her, and I don't want her to think I'm a bad person."

"Then, go." Mrs. Hinze stood, then bent down and placed a soft kiss on the top of Vern's head. She'd not done that in many years.

"Yes, Son," Mr. Hinze added. "*Go.*"

Vern didn't need any more encouragement. He jumped to his feet, raced through the kitchen, grabbed his coat, and flew out the back door.

If ever there'd been a need to pray, it was now. And though he wasn't sure if he was going about it right, he decided to ask God for only one thing and looked heavenward. "Just keep her quiet long enough to hear me out. All right?"

No booming voice came from above with an answer, but he hadn't expected one anyway. Still, he felt better having asked for help.

He headed for the livery.

CHAPTER 9

Margaret carried the box of rolls into the kitchen and left them with the cook, then sought out Mrs. Archer. She found her in the back room that had previously been used as an office alone, but now doubled as a nursery. Mrs. Archer's father sat in a corner chair, and the man was gleefully cooing at the tiny baby in his arms.

"Are you Papa's boy?" Mr. Linderman gazed at the child so lovingly, it stung Margaret's heart.

She turned away.

"Margaret?" Mrs. Archer walked up behind her. "Is there something you need?"

Margaret shifted enough to see her, yet made a point not to look at the baby. "Yes'm. Your husband and I just returned from the bakery. I gave the rolls to Mr. Green."

"Thank you." She cautiously eyed her. "I can see you have more to say."

"Yes'm. I forgot to pay for them."

"I see . . ."

Mr. Linderman laughed. "You're the finest baby boy in the country." His laughter died to a low chuckle. At first, Margaret believed he'd laughed at her, but the man seemed oblivious to everything but the infant.

Mrs. Archer shot him a smile, then returned her attention to Margaret, with a much more serious expression. "We've been doing business with Mr. and Mrs. Hinze for years, so I doubt this will harm our relations." She glanced at the clock on the corner shelf. "There's no time to send you back now. You need to prepare for the dinner crowd. I'll have Eustace take you again tomorrow."

"I'm sorry for the trouble."

"It's fine. We all make blunders now and then." She looked over her shoulder, then giggled. "Have you ever seen a prouder grandpa?"

"No, ma'am, I never have." Margaret wanted to run, but she kept her feet firmly planted. "I'd best get busy. Thank you for your understanding."

Mrs. Archer laid a hand on Margaret's upper arm. "You've become invaluable to us." Her smile grew, and this time it was directed at her. "I imagine you saw Vern while at the bakery. Is he doing well?"

She firmed her jaw. "He got in a bit of a scuffle and cut his eye, so he wasn't at his finest."

"Oh, my." Her face drew up with concern. "What sort of scuffle?"

Margaret's thoughts spun. She'd have been wise to say nothing at all. "I don't fully know. I didn't pry."

Mrs. Archer nodded. "That's commendable. Knowing Vern's character, I'm certain whatever happened wasn't his doing."

Margaret pinched her lips together. Maybe it had been wrong to keep the truth from Mrs. Archer, but since it wasn't hers for the telling, she felt it wise to say as little as possible. Even so, white lies weren't any purer than outright falsehoods and just as sinful.

"Clara?" Mr. Linderman coughed, then groaned. "I think your boy needs to be changed."

She laughed and leaned close to Margaret. "Now he's *my* boy." Another joyful giggle. "I'll tend Matthew, while you prepare for our guests. You're a gem, Margaret." She gave a brief hug, then flitted away toward her son.

The hug was unexpected, yet it happened so quick it didn't trouble her. At least now she could leave the uncomfortable setting and put her mind on business. If only she didn't have to go back to the bakery tomorrow . . .

She wandered through the restaurant and checked every table, making sure all linens were clean and crisp, and every place was set with the appropriate dinnerware and utensils. To guarantee everyone would be plenty warm, she added several logs to the fire in the central fireplace, then poked around them to get the flames proficiently rising. Once confident all was in order, she returned to the kitchen.

Unlike earlier, she paid close attention to everything around her. "The food smells wonderful, Mr. Green."

He sipped from a spoon. "It tastes even better." After setting the spoon aside, he lifted the bottom of his long apron and dabbed it across his mouth. "I assume Edwin is *sleeping it off* upstairs?"

"Yes. And his brother and Mrs. Archer are entertaining the baby. I suppose they're relying on the two of us to tend the restaurant."

"We should ask for more pay." He winked, then laughed.

"Perhaps." She offered a simple smile, somewhat bothered by his flirtatious action. "I'd best be getting to my station. Hopefully, Miss Cynthia will arrive soon, or I'll be waiting tables along with all my other responsibilities."

She left the kitchen, then came to an abrupt stop.

Vern stood near the front door.

Seeing him added stress to the situation, so she marched across the floor to deal with him head on. "I don't have time to speak with you right now, so you should go."

"Hello, Margaret." He folded his arms and didn't budge.

"Did you not hear me? I said, *go*."

"You're not doing well with that *pleasantness* you claimed to be working on. What makes you think I came to talk? I might be a hungry patron."

He certainly had a way of putting her in her place. "Forgive me. May I show you to a table?"

"No. I came to talk to you."

She stomped her foot. "You infuriating man!"

He calmly set a sheet of paper on the front station counter. "This is a bill for the rolls. Seems in your haste, you didn't pay."

Utterly flustered, she hurried around to the other side of the counter and retrieved the proper amount from the money drawer that she'd returned from her satchel. She set the coins beside the bill. "There. Now, go."

He pocketed the money. "Not yet."

"Why? Isn't it obvious we can't have a single conversation without arguing? Why torment ourselves by attempting friendship?"

He moved closer, and she was grateful for the barrier that separated them.

"When you're raised in a public business," he boldly said, "you learn a lot about people. Folks usually don't get angry with each other, unless they truly care. Considering how mad you are at me right now, I'm guessing you like me a lot. Maybe more than you're willing to admit."

"Ugh!" She glared at him. "You're a thorn in m' side, Vern Harpole. I thought I could trust you, but you lied to your own mum." She wiggled a finger at his injury. "How can I be a friend to a man who lies and gambles?"

"What happened to the woman who told me she knew we were both in pain and could help each other through it?"

"Pain doesn't make a man do terrible things."

"Are you sure about that?" His blue eyes penetrated hers. "Pain drives us in different ways, but I'm not a bad person. I play pool because I want to do something more with my life, and I need money to do it. I swear to you, I don't cheat. I win fairly. As for the lying . . ." He blew out a long breath. "It was wrong, and it won't happen again. But I've *never* lied to *you*."

"How can I be certain?"

"You can't. Still, I'd like to continue what we started and keep working on that friendship. Eventually, I hope to regain your trust."

"I don't know . . ."

His gaze intensified. "Will you at least come to Thanksgiving dinner? Mr. and Mrs. Hinze would like you to join us."

"I'd think by now they'd see me as a bother."

"Be thankful they didn't have you arrested for thievery." He grinned, wiggled his brows, then winced. "Ouch. I shouldn't have done that."

When he went to touch his brow, she grabbed his hand and stopped him. "Don't make it worse."

He gently smiled. "You *do* care."

She jerked her hand back. "You have a way of needling me, but I'd be lying if I said I didn't find some enjoyment in our time together."

"Then, you'll come for Thanksgiving?"

"On one condition." She lifted her chin high.

He cast a wary gaze. "Okay . . . What is it?"

"You have to go with me to Mass on Christmas Eve."

"All right."

He answered so fast, it caught her off guard. "You have no objections?"

"Nope." He stood tall, then seemed to think better of it and leaned nearer. "Will it be a problem that I'm not Catholic?"

"Of course not. The church wouldn't grow if we couldn't enlist non-believers."

The front door opened, and a group of four walked in. "Welcome to Linderman's," she *pleasantly* acknowledged them.

The tallest man in the group nodded in response.

She returned her attention to Vern. "I'm needed elsewhere. Will you come for me on Thanksgiving?"

"Yes. I'll pick you up at the boarding house at one o'clock. Mrs. Hinze wants to eat at two."

"I'll be waiting. Is there anything I can bring for the meal?"

"Just yourself." He bowed in an overly animated fashion, then spun on his heel and left.

The sight tickled her, but she held in her laughter, needing to remain professional for the current guests.

An unexpected weight lifted from her shoulders. Yes, she'd been angry, but she didn't want to be. And since he'd so willingly agreed to attend Mass, maybe she had been right about him and he was indeed a good man.

* * *

"Who's hungry?" Broadly grinning, Mr. Hinze set the platter holding the golden-brown, roasted turkey on the service counter.

Vern rubbed his hands together. "*I* am."

Every year prior, the three of them had eaten Thanksgiving dinner at the table in the kitchen. Since Margaret had joined them, Mrs. Hinze thought it would be nicer to dine in the shop. Vern found it a little unusual. Then again, no one would be peeking through the store window or strolling out and about on the street. All businesses were closed. A welcomed calm after the wild storm.

They'd baked more bread, rolls, pies, and pastries in the last four days than they had in the past two months. Vern had worked up an enormous appetite for something other than bread.

"It smells delicious," Margaret said. "'Tis an American custom I can appreciate. I've always loved turkey."

"I'm happy to hear it," Mrs. Hinze said. "Dietrich, slice a large portion for Miss Jordan."

He glided the carving knife through the meat, and trickles of savory juice seeped from every cut. Vern's mouth watered at the sight.

The large platter wouldn't fit on the table. It already overflowed with bowls full of potatoes and assorted vegetables. Yet, as hungry as he was, nothing pleased him more than having Margaret sitting beside him.

He'd dressed in his best white cotton shirt and stylish striped pants, and though he wore a black tie, he and Mr. Hinze agreed to forego their coats for comfort. He hoped Margaret recognized the effort he'd made to look his best. He definitely appreciated how *she* looked.

Her pale green dress brought out the color of her eyes, and it was lined in feminine white lace. She'd twisted her hair in a long thick braid down her back, and topped it off with a pretty hat that perfectly matched her gown. He could stare at her forever . . .

Mr. Hinze set a plate in front of her with the sliced turkey on it, then served the rest of them in turn. Lastly, he got his own portion and sat. They passed around the bowls, and soon, their plates were full.

"Will you offer a blessing, Mr. Hinze?" Margaret asked.

Having never heard the man pray, Vern expected him to decline, but he lifted his head high and nodded. "Gladly." He folded his hands and bowed his head, and the two women did the same.

Vern matched their actions, yet kept his eyes lifted enough to watch everyone at the table.

"Lord," Mr. Hinze reverently said, "Bless this meal that my wife so beautifully prepared. We thank You for the abundance You've given us, and for each other. Thank You for bringing Vern into our lives all those years ago, and for our new friend, Miss Jordan. May her life be fruitful and fulfilling." He breathed deeply and seemed to be inhaling the food. "Now, may we enjoy this food, and may it bless our bodies and keep us strong. Amen."

"Amen," Margaret whispered and crossed herself in an unusual way.

As she opened her eyes, she met Vern's gaze, so he decided to be bold. "Why did you cross yourself like that?"

"'Tis a Catholic's way of showing additional reverence to God. 'Tis symbolic of the Father, Son, and Holy Ghost, and in many ways, 'tis a prayer in itself."

"That's beautiful," Mrs. Hinze said. "I've seen people cross themselves, but I hadn't heard an explanation of it before."

Vern had a lot to learn about Margaret *and* her faith. "I suppose I'll see others doing that at Christmas Mass?"

"You will indeed." She lifted her fork and took a dainty bite.

Though tempted to shovel in a mouthful of dressing, Vern politely ate and savored each morsel. "This is better than ever, Mrs. Hinze."

"Thank you, Vern." She smiled at him, then looked at Margaret. "How long have you been in America, dear?"

Vern held his breath, hoping she wouldn't become defensive.

"A little over six months."

"Vern told us you live alone and have no other family here. What brought you to Kansas City?"

Margaret set her fork aside, then sipped from her water glass. "I had a second cousin in Pittsburgh, Pennsylvania who was supposed to take me in. Sadly, when I arrived at her address, I learned that she had died."

Mrs. Hinze gasped. "Oh, my heavens. I'm so sorry for your loss."

"'Twas difficult to accept, for I had no one else to turn to and no other destination."

Finally, Vern had a better understanding of her recent past. "What did you do?"

"I didn't care to stay in Pittsburgh, so I boarded a steamboat heading west and stayed aboard until it came to a city that appealed to me." She lowered her head. "'Tis the most foolish thing I've ever done."

"And you chose Kansas City," Mr. Hinze proudly stated. "I understand why. The city is prospering."

Margaret picked up her fork and poked it around her food. "I believe something deeper led me here. When I came upon St. Patrick's parish, the priest directed me to Miss Polly's. From there, I found employment at Linderman's, and here I am."

"You may have thought you acted foolish," Vern said. "But I'm glad you stayed on that steamboat till you got to Kansas City."

"I agree," Mrs. Hinze said. "*We* truly love it here, and I'm happy you've made it your home. However, I'm confused as to why you left Ireland. Surely, you have family who misses you."

Margaret's face shadowed over, and she lowered her eyes.

"You came to help your cousin," Vern quickly said. "Isn't that right?"

"In a manner of speaking," Margaret whispered. "If you don't mind, I'd rather not talk about it any longer. I don't want m' troubles to dampen the spirits of this fine holiday."

Mr. Hinze lifted his water goblet high. "It *is* a fine holiday and I'd like to propose a toast to newfound friends and the blessing of our prosperity."

"To friends and prosperity," Vern repeated and raised his glass.

Mrs. Hinze smiled and did the same, and lastly, Margaret added her glass. They clinked them together at the table's center, then each took a hearty drink.

Margaret shyly returned her near-empty goblet to its place on the table, then cut her eyes toward Vern. She mouthed *thank you*, and the simple act set his heart soaring.

He doubted her cousin had anything to do with her reason for coming to America, but he hadn't made the comment with the intent of lying. He wanted only to help her out of an uncomfortable topic of conversation, and he thought he'd succeeded.

Whatever reason had brought her here, he was simply glad she'd come. He hoped in time, her pain would subside, just as his had lessened over the years.

He needed to believe that even bad things happened for a reason. If his mama hadn't left him, he wouldn't have been raised in a fine home, and he never would've met Margaret Jordan.

As he looked into her pretty face, he saw his future.

Convincing her she belonged there was a challenge he'd happily undertake.

CHAPTER 10

An inch of cold white crystals blanketed the ground, and tiny light flakes continued to fall.

Vern had wrapped a wool scarf around his neck, but his face was exposed to the elements and his nose was likely red as a beet from the cold ride. He'd arranged to show Margaret around Kansas City, and he hoped the frigid air wouldn't change her mind.

Before ascending the steps to the front door of the boarding house, he stomped the snow from his boots. The last thing he wanted to do was upset Mrs. Williams again by dirtying her porch in any way.

He bravely knocked, and to his relief, Margaret opened the door. "You're punctual, Vern." She smiled, glanced nervously behind her, then faced him again. "I told Mrs. Williams you were coming, and she said as long as you wipe your feet, you're allowed in the parlor."

"Are you sure?" The idea of warming himself by the fire was appealing, but . . .

"Come in, Vern." She stepped aside and widened the opening of the door. "Wipe your feet there." She gestured to a small rug beside the entrance.

He did as she instructed, then entered the house. It was fancier than he'd imagined with abundant trinkets, elaborate furniture, paintings, and other wall hangings. As he followed Margaret to the parlor, he was grateful no one else lingered about, and the way she kept darting her eyes around the room, he believed she felt the same.

The crackling fire beckoned him. He eagerly moved to stand in front of the hearth, took off his gloves, and put his bare hands to the flames. The warmth rose to his face and he relished it.

"It's colder outside than I thought it would be," he said without turning away from the heat. "Do you still want to ride around the city?"

"I don't mind the cold. I set aside a blanket to take with us. If *you've* changed your mind—"

"No." He turned and put his back to the fire. "I want to go, and I'm glad you agreed to, but aren't you concerned about people seeing us together?"

"You're m' friend. If anyone reads more into it than that, let them. We know the truth."

He nodded, yet couldn't help wonder if she understood that his feelings for her went much deeper. Maybe in time she'd see *him* differently, too.

"Are you ready to go?" she asked.

"If you are."

"I am." She put on some long white gloves, then lifted a coat that was draped over the back of a chair and thrust an arm into one sleeve.

He hurried across the room to help her.

She laughed. "I've been doing this m'self for years. But thank you for assisting me." She stepped away and buttoned her coat up to her neck, then wrapped a scarf around it as well.

He put his own gloves back on, then headed for the door and opened it for her.

She paused at the entrance and grabbed a blanket that lay folded on a table beside it. "Goodbye, Mrs. Williams," she called out over her shoulder as she walked out.

He glanced behind him and caught sight of the old woman's head protruding from a room in the hallway. When she noticed him looking at her, she grunted and disappeared.

He hurried onto the porch. "Mind the steps. They're a bit slick."

Margaret stood utterly still and lifted her face to the falling crystals. "The snow has made the city so beautiful. It covers the ugly mud and bare branches like icing on a cake."

"You're in a fine mood this afternoon." He took her arm to help her down the steps and couldn't help but smile when she didn't pull away.

"I appreciate every Monday. There's something to be said for days on which you can do whatever you please."

When they reached the pathway to the road, she released him and increased her pace. He followed behind her, wishing she hadn't separated herself from him. Still, he was doing all he could to abide by her boundaries.

The severe cold prevented the snowflakes that had landed on Betsy from melting, but she seemed unbothered by it. Animals weren't as sensitive to the elements as people. Regardless, he brushed some of the powdery snow from her mane.

When he turned around, Margaret had already climbed into the buggy.

He moved in beside her, and she tucked the blanket around them. He appreciated the warmth, as well as the closeness to her, but this all felt a little too comfortable. If she was trying to raise his hopes for something beyond friendship, she'd succeeded.

With a light heart, he clicked to Betsy and steered her toward the river. They passed Linderman's, and as they went by the old hotel, he shuddered, and his good mood plummeted.

"Is the blanket not helping?" Margaret asked. "You shivered."

"The cold didn't cause it." He kept his eyes on the road. "I shouldn't have come this way—that hotel always upsets me."

"The Crestmore?"

"Yes."

"Why?" She lightly touched his arm, causing him to jump. "You truly are on edge."

"I'm sorry. It's hard to talk about."

"I understand. If it upsets you so much, you don't have to explain."

"Well . . . I . . ." He glanced at her, then faced forward again. If he wanted her to trust him enough to open up to him, maybe telling her more about himself would help. "I don't mind telling you, even though it's painful."

"It might help for you to share it, but only if you're certain you want to."

"I am. I think it's important that you know." He took a big breath. "It was the last place I saw my mother. We were staying in room number sixteen. One evening, she added a large amount of liquor to my cider so I'd sleep through the night, then took me to the porch of the bakery, and left me there. I woke up with Mr. Hinze staring down at me, wondering what I was doing there."

"I'm so sorry, Vern."

When he pushed himself to look at her, she sniffled and turned her head.

"No, *I'm* sorry. You were happy when I picked you up, and now you're not. I should've gone a different direction."

"I'm still happy." She slowly faced him. "But I hurt for you. How did you ever overcome it?"

"I worked hard, and that kept my mind off it *somewhat*. One's thing's for certain, I'll never drink alcohol because of it. Anything that makes you oblivious to what's going on around you shouldn't be legal."

She solemnly nodded. "I'm happy to hear you say that. Spirits can taint the finest of souls."

"That's an odd word for it. Most folks around here just call it *booze*."

"Well, whatever the term, it was wrong for your mum to give it to you."

"You're right. I won't do that to *my* kids—if I ever have them." He cast a quirky smile, feeling heat rush into his cheeks. "As for how I've dealt with it," he hastily changed the subject, "more than anything, Mr. and Mrs. Hinze taught me how to care and trust again. Even so, a day doesn't go by that I don't wonder where my mother and sister are."

"Since you've never mentioned a father, I assume your da is dead?" She said it matter-of-factly, but with a gentleness he appreciated.

"Mama said he died in the war. I never knew him, so I honestly don't wonder about him—unlike her and my sister. I think about *them* all the time."

"Tell me about your sister."

"Her name's Virginia. She was sixteen when she and Mama left me." He quickly calculated. "That would make her twenty-five now."

"A few years older than me." Margaret stared straight forward. "What would compel a mum to leave her son and keep her daughter?"

"I wish I knew." He blew out a breath that floated in front of him as a white puffy cloud. A cigarette would be helpful about now, but he doubted Margaret would appreciate the smoke. "Will you tell me about *your* mother? Or your *mum,* as you say."

"She was kind enough."

"Did she die?"

Her head dropped down. "She was living when I left Ireland, as was m' da. I no longer correspond with m' family, so I can only hope they're thriving."

"Why don't you write to them?"

She turned her head painstakingly slow toward him. "I appreciate your openness about *your* life, but there are things about mine I *never* want to share. Please, try to understand."

He stared into her beautiful eyes that had pooled with fresh tears. The painful sight shot straight to his heart. Whoever or whatever had hurt her had cut unimaginably deep. "All right. I won't push you to tell. Still, if you change your mind, I'm here to listen."

"I won't." She swiped across her face and dried the fallen tears with her glove.

If only she'd allow him to hold her and give comfort. But even if they weren't out on the open road in a buggy and were alone inside a building somewhere, he knew she wouldn't let him get any closer.

He steered Betsy down a side road that led to the center of town. It had been decorated for Christmas and signs of the upcoming holiday were everywhere. Wreaths made from fresh boughs, donning large red bows, circled every street lamp. Several businesses had erected Christmas trees bearing fancy ornaments and candy canes.

One of the churches had a life-sized, cut-out wood scene with shepherds, angels, cows, and sheep all huddled together in a large barn. Vern had seen it in years prior, and had been told that the reason for Christmas was the celebration of the birth of a baby named Jesus. The child Christians worshipped.

"What a lovely nativity," Margaret said as they passed it.

"Nativity?"

"A representation of Jesus' birth." She shifted her knees slightly toward him. "Do you not know His story?"

"I've heard carolers sing songs about Him, so I know He was born in a barn. And, I understand He was more than just a simple baby. He grew up to be someone folks worship. People like you and the Hinzes, though they don't go to church as much as you do."

"Jesus is God's son, born of the blessed Virgin Mary, and Savior of us all. Without Him, our lives would be hopeless." She set her gloved hand on his arm. "If not for m' faith, I doubt I would be sitting here with you. 'Tis the only thing that's given me the strength to move on with m' life."

She'd said that very thing before, along with a similar touch. Previously, she'd pulled away immediately. This time, for several long incredible moments, she remained still.

Her gentle touch and impassioned words sparked a stronger desire to know even more. "When I go to Mass, will I hear the whole story? It's hard to believe a child could come from God and a . . ." He took a deep breath. ". . . a *virgin,*" he whispered. Though *she'd* boldly spoken, the word felt a bit too delicate to repeat.

Margaret softly smiled and smoothed the blanket on her lap. "God is all powerful. He can do anything."

"When you speak about your beliefs, you come across so self-assured. I wish you'd trust me enough to talk as openly about your life. If you believe God can do anything, maybe He brought us together, so you could tell me about Him, and so I can help you, too. You said we can ease each other's pain, but I can't help you, if you shut me out."

Her features hardened. "I don't care to tell you everything, but that is by no means *shutting you out.* I've been more open with you than anyone in a very long while." She huffed. "You said you wouldn't push me to tell, yet you're doing just that."

"I'm sorry. But I see so much pain in you, it makes *me* hurt. I only want to help."

She lowered her eyes. "You *are* helping." As she lifted her gaze, a single tear trickled down her cheek. "I know I'm not the easiest person to put up with. Even so, I'd like you to continue being my friend."

"I intend to." He chuckled. "You sometimes aggravate the fire out of me, but I care about you, Margaret."

More than you realize.

She cast one of her most beautiful smiles ever, then silently faced forward.

His hand twitched, holding the reins. He wanted to reach over and link his fingers with hers, but he kept them tightly entwined around the long leather straps.

Oscar had told him time and again how foolish he was for keeping his sights on an unattainable woman, and that it would only cause him inner turmoil as well as physical pain. Sure, he could have Minnie if he wanted her, and likely Mrs. Pennington's niece, too. But ever since he'd first laid eyes on Margaret Jordan, only *she* filled his dreams and held his desires.

Foolish as it might be, he chose to be patient.

* * *

Christmas memories were by far some of Margaret's favorite recollections. Even now, she could easily envision the Christmas candle positioned for the blessed holiday in the window of her parent's home. It was the symbol telling all who passed by that there was a place for Jesus in their home, though there'd been no room for Him at the inn in Bethlehem.

Margaret had lit her own candle. Instead of putting it in the window, she'd placed it on her nightstand. She stared at its flickering light, hoping it might help her stay awake.

Midnight Mass was another beloved tradition, yet the late hour proved to be difficult. On any other night, she'd already be sleeping.

She checked her clock.

Eleven fifteen.

Time to go downstairs and wait for Vern.

She watched the candle a few seconds longer. "Happy Christmas, Mum and Da." A slight ache wrenched her heart as she blew out the flame, but she threw aside all ill feelings. This night was meant to be joyfully celebrated.

As quietly as possible, she crept down the stairs and to the front door. She'd informed Mrs. Williams that she'd be attending Midnight Mass, and as much as the woman had complained about the late hour, she didn't tell Margaret she couldn't go. And if for some reason she'd done so, Margaret would've voiced her feelings and gone regardless. Mrs. Williams might very well be the proprietor of the boarding house, yet that didn't make her Margaret's keeper.

She donned her gloves, coat, and scarf, then went out the door.

As she gazed down the road, she smiled at the lovely sight. The street lamps glistened and illuminated the softly falling snow. Her spirits lifted even higher when she spotted Vern's buggy coming nearer.

She carefully descended the steps and walked across the white-crusted ground to the edge of the property.

Vern pulled the buggy to a stop. "Hello, Margaret." He started to get down, but she held up a hand to stop him.

"I can put m'self in." She climbed up and sat beside him. "Happy Christmas, Vern."

He grinned. "Don't you mean *merry* Christmas?"

"'Tis the same greeting. However, in Ireland we say *happy*."

He leaned close. "You're in America now. But please don't change how you say it. It's what makes you, you." His smile stretched incredibly wide. "Happy Christmas, Margaret."

Every bit of melancholy she'd been feeling vanished. Vern had been more than patient with her. Yes, he tended to needle her, but he also made her happy. She fully understood his youthfulness, yet with each passing day, he became more of a man.

Several times, she'd considered asking him to leave her be and forget about her. It would make both of their lives easier and remove the complications of having to build on a relationship. Yet, selfishly, she wanted him near. He'd helped alleviate her loneliness and gave her something to look forward to.

She directed him to St. Patrick's and when they arrived, many others were already congregating. The street was lined with buggies and wagons, and laughter from excited children surrounded them.

"I'm surprised to see so many kids up this late," Vern said as he rechecked the brake, then stepped to the ground. "Don't they know they need to be asleep for Santa Claus to come?"

"They'll sleep soon enough. For now, their anticipation of the coming joy is overwhelming them." It was easy to understand, because she used to feel that way.

She turned to get out of the buggy, only to find Vern reaching upward.

He wiggled his fingers. "For once, let me help you. The ground's slick."

"Fine." Heart pounding, she took his hand. A good thing, too. The instant her feet touched down, she slipped ever-so-slightly.

Vern steadied her, chuckling. "You'd have found yourself on your rump if not for me."

"Not a pleasant thought." She fully righted herself, stood tall, and released him. "Thank you."

She caught sight of Mrs. Hendricks watching them, and when their eyes met, the old woman cast a knowing gaze.

Margaret shook her head, but said nothing. Maybe Mrs. Hendricks would understand that her assumption was misconstrued. If not, the entire church body would soon be under the impression she had a beau.

It shouldn't bother her. In all honesty, it could make her life easier. She often believed her fellow parishioners thought she was odd and distant. Of course, she had given them good reason, since she'd kept to herself for the most part. They might change their opinion of her and see her as normal if she had a man in her life.

Man . . .

Vern wasn't even eighteen yet.

It might be better to pass him off as a youth she was mentoring.

"Margaret?" Vern tapped her on the shoulder.

"Yes?"

"You must be really tired. I've been talking, and I don't think you heard a single word I said."

"Forgive me." She shook her head to dismiss all her silly thoughts. After all, she'd brought him here to worship, and what others perceived shouldn't matter. "I am indeed weary. Let's go in and find a seat."

He smiled and nodded, then followed her into the church. She loved the simplicity of St. Patrick's. The small, white wooden structure reminded her of her church in Ireland, and additionally, it was made up of many Irish immigrants. They'd named it after Patrick, the patron saint of Ireland, and although Kansas City boasted other fancier churches, it was no wonder she'd been drawn to this parish.

Already, the pews were rapidly filling. She guided Vern to one in the center of the sanctuary. He looked a scant uncomfortable— or more curious than anything. At least he'd kept his promise and attended.

She prayed he'd find something greater in attending Mass than simply a means to appease her.

He yawned, but quickly covered his mouth. "Why is the service held so late?"

"To celebrate Jesus' birth," she whispered. "'Twas believed He was born at midnight."

"If I fall asleep," he said directly into her ear in a hushed tone, "will you ever speak to me again?"

"Likely not, so you'd best perk up."

He straightened his posture. Because there were so many in attendance, they'd been crammed together on the seats, and he was closer to her than he'd ever been before. She appreciated his warmth, but otherwise wished they had a little more distance between them.

She tipped her head toward the altar. "'Tis time."

He startled and his eyes darted every which way when several loud musical chords resounded through the building.

She casually gestured to the organ with its multiple rows of metal pipes. The organist continued playing the beautiful melody as everyone stood. Vern followed suit, all the while shifting his eyes in every direction.

She was accustomed to seeing the robed people walking up the center aisle, yet Vern stared at them as if they were unreal. They held flickering candles and sang along to the tune being played. *O Come All Ye Faithful*. The congregation joined in, and their jubilance filled the sanctuary.

Vern's expression changed. He appeared *enthralled*. "It's beautiful," he whispered in her direction.

She nodded and remained quiet, choosing to listen rather than add her own voice. She'd not been moved to sing in a long while and prayed for God's understanding. She hoped He'd be satisfied with her heart and mind alone singing His praises.

Several other songs followed, including one of her favorites, *Hark! The Herald Angels Sing*. When it ended, they all sat as the priest stepped to the podium by the altar.

"In the name of the Father, the Son, and the Holy Ghost, peace be with you." As Father Tierney spoke, he crossed himself and Vern nudged her.

She reprimanded him with her eyes, but smiled at the same time. And as the priest welcomed everyone and wished them a blessed Christmas, she found herself more fascinated by Vern's awe than the service itself. Maybe her action was a sacrilege, yet she couldn't help herself.

"A reading from Luke," Father Tierney said and lifted his chin high. "In those days a decree went out from Caesar Augustus that all the world should be enrolled."

Vern stared at the man and took in every word as the priest continued to recite the passage. Margaret couldn't count how often she'd heard this scripture read and knew most of it by heart. But she'd never *felt* it stronger than she did now, taking it in for the first time through Vern.

"And she gave birth to her first-born son . . ." The priest's words shot directly into Margaret's heart. ". . . and wrapped him in swaddling clothes, and laid him in a manger, because there was no room for them in the inn."

She shut her eyes, thinking not only of what she'd given up, but once again envisioning the lit candle in her parent's home. Last Christmas, she'd been there with them, yet they'd scolded her for spending too much time searching for what she'd lost. By their account, it had been too many wasted years of foolishness.

She shook her head to put her mind right and placed her attention solely on Father Tierney as he completed the passage.

Once finished, he cast the most radiant expression. "What I wouldn't give to have been there that night to see our Lord in the newness of His life. How many times have we heard this account and haven't fully grasped the depth of it?" He braced his hands on the podium and leaned forward. "I ask you now to close your eyes and imagine yourselves there." With a drawn-out pause, he gazed around the sanctuary, and with a slight wave, encouraged everyone to do as he asked.

Margaret turned her attention toward Vern, who had honored the priest's request. She took a deep breath and did the same.

The congregation became utterly quiet and reverent.

"Inhale the earthy scent of straw and animals," the priest went on, "and feel the coolness of the night on your face. The only sound you hear is the faint breathing of the barn animals, and the soft noises made by a tiny, newborn baby.

"All of you men, put yourself in Joseph's shoes. Imagine the panic he felt while searching for a place his wife could give birth. The city overflowed with travelers, and there was no room for them to go anywhere other than a stable. He wanted something better for Mary and the coming baby, but was led to the simplest of places. And now that the child had arrived, he stood proudly watching Him in the arms of His mother.

"I'd like for you ladies to picture yourself in Mary's place. A young woman, chosen by God to bear His son, and when the pains of birthing came upon her, she, too, must have felt fear and uncertainty.

"Imagine how overwhelming it was the first time she held the infant, Jesus, in her arms. Surely, she knew His life wouldn't be easy by any means, but her love for Him conquered every fear. She cradled God's greatest gift and held Him pressed close to her heart. I find it hard to comprehend the awe of that moment and the trust in God that both she and Joseph so faithfully bore."

The ache in Margaret's heart grew. This was too much. Her parents had thought it best for her to leave Ireland and start anew, yet did they realize how alone she'd be? She'd been sent away with no one.

Of course, they'd expected her to be with Cousin Mary. Even if she'd found her alive, a cousin she knew nothing about couldn't have filled the void inside her.

Her chest tightened further. If she didn't put her mind back in the proper place, she'd crumble and ruin everything for Vern. He deserved better.

She froze, feeling wholly lost. Every part of her began to ache. This wasn't supposed to happen. Not here. Not now.

She prided herself in being strong, but she'd never felt weaker.

"Margaret?" Vern lightly pushed his arm against hers. "Are you all right?"

She couldn't breathe. "No."

The congregation stood, and she didn't know why. She'd become so lost, she hadn't realized the priest's message had ended. Unable to stay another second, she took the opportunity to move from the pew and into the aisle.

As she left, she felt the eyes of everyone around her, following her down the aisle. They wouldn't understand her reason for leaving, but she didn't care. God knew everything, and nothing else mattered.

The minute she stepped outside, she deeply inhaled the crisp night air. It stung her lungs, reminding her she was alive. Still, she couldn't deny a part of her had died, and she'd buried that bit of herself in Ireland.

Vern took hold of her arm. "Are you sick?"

She couldn't look at him. "Please, take me home."

"All right." He kept hold of her, then guided her to the buggy and helped her into it.

The instant the horse started down the road, she burst into tears. She sobbed all the way home, and poor Vern simply drove the buggy and let her cry. She had no doubt she'd upset him, but she couldn't calm herself enough to talk to him and ask his forgiveness for ruining Mass.

He pulled in front of the boarding house and stopped the buggy, then turned sideways on the seat and faced her. "What's wrong, Margaret?"

She sucked in a large breath and wiped across her cheek with her coat sleeve. "I'm not who you believe me to be."

"You're wrong. I know you're troubled, but I really care about you. I think you're a wonderful woman."

"I'm no good. If I was, I could sing along with the congregation and set a decent Christian example for you." She sniffled, then looked him in the eyes. "I've seen how you look at me, and I know you feel something stronger than friendship. You deserve better than me, and I don't want you to come around any longer."

"Why?" The pain in his expression pierced her soul. "What did I do? I thought everything was fine. The service was beautiful, and—"

"It's not you, it's me! I can't keep pretending."

"I don't understand."

She clenched her fists. "I had a baby, Vern!"

As fast as she could, she got out of the buggy and pushed herself toward the safety of the boarding house. She didn't dare look back.

Now that he knew, he'd never gaze at her with any form of longing, but his disappointment was the least of her worries. She doubted she'd ever see him again.

CHAPTER 11

Vern's heart dropped in his chest like a leaded weight, and he could do nothing more than stare vacantly in the direction Margaret had gone.

A baby?

He'd assumed she was chaste—as virtuous as the Blessed Mother he'd just learned about.

The thought of her entwined with a man sickened him. She'd said nothing about having been married, so he could only assume . . .

Was she no better than the harlots who peddled themselves down by the river? Or like Minnie, who bore the worst kind of reputation? Oscar had said she'd been known to have cavorted with several *dozen* men. He'd wanted Vern to learn from her, but Vern wanted someone who knew nothing about intimacy, so they could become educated together. Two people who were both blissfully ignorant and curious.

He grasped the reins tighter and tighter and finally gave them a little snap to get Betsy moving. He needed to distance himself from Margaret.

But the farther away from her he went, the worse his heart hurt. Worse yet, his mind spun with so many questions, it made him light-headed.

She'd said there were things she didn't want to talk about, but a baby was more than a *thing*. She'd created a *person*.

Maybe that was why she'd left Ireland. She'd abandoned her child, just as his mama had done to him. No wonder her parents didn't correspond with her. They were ashamed of what she'd done. And since she'd been told by Mrs. Archer about his circumstances, maybe it was guilt that had driven Margaret to apologize to him. She'd *befriended* him only to make herself feel better.

"I should've listened to Mr. Hinze," he mumbled into the frigid air.

The man had warned him there was likely something wrong with Margaret—considering her age and lack of a husband.

A woman as pretty as her should be married by now.

She was *too* pretty. That was the problem. And she'd flaunted herself, enticing men, only to grow a child, then toss it away like trash.

How could she be so heartless?

He found himself driving mindlessly down the wrong road. This wasn't the way home.

Music floated into the air and penetrated his mind. The voices sounded incredibly joyful, and he realized his senselessness had returned him to St. Patrick's. Even being outside the building, he could make out the words being sung.

Joy to the world, the Lord is come, let earth receive her King!

His chest constricted and suddenly, unexpected tears emerged. He couldn't recall the last time he'd cried. But why now? Why *ever*? Men weren't supposed to cry.

Let every heart prepare Him room, and heaven and nature sing!

He hadn't heard Margaret sing a single word, and just as she'd confessed, her silence had set a poor Christian example. He'd thought she was good, yet every thought he'd had of her since she'd blurted out her unforgivable revelation was horribly ugly.

He pulled the buggy to a stop outside the church and let the music wash over him. He'd drunk in the priest's words like life-giving water in its purest form. He'd wanted what Margaret had—the understanding of a Savior meant for all mankind. She'd led him to this very place, and from the moment the service had started, he'd felt he belonged. He'd craved something within the walls of St. Patrick's that he'd never even known was absent in his life.

Joy to the world, the Savior reigns! Let men their songs employ!

The powerful music spoke to him and softened his anger.

I shouldn't judge her.

There had to be more to her story, and it was wrong to presume the worst.

All his life, he'd wanted to believe *his* mother had good reason for leaving *him* behind. He'd give anything to see her again and have the opportunity to ask *why*. Shouldn't he afford Margaret the same consideration?

Part of him wanted to go straight back to the boarding house and force her to tell him everything. A bigger part of him urged him to go home. Maybe Mr. and Mrs. Hinze could offer sound advice. They'd always done what was best for him and tried to lead him into making good choices. For something this important, they wouldn't steer him in the wrong direction.

But was it right to tell Margaret's secret?

He shivered, yet otherwise sat unmoving, staring at the snow-flakes as they passed his line of sight.

Betsy pawed the ground.

"All right, girl. Let's go home."

Mr. Simpson had been kind enough to allow him access to Betsy at the late hour. A few extra pastries had sparked some Christmas spirit in the man and he'd obliged the request.

One day, Vern wanted his own horse with a barn to put it in, and a big house with a faithful wife and lots of children. He'd hoped Margaret would be a part of that dream, yet everything had shattered. He felt almost as sick inside as the day he'd woken up on the front porch of the bakery.

Whenever he'd wondered whether or not his mama was dead, Mrs. Hinze had always told him to hold onto hope. He doubted she'd say the same about Margaret's situation—not if he told the truth. Mrs. Hinze would probably try to push him toward Mrs. Pennington's niece. A young woman Vern hadn't even met.

The idea didn't appeal to him in the slightest. As tainted as Margaret might be, his heart still held onto her.

Oscar had been right. He was hopeless and foolish. A disastrous combination.

* * *

Before going to his room, Vern lit up a cigarette, then sat on the front porch and savored every puff. The simple act soothed him, and he hoped it would also calm him enough to manage some sleep.

He'd half expected to find Mr. and Mrs. Hinze waiting up for him, but he was relieved to discover they'd gone to bed. Maybe by morning, he'd know what to tell them.

Christmas morning . . .

A smile oddly emerged, prompted by a happy memory. He'd never forget his first Christmas in the care of the Hinzes. Mrs. Hinze had flitted around the bakery for days, humming Christmas carols and decorating with fresh boughs and pretty hand-painted ornaments. The tunes she'd hummed were different from what he'd heard at St. Patrick's, but just as beautiful in their own right.

And on Christmas morning, he was given two presents. A bright red scarf she'd knitted, and a wooden boat Mr. Hinze had whittled. Vern had cried then, too. Happy to have gotten gifts at all, but also confused. As a young, recently abandoned boy, his tears hadn't been frowned upon. If anyone saw him do it now, they'd likely not be so understanding.

"Vern?"

Mr. Hinze startled him from his thoughts. "Hey, Mr. Hinze."

"You should be in bed, Son." He tightened his robe, crossed the porch and sat beside him, then studied his face. "Something's troubling you."

Vern took a long drag, using the time to decide what to say. He blew the smoke out just as slowly.

"Did something happen with Miss Jordan?" Mr. Hinze asked before he could answer, and his eyes widened as he spoke.

"What?" Surely, he didn't think he'd done something improper.

"I can tell you're out of sorts. You look as if you're feeling guilty about something, so I assumed—"

"That I took advantage of her?" Vern inhaled a faster puff, then pitched the butt on the porch and snuffed it out with his foot. "How could you think that?"

"That's not what I said *or* thought. From my understanding, you and she were at church for God's sake. I know you wouldn't do anything out of line there, or honestly, *anywhere* for that matter. I merely thought perhaps you two had another argument and you possibly felt bad about upsetting her. Especially at Christmas."

Vern bent forward and put his head in his hands. "I'm sorry." He fisted his hair with both hands and cinched his fingers around it. "I'm so confused. I don't know what to do."

"Tell me what happened. Maybe I can help." The man lightly patted his back.

He trusted Mr. Hinze more than anyone, and if he asked him to keep this between them and no one else, he knew he'd do it. Besides, if he *didn't* talk about this, he might burst.

"You were right about Margaret," he whispered.

"In what way?"

Vern breathed deeply, sat upright, and grasped the edge of the bench. "There *is* something wrong with her." He turned his head enough to see the man. "But if I tell you what it is, you can't repeat it to anyone."

"Of course. Whatever you say will stay between us."

Vern's heart beat harder. Maybe it cautioned him that this was a betrayal, but he couldn't hold it in. "She told me she had a baby."

"Oh, Son . . ." Mr. Hinze repeatedly tapped Vern's leg, slow and steady. "No wonder you look the way you do." His eyes searched Vern's face, and he stilled his hand. "Where's the child now?"

"I don't know." He lowered his head. "Truthfully, I don't know much of anything. She blurted it out and left me, along with telling me she was no good and I deserved better."

"So, she said nothing of the baby's father?"

"No." He wrapped his arms around his midsection and hugged himself. "I feel so sick inside. The night started off perfectly, and I really liked St. Patrick's. I think I finally understand what Christmas is all about." He cut his eyes toward Mr. Hinze, who nodded for him to continue.

"There was a lot of incredible music, and Father Tierney read the story from the Bible of how Jesus was born. After that, he asked everyone to close their eyes and try to imagine what it would've been like to be there in that stable. He said the men should picture being Joseph and the women being Mary. It must've gotten her thinking about her own baby, because right after that, she got up and left, and I followed her outside."

Vern shook his head and sat back again. "She's a mess, Mr. Hinze—hurting something awful. And when I drove away from the boarding house, I thought the worst of her. I figured she was no different from my mama. Just a woman who didn't hesitate leaving her child behind."

"And what do you think *now*?"

Vern appreciated how calmly Mr. Hinze had been taking the news. It made it easier to talk about. "I need to know more. I doubt she'd hurt so badly if she didn't care about her baby."

The man firmly folded his arms—a gesture Vern knew well. "Please, don't tell me you want to go back to her?"

"Not tonight." He sat defensively rigid. "And probably not to-morrow—or today, that is. The sun will be coming up soon enough. It's Christmas and I know Mrs. Hinze has been working hard to make it a special day. I don't want to ruin that for her by running off to see Margaret and likely getting even more upset." He looked straight at Mr. Hinze. "But eventually, I've got to see her and get some answers, or it'll keep weighing on my mind and troubling me. And as much as I hate to do it, we'll need to tell Mrs. Hinze about this. We promised not to keep things from her, and she won't understand why I'm hurting. I can't lie to her."

"Poor Annie." He huffed. "Can you try to act as if nothing happened until the holiday is over? This will hurt her terribly."

"Why? This doesn't affect her."

"Not directly, but it affects you." His eyes narrowed. "When *you* hurt, *she* hurts." He briskly rubbed up and down his arms and stood. "We should go inside. It's freezing out here, and we both need our sleep. As you said, the sun will be up soon—Annie with it."

Vern slowly got to his feet. "Will you promise me something else?"

"What?"

"Try not to think too badly of Margaret. Until we know the truth, I don't want you to dislike her."

The man's features tightened. "I'm sorry, Son, but I still feel she's wrong for you. Even as just a friend. I was concerned from the instant I met her, and knowing what you told me only deepens my apprehension."

"But I've seen the good in her." When Mr. Hinze's cautious expression didn't waver, Vern dropped his gaze. It was impossible to fully defend her, when he himself had thought poorly of her such a short time ago.

Mr. Hinze wrapped an arm around his shoulder. "Get some sleep, and maybe you'll see things more clearly in the morning."

"Yes, sir." With a heart heavier than ever, Vern walked inside, then trudged up the stairs to his room.

He doubted he'd sleep a wink.

* * *

"Merry Christmas!"

Mrs. Hinze's cheery voice roused Vern from a restless slumber. She poked her head into his room and jingled a string of bells. "There's hot schnecken and coffee in the kitchen!"

There was *always* schnecken and coffee in the kitchen, but Vern wouldn't douse her enthusiasm by pointing out that fact. "Merry Christmas, Mrs. Hinze," he mumbled, half-asleep.

She tittered. "I can't wait for you to tell me all about St. Patrick's! Hurry and get dressed." Giggling like a little girl, she flitted away.

Somehow, he had to plaster on the jolliest expression possible and not ruin her joy.

Morning had come, and *nothing* had become clearer. Even more so than last night, he wanted to see Margaret.

While remaining flat on his back in bed, he grabbed his pillow and held it over his face. Maybe he could hide from the world.

"Son?" Mr. Hinze walked in. "Annie's waiting."

Vern lowered the pillow. "She was just here. I haven't even had time to get out of bed yet."

"You know how much she loves Christmas morning. She's excited to give you your presents."

"All right. Give me five minutes and I'll join you."

He eyed Vern cautiously. "Smiling?"

After almost no sleep at all, Vern flashed the finest one he could. "Don't worry. I won't say a word about Margaret's *situation*."

"Good." He pivoted and headed for the hallway, then stopped in the doorway and faced him again. "Thank you, Son." With a pat to the doorframe, he left.

Obviously, Mr. Hinze hadn't stopped worrying about his wife's delicate feelings. And considering the man's reaction to Vern's enlightenment, he started wishing he'd kept everything to himself. It would've been best for everyone.

* * *

Margaret hadn't bothered changing into her nightgown before going to bed last night. She'd flopped onto her mattress fully clothed and hadn't budged since.

Thank heavens she didn't have to work today.

Where had her good senses gone? In order to have the clean start her parents had claimed she needed, she'd internally vowed not to tell a soul in America about her past, or more specifically, the child she'd birthed. The baby she'd never been allowed to hold.

When Father Tierney had spoken so passionately about the Savior's birth and what it must've been like in that stable, it had broken her—ripped her heart in half.

She'd never claimed to be as righteous as the Blessed Virgin, but she'd done all she could to please the Lord and follow His example. So why did it feel as if God had turned His back on her now?

No. She didn't want to think about it. Too many times had she already relived that horrible night.

Her mum had told her she had a greater purpose, and that she needed to let go of her anger and forget what had happened. Yet it hung over her like the darkest of shadows, and she couldn't simply wash it away or *let it go.*

"That's why I'm *here.*" She sat up, put her feet on the floor, and stood.

With no enthusiasm whatsoever, she trudged across the floor to the water basin and splashed some of the cool liquid on her face. She'd stopped crying as soon as she'd reached the front door of the boarding house, but she'd wept so hard, her tender, swollen eyes carried the effect of the shed tears.

At least she'd had the sense to decline Vern's invitation to Christmas dinner. Mrs. Williams had already told her about a traditional boarding house celebration put on by her and her daughter for all the residents. She'd made it clear she wanted Margaret to attend.

Even so, Margaret doubted she'd leave her room today. Not only was she not hungry, she didn't want to see anyone.

Except Vern.

Regardless of his youthfulness and sometimes troubling disposition, she adored him. Something unexplainable kept drawing her to him.

She dropped down onto the edge of her bed and limply sat there, staring at the wall.

If she had the chance to explain about the baby, maybe he'd be understanding. Yet, in order to do that, she'd have to verbalize what had happened that night. The mere thought of it sickened her, so how could she bring herself to say the words out loud?

There was an alternative—one she'd done before.

She could pack her things and leave. Board the next train, stagecoach, or steamboat leaving Kansas City and go somewhere else. *Any*where else.

She'd saved a little money, so it was doable. However, the holiday posed a problem. All forms of transportation would be halted.

She'd have to wait.

For now, she'd keep to herself, and if Mrs. Williams came to fetch her, she'd claim to be ill. That would keep the old woman away and allow Margaret complete privacy.

She flopped backward and shut her eyes. Unfortunately, the simple idea of leaving brought on a reemergence of tears. She let them fall silently down her cheeks and onto the bedding below.

"Happy Christmas, Margaret," she whispered, then curled into a ball and simply tried to breathe.

* * *

"Merry Christmas!" Mrs. Hinze grabbed Vern the minute he stepped off the final stair and hugged him.

"Merry Christmas, Mrs. Hinze." He delivered his reply with greater vigor than the earlier one and plastered on his best smile.

It was obviously convincing, because her happy expression didn't dim in the slightest. She took his hand, shuffled him to the kitchen table, and shoved a plate into his grasp. "Get some schnecken and a cup of coffee, then come upstairs to the tree."

The common room on the upper floor was small, and they only used it on Christmas morning. On any other day, they gathered in the kitchen. He figured she'd put a tree there if Mr. Hinze would allow it, but it'd be bad for business if the needles got into the bread, or if the pine smell overpowered the fresh-baked aroma.

Vern dutifully loaded his plate, then poured a cup of coffee and returned upstairs to the sound of Mrs. Hinze humming. She'd moved a chair close to the five-foot tree and sat there, beaming. Several brown paper-wrapped packages lay at her feet.

Three days ago, he'd placed the gifts he'd gotten for the two of them at the back of the tree, along with one for Margaret. All the activities Mrs. Hinze had planned would give him a good excuse not to take it to the boarding house today. And if all went well, he'd find a way to keep their conversations far from the subject of Margaret Jordan.

Mr. Hinze positioned another chair across from his wife and sat, holding his own plate of schnecken. Though a family tradition to eat it every Christmas morning, they had to be tired of it. Vern loved the pastry the first time he'd tasted it and for a good while after, but smelling it day in and day out had diminished the specialness of the sweet bread. Regardless, he happily ate it to appease Mrs. Hinze.

Just as he'd done since he was a boy, he took a seat on the floor in front of the tree. He secured the pastry plate on his lap, and set the steaming cup of coffee beside him.

Mrs. Hinze extended one of the wrapped packages. "You first."

He took it from her and loosened the strings that held it together. From the feel of it, he could tell it was an item of clothing.

"It's a shirt," she said, before he'd finished opening it.

Mr. Hinze grunted, grinned, and shook his head.

Vern laughed. "Thank you." Once he got the paper removed, he uncovered a finely sewn blue cotton shirt. He held it in front of himself. "I like it."

"Mrs. Pennington recommended the most incredible seamstress. She makes clothes for Mrs. Pennington's niece as well." The way she said it, Vern swore she was still trying to push him in the niece's direction. Once she learned about Margaret, she'd be relentless.

"That's good." Vern decided to keep his reply simple, and he smoothed the front of the shirt flat against his chest. "I think it'll fit, but I'll try it on later, so we can finish exchanging gifts. Thank you again." He smiled at her and Mr. Hinze in turn.

Mr. Hinze handed him a smaller package. "I had *this* made for you."

"You both always do too much." He quickly opened the little parcel and stared at the well-crafted leather wallet.

"To hold all that money you're going to make," Mr. Hinze said. "I decided you needed to start carrying your cash like a man. You've grown beyond being a boy who shoves bills into his pockets."

Mrs. Hinze leaned close and eyed the wallet. "Mr. Simpson did a lovely job." She lifted her gaze to meet Vern's. "I want you to be certain every dollar you put in there is earned honestly."

"It will be." He waved the thing in the air. "I love this. Thank you."

Mr. Hinze reached under the tree and passed over a package to his wife.

She giggled and took it, then wildly tore off the paper. "Oh, Dietrich . . ." With a dreamy sigh, she lifted the dress high. "You ordered this special, didn't you?"

"Yes. From *Strawbridge and Clothier*, just as you wanted."

"That's fancy," Vern said. "I've never seen so many ruffles." The bright turquoise gown was dotted with a pattern of roses and an abundance of lace. "It'll look beautiful on you, but where will you wear it?"

"Wherever she pleases," Mr. Hinze said. "Even behind the shop counter if she'd like."

She held a hand to her face and shook her head. "I couldn't. I won't risk staining it. Perhaps you can take me to dinner at Linderman's, and I can wear it there." She grinned in Vern's direction. "Maybe we can go on a night Margaret can join us."

Vern gulped. "You and Mr. Hinze should go without me. The two of you rarely have the opportunity to be alone."

Mr. Hinze retrieved another package and gave it to her. "There's more."

"No. You shouldn't have done all this." Though she said it, she wasted no time opening the wrap. She held up a hat that perfectly matched the dress, including the large red rose adorning one side of it. Beaming as bright as the North Star, she put it on and tied the large turquoise bow under her chin.

"Beautiful," Mr. Hinze whispered.

She promptly kissed his cheek.

Vern took the opportunity to remove his gifts for them from the back of the tree, and also shoved the one for Margaret out of sight. "I'm afraid my presents to you aren't so elaborate, but they're given with love." He gave them their appropriate packages, and they opened them simultaneously.

"My favorite brand of tobacco," Mr. Hinze said. "Thank you, Vern."

"I wanted to get you some machine-rolled cigarettes, but they're hard to find. For now, I guess we'll keep on rolling."

"I've been doing it a long time. That's fine by me." He tucked the pouch of tobacco into his pocket.

"Vern." Mrs. Hinze cast a gaze similar to the way she'd admired the dress. "What about this isn't elaborate? It had to have cost you a fortune." She ran her fingers along the broach. "It's the Christmas star, isn't that right?"

"Yes. I didn't know much about it when I bought it. I just thought it was pretty and something you'd like. It has more meaning now."

"I love it, Vern. I take it you learned about the Star of Bethlehem at St. Patrick's last night?"

"Yes'm. Merry Christmas, Mrs. Hinze. I hope every year when you wear that, you'll think of me."

She fanned her face. "Don't start talking that way. The last thing I want today is to think about you leaving." She held the broach over her heart. "That being said, I'll treasure this forever."

Mr. Hinze looked his way and smiled, likely grateful for the quick change of subject.

"There's only one more gift," Mrs. Hinze said, reaching way back under the branches.

Vern nearly stopped her, until he realized she was withdrawing a different package than Margaret's. She handed the small box to her husband. "With my love, Dietrich."

He chuckled as he revealed what was inside. "A pipe?"

"Vern's tobacco will work for that, won't it?"

"Not exactly. It's processed differently, and pipe tobacco is moister. But what inspired you to buy this for me?"

"You're getting on in years, and I've always thought a pipe is more sophisticated-looking." She bit her lower lip. "Do you hate it?"

He put it in his mouth and posed with his chin lifted high, then grinned and withdrew it. "Not in the least, Annie. I'll be happy to give it a try."

"I can buy you some pipe tobacco," Vern said, a bit surprised he'd not remarked about his wife's *getting on in years* remark. Even in a jesting *Christmassy* way. "After all, I spent a whole lot more on your wife than I did on you."

Mrs. Hinze stood tall and proud. "I feel very spoiled. Thank you both." Her smile had returned full force. "I'd best get to the kitchen and start preparing our Christmas dinner. The goose won't roast itself."

She carefully folded the fancy dress and placed it back under the tree, along with the hat and pin. Then, happy as ever, she left the small room.

Vern watched her leave. "I'd say we did good," he said as soon as he heard her reach the bottom step.

"Better than good." Mr. Hinze patted him on the back. "And if we can keep this going until tomorrow, I'll say we succeeded."

"By protecting her *delicate feelings*?"

"Not exactly. Annie is a blessing I'm grateful for every day of my life. I love to see her happy, and since we don't know how many more Christmases we'll have with you, I wanted to make this one an extra special memory for her to cherish. So, thank you for helping me achieve it."

His sincerity tugged at Vern's heart. "I can't begin to tell you how much I want what you two have with each other."

"I want that for you, too." His expression turned utterly serious. "Give it time, Vern. The right woman is out there for you somewhere." He gave him another pat, then left the room.

Maybe he realized Vern needed to be alone to contemplate his words. Or perhaps the man just wanted to go and be with his wife —the love of his life.

Vern knelt in front of the tree, then bent low and retrieved Margaret's gift. He took it to his room and tucked it safely in the back corner of his bureau drawer. One day, he'd know when the time was right to give it to her. For now, he'd enjoy the company of the people who'd raised him, loved him, and were teaching him how to be a respectful, independent man.

As he descended the stairs to the lower floor, his thoughts shifted to Margaret.

He prayed *she'd* found a way to enjoy the celebration of Jesus' birth today, yet he feared her troubled heart might keep her from it.

CHAPTER 12

The busyness of the Christmas holiday carried over into preparations for the coming New Year celebrations.

There'd been no time at all for Vern to even *think* about when to see Margaret. After enjoying a somewhat relaxing Christmas Day, he and Mr. Hinze hit the ground running the following morning. Specialized orders were brought in the moment the bakery opened.

Mrs. Hinze remained in the shop, while Vern and Mr. Hinze baked up a storm of goods. Whenever the kitchen door opened, Vern knew another order had come in.

He wiped his sweaty brow with the back of his arm, taking care not to get flour from his hands on his face, or worse yet, into his eyes. "Are we being punished for enjoying a day off to celebrate Christmas?"

Mr. Hinze chuckled, while vigorously kneading. "If good business is punishment, then I'll happily accept the reprimand."

The kitchen door opened, and Mrs. Hinze peeked her head through the crack.

"Another order?" Vern asked.

She frowned. "No. Mrs. Archer is here, and she's asked to see you."

He shot a glance at Mr. Hinze, whose enthusiasm plummeted. Not only had Vern not had time to see Margaret, he'd also not had the opportunity to tell Mrs. Hinze about the evening at Mass. Once she learned she'd been kept in the dark, she'd surely be upset.

"Me?" Vern pointed at himself.

"Yes. She said it involves Margaret." She faced her husband. "I believe it's serious in nature, so . . . should I invite her to come here to the kitchen, or would it be best for Vern to speak with her in the shop?"

He punched a fist into the dough, then yanked his shoulders back and stood erect. "Have her come here. I can't leave the ovens, but if it's something that needs to be said privately, Vern can take her upstairs to the common room and speak with her there."

"All right." Her lips twitched into a smile. "I'm glad I straightened the room this morning." She shut the door, then several seconds later, it reopened for Mrs. Archer. Mrs. Hinze returned to the front counter, where several other customers could be heard conversing.

Mrs. Archer hastened across the floor to Vern. "I know how busy you are, but I'm beside myself, and coming here was the only solution I could think of." She glanced at Mr. Hinze. "Forgive my intrusion."

"It's fine. What can we do to help?"

She faced Vern again. "I know you and Miss Jordan have been spending time together. Were you aware of her plans to leave Kansas City?"

The words slapped hard. "What?"

"My assumption was right." Her features drew in with worry. "You didn't know."

"Is she already gone?" His heart raced and his feet wanted to follow just as fast, right out the door.

"She came to the restaurant a short while ago to tell me she couldn't work any longer, and that she was leaving the city. I'm quite sure she's already at Union Depot, waiting on a train." The poor woman had never looked more distraught. "I'm being selfish, but I need her. Ever since little Matthew was born, I've relied on

Miss Jordan to help run the business. She's a gem I can't afford to lose."

"Did you tell her that?"

"Yes, but it made no difference." She firmed her jaw. "Miss Jordan can be headstrong. When she makes up her mind about something, she rarely wavers."

He knew that fact well. She had a feistiness about her that could be infuriating, but was also part of her charm. "Why come to me?"

"Because I know she cares about you. Did the two of you have a falling out?" She shook her head and waved her hands. "Don't answer that. It's none of my concern, yet if you did . . ." She leaned close. "Tell her you're sorry and ask her to stay. Please?"

Mr. Hinze roughly cleared his throat. "My son has nothing to apologize for. If Miss Jordan has decided to leave, it's not up to him to stop her." He puffed out his chest. "There must be plenty of others in this vast city who you can train to take her place." The man returned to the mound of dough on the kneading table and began pounding away at it once more.

"At present, I haven't the time or energy to teach someone new. We have multiple dinner parties scheduled through the New Year." She released a long, sad sigh and lowered her head.

Vern could scarcely stand still. "Are you sure she's at Union Depot?"

Her head popped right up. "Yes. She said she had a train to catch, so where else would she go?"

He shifted his attention to the Mr. Hinze—the man he respected more than any other. "I know you need me here, but I can be quick."

"I can take him," Mrs. Archer rapidly added. "Eustace is waiting with our buggy outside."

Mr. Hinze huffed. "Go on, then." He held up a single finger. "Come back as fast as you can. And if that young woman is insistent on leaving, you have to let her go."

"Yes, sir." Vern threw off his apron, grabbed his coat, and sped through the door. He passed Mrs. Hinze without saying a word.

Once he got to the buggy, Mrs. Archer arrived as well, obviously driven by just as much eagerness.

They rode silently to the train station, but Mr. Archer kept the horses moving fast. Vern assumed his wife had voiced her frustration and the man was doing all he could to keep her satisfied.

Since Linderman's served only lunch and dinner, unlike the bakery, mornings at the restaurant didn't involve direct contact with customers. If they did, the Archers wouldn't have been able to leave and seek his help. And if that had happened, by the time he learned Margaret had left, it would've been too late for him to do anything about it. Exactly as it had been all those years ago with his mother.

He hoped it wasn't already too late.

* * *

Margaret dropped her money on the ticket counter. "I'd like to go as far as this will take me. And just a regular passenger seat, please. Not a sleeping car."

The booking clerk studied the combination of coins and bills, then looked her in the eyes. "You don't have a specific destination?" He wrinkled his nose, lifting his black mustache.

"No, sir. I want you to give me a ticket and tell me which train to get on, but don't tell me where it'll take me. I don't care to know."

His head drew back. "Are you in some kind of trouble?"

"'Tis my business and not yours. Please, just do as I asked."

"All right." He counted the money, then ran his finger along a schedule in front of him. "How soon do you want to be on your way?"

"As quickly as possible."

"Hmm . . ." He glided his finger over the list again, then tapped a particular line. "You sure you don't want to know where?"

"Quite." She lifted her chin, acting as confident as possible.

"What if you don't care for the destination when you get there?"

She leaned over the counter. "Send me anywhere but Hades, and I'll like it perfectly fine." With a brisk nod, she stood fully upright once more.

He lightly chuckled. Though she'd been completely serious, her remark seemed to have humored him.

He produced a ticket and handed it to her. "The train won't be leaving the station for another hour, so I hope you don't mind the wait."

"An hour is acceptable."

He rubbed his chin. "I can't help but ask, what's so wrong with Kansas City that you want to leave?"

She nervously tapped her foot. "You ask too many questions." As confidently as she could manage, she took the ticket and tucked it into her coat pocket. "Which train?"

"Number five." He pointed. "You can wait over there, and when the train comes in for boarding, you'll go out that door to the loading platform. But I have to warn you, when they call for passengers, they'll name the destination. You'll know then where you're headed."

"Fine. Until then, I'll enjoy contemplating where it might be." She gave him another curt nod. "Thank you."

She headed in the direction he'd indicated, then took a seat on a long wooden bench similar to the pews at St. Patrick's. Wherever she went, she hoped to find a place of worship as inviting as it had been. It bothered her not having had the opportunity to tell Father Tierney goodbye, but it was probably for the best. He'd surely noticed the way she'd left in the middle of Mass and would likely question her about it. Avoiding that conversation suited her.

As calmly as she could, she placed her carpet bag beside her and folded her hands on her lap, then thought better of it and checked the satchel at her wrist, counting the remaining money within it. She'd not given the ticket clerk *all* of her money and hoped she'd kept enough for later use. She'd need funds to arrange lodging somewhere.

Hopefully, she'd spent a sufficient amount to get her far enough away to alleviate the temptation to return. As fond as she'd grown of Kansas City, she hated the idea of coping with the hateful looks and nasty murmurs she'd be forced to endure once everyone learned her secret. Now that she'd told it, it wouldn't take long for it to spread. People thrived on gossip.

With every passing minute, the station became busier. Probably holiday travelers going home, or possibly new arrivals coming to spend the New Year with family. People bustled in and out of numerous doors and shuffled hurriedly across the floor.

She'd not set foot in Union Depot before today, and its vastness and beauty overwhelmed her, with its tall ceilings and fantastic archways. Unfortunately, her poor mood crushed her appreciation of its fineness.

The weather had become so cold, the idea of traveling by steamboat—as she'd done before—didn't appeal, nor did the thought of riding in close quarters with others inside a stagecoach. Although she couldn't afford a sleeping car, she hoped with so many seats available on a train, she could avoid conversation.

Would she go east or west, north or south?

Feeling a rush of uncomfortable warmth, she removed her scarf, then unfastened the top buttons of her coat. Several men passed by, tipped their hats, smiled, and kept going. Thank goodness they didn't pause to converse, or worse yet, sit near her.

She shut her eyes and prayed running away was the right decision.

The sense that someone else was near popped her lids open again. If one of those men had come back . . .

"Margaret?"

No . . .

Though not wanting to see him at all, she begrudgingly faced him. "Vern? What are you doing here?" The pain in his eyes didn't help her disposition. The sight cut a deeper hole in her heart and worsened the ache.

"I came to find you," he said with sincerity, "and thank God I did. Why are you leaving Kansas City?"

She faced forward and squared her jaw. "'Tis a foolish question. You know very well why."

"No, I don't. Mrs. Archer is beside herself, wondering how she'll ever replace you, so she came to me for help. And I'm glad for that, or I wouldn't have known you were leaving and been given the chance to talk you out of this."

"Don't even try, Vern. I'm going, and you can't stop me."

"I won't force you to stay, but I don't want you to go."

Her heart constricted, and all the pain she'd been feeling doubled. She scooted farther away, then shifted in the seat to face him. "I saw how you looked at me when I told you m' secret. I don't believe you want me anywhere near you any longer. Surely, Mrs. Archer asked you to say all those things."

"She thinks I'm the only person who can convince you to stay, because she knows we care about each other. But it's not because of her that I'm here. The second she told me you were leaving the city, I wanted to race out the door and find you." His eyes misted over. "I know you have more to tell me about . . . well . . . you know. And when you're ready, I'm here to hear it. I don't understand why you think running away from me will help."

"Running from *you*?" She rubbed across her aching chest. "'Tis not you I fear, but the hatefulness of others when they learn the truth. I'd do Mrs. Archer little good if every patron who came into the restaurant whispered ugly things about me. I'd have no respect from anyone, and I'd end up hurting Linderman's, not helping."

His head tipped to the side, and his features scrunched tight. "How would they know?"

"Gossip travels faster than wildfire."

"Only if it's told." He straightened his posture. "Do you think *I* told?"

"Are you saying you didn't?" She widened her eyes, challenging him.

"Well . . ." He swallowed hard, then breathed a bit faster. "I told Mr. Hinze, but no one else. Not even his wife. Yet, I'll be honest, I intended to tell her."

She patted her lap with both hands. "There you have it. That's exactly how it starts. One person tells another, then another, and it never stops."

"You're wrong. I trust them more than anyone. If I ask them not to tell, they won't."

"I trusted *you*, and you told."

"Yes, but you didn't say I couldn't—or *shouldn't*." He rapidly licked his lips. "You have to understand, when you said what you did, it tore me up inside. It hurt worse than any physical pain I've ever had. Worse than that punch in the eye. I *needed* to talk about it."

"Then why not come back to *me*? Discuss it in depth with me alone?"

"Are you serious?" He folded his arms and grunted. "You sent me away. You made it clear you didn't want to talk about it at all. *I'm* not at fault here."

"Shh . . ." She put a finger to her lips, then darted her eyes around the depot. Fortunately, it appeared as if nobody was paying them any mind. "Fault is oftentimes misconstrued," she forcefully whispered. "You don't know everything, Vern Harpole."

"No, I don't. And I suppose I never will. Because you're going to leave on a train to only God knows where, and I'll be left here, wondering." He looked behind him, then at her again. "Good thing Mrs. Archer's husband is with her. I've never seen her so out of sorts. She relies on you, Margaret."

She looked in the direction he had, and sure enough, there stood Mrs. Archer clinging to her husband's arm, appearing as frightened as a rabbit. When she'd told her she was leaving, she'd asked her to stay, but Margaret had been so determined to go, she'd not paid attention to the woman's pleas.

"If you play your cards right," Vern said, "you might even get a raise in pay. If you're that valuable, they'd be foolish not to offer it."

"Play m' cards right?" She eyed him cautiously. "Have you taken to card-playing along with pool?"

"I've considered it. After all, a man needs *something* to occupy his free time. Especially when the woman he'd rather be spending it with decides to move away."

"You're not in your right mind."

"Because I occasionally like to gamble?"

"No." She stared downward. "Because you said you want to spend time with me, even after knowing m' secret." She forced herself to look him in the eyes, and kept her voice barely above a whisper. "I lost my virtue, Vern, and it's something a woman can't regain. You deserve someone pure."

"I don't know what I deserve, but I *do* know I care about you. I didn't come back to you right away, though I intended to eventually. Not only did I need a few days to sort through what you told me, but I wanted to give you the opportunity to calm down and *maybe* be willing to tell me more. So, never think I don't care. It's just the opposite. I probably care too much. Regardless, if you leave, none of it matters anyway."

He *sounded* sincere. But why should that be enough to make her reconsider? She shouldn't care about him at all. He'd been complicating her life from the day she'd met him.

Still . . .

"Do you plan to tell your mum my secret?"

"I've kept important things from her before, and it only ends up hurting her. So, yes, I'll probably tell her—only because she needs to know why I've been hurting. I put on a false face for Christmas, but I can't keep it up forever."

"I didn't mean to hurt you, yet I suppose news like I shared would pain anyone. Especially the way it came out. I told you it would be best to forget me."

He sadly shook his head. "You still don't understand. It's not the news that hurt me the worst, it was you telling me to go—not wanting me around anymore."

Yes, he cared too much, and though she hated to admit it to herself, it touched her deeply, in a good way. "Are you certain your parents will keep this to themselves?"

He placed a hand to his heart. "If I ask them to, I swear they will."

She lowered her head and focused on the depot floor. "They'll never see me the same way, nor will you. I don't know if I can live with that."

"You're being silly, Margaret, and you don't listen very well. You're the same woman I met three months ago." He let out a slight laugh. "Hard to believe so much has happened in such a short amount of time. You make being a friend quite an adventure." He chuckled a little more, then his expression sobered. "Don't go. Please?"

She withdrew the ticket from her pocket. "I don't even know where this will take me."

"You didn't ask?"

"I told the ticket clerk not to tell me. I just laid out m' money and paid for the ride. So, you were right when you said I was going where only God knew." A laugh escaped her. "You see, I listened better than you thought."

He snatched the small piece of paper from her grasp and studied it. "Oh. *No*. You don't want to go there." He got to his feet and headed for the ticket office.

She jumped up and hastened after him. "You can't swipe m' ticket away. I need it."

"No, you don't."

"Yes, I do!"

He stopped in the middle of the floor and glared at her. "No. You. *Don't*."

She fisted her hands on her hips, then deflated and let her arms fall to her sides. "You truly want me to stay?"

With a much softer expression, he nodded.

People passing by cast odd looks, but they kept walking—all with a greater purpose.

She held out her hand, palm up. "May I have m' ticket please?"

His shoulders drooped and he eyed her warily, then he did as she asked and laid it on her palm.

She marched to the ticket window and set it on the counter in front of the man who'd issued it. "I changed m' mind. I've decided not to leave Kansas City. May I have a refund?"

He looked beyond her, and she turned to see what he was staring at, only to find Vern watching them with more uncertainty in his gaze than she'd seen on Christmas Eve.

She returned her attention to the clerk. "M' refund?"

He obliged her, and she tucked the money into her satchel. She intended to put it back in the hiding place in her room at the boarding house. It would remain there until she decided whether or not staying had been the right decision.

She walked over to Vern. "Can you give me a ride to Miss Polly's?"

"*I* can't, but I think the Archers can." He pointed over his shoulder.

She nearly laughed. Dear Mrs. Archer's elation boiled out of her. The woman was practically dancing on the depot floor, no doubt realizing she'd changed her mind about going. "I hope Mrs. Williams hasn't already rented m' room."

"It's unlikely, but if she has, there are other boarding houses in Kansas City. If need be, I'm sure Mrs. Archer will give you a place to stay till you find another one."

A heaviness lifted from her shoulders as she walked alongside Vern toward the Archers. "I'm staying, Vern, but please don't pry me with questions. For now, can you be content talking to me about anything other than *that?*"

"I'll be your friend, and whatever you choose to share with me, will suit me fine. I won't pry."

"Good." She stopped and grabbed hold of his arm. "And please, beg your parents not to speak of it."

"I won't have to beg. They're good people, Margaret. They'll respect your privacy."

"Thank you." She released him, and they continued on.

Mrs. Archer hugged Margaret so hard it took her breath, and she kept an arm around her all the way to the waiting buggy. Maybe she feared it was the only way to ensure she wouldn't change her mind and race back into the depot.

Mr. Archer helped her onto the seat, and Mrs. Archer sat beside her. Because there wasn't enough room for Vern, he perched on the tail board. It wouldn't be the most comfortable ride for him, but he didn't complain. Maybe it was best they had some distance between them. Now that all of them were together, an air of discomfort flooded over her. She assumed he felt it, too.

As the buggy departed the station, conflicted emotions took hold. She was happy to be staying, yet worried her secret would surface.

Ever since she'd been so brutally scarred and spurned, trusting anyone at all had become an issue. But something about the way Vern and the Archers had come to stop her from leaving town warmed her. Maybe the time had come to let her guard down and allow herself to be cared for.

The New Year could prove to be the perfect opportunity to reevaluate her life and her future.

She shivered.

It wouldn't be easy.

CHAPTER 13

Vern stood for a brief moment on the bakery porch and watched Margaret ride away with the Archers, then hurried inside and went straight to the kitchen.

As he passed Mrs. Hinze, she cast a questioning gaze, but he had no time to talk at present, nor was he ready to.

He hung up his coat and donned his apron, then washed his hands and got busy. "More orders?" He gestured to the small sheets of paper on the far counter.

"Yep," Mr. Hinze said. "But nothing we can't manage." He pushed the long wooden paddle under the bread in the oven and slowly withdrew it. Perfectly browned and beautiful.

Vern had learned to appreciate a good loaf of bread, though he rarely ate much of it. It was their life's blood, and if they prepared it poorly, they'd pay a miserable price.

"So . . ." Mr. Hinze positioned the bread on cooling racks, then returned the paddle to its place. "Did she leave?"

"No, sir. She decided to stay." Vern grabbed a bowl to mix glaze for the soon-to-be-done sweetbread.

"I see . . ." The man let out a long breath. "Did she say anything else about *the baby*?" He whispered the words.

"No. I honestly didn't expect her to. She may never be ready to tell me the details. And I have to confess, it bothers me not to know." He measured out the proper amount of confectioners' sugar, then went to the icebox for the milk he needed.

Mr. Hinze said nothing and kept working.

Vern had assumed he'd have a lot more to say, yet the man seemed exceptionally sullen.

"Are you upset because I left?" Vern finally asked after too many quiet minutes had passed.

"Not exactly." He rolled out a ball of dough, brushed on a mixture of cinnamon and sugar, then cut the pastry into strips. "I'd hoped she'd already gotten on that train."

"What?" Vern stopped mixing and stared at him. "Why would you want that?"

"Because she's not right for you, Son. Any woman who'd get herself into that kind of trouble is bad news. You deserve a *good* girl."

"I'm so tired of being told what I *deserve*!" He snapped his mouth shut, immediately feeling terrible for raising his voice. "I'm sorry, sir, but everyone keeps telling me I deserve better—even Margaret herself. Doesn't what I *want* matter more?"

"You'd want a woman like that?"

"Like what? She's beautiful, kind, and . . . spunky. I like that about her."

Mr. Hinze rolled the dough into pinwheels and placed them in the baking pan, frowning all the while. "She's tainted, Vern."

"Aren't we all—in one way or another?"

"You know what I mean." He lifted his head from his work and looked directly at him. "If you continue to pursue her, you'll be playing with fire. How do you know her child's father won't come searching for her? Or perhaps, there are other men, too. Just because she goes to church doesn't mean she's good."

"You don't know her," Vern said as forcefully as he could, without raising his voice.

"Neither do you."

Mr. Hinze kept his eyes on Vern as if expecting another outburst, but Vern couldn't utter a word. He decided to put all his attention on the glaze—and whatever else needed to be done to fill the orders—and keep his muddled thoughts to himself.

A full hour ticked by in total silence.

"Annie is full of questions," Mr. Hinze said, startling Vern from his thoughts. "Once we close for the day, all of us should talk. Annie needs to know what happened."

"Will she be as judgmental as you?"

"Vern. Try to see things from my perspective. We only want what's best for you."

He sluggishly nodded, but felt sicker inside than ever. "I know you care, but can't you at least try to trust *my* judgment? If you're this negative when we tell your wife about Margaret, she'll think the worst of her before any of us have given her the chance to explain. Has it crossed your mind that maybe Margaret was *molested*?" He barely breathed out the word, hating to think it, let alone, say it.

The man's face shadowed over and he stood motionless. "It honestly didn't. Do you think it's a possibility?"

"Considering how she behaves—all distant and mistrusting—yes, I do. Sadly, it makes more sense than any other scenario. And if that did happen to her, she's gone through hell. She *needs* a good friend."

"If you find out it's true, it still doesn't explain what became of her child."

"Maybe she gave it up." Vern stared vacantly at the bowl in his hands. "What woman would want to look at a child every day of her life who reminded her of the awful way it came into the world?"

"But the child isn't to blame."

"I know." He lifted his head and met the man's gaze. "Better than most anyone. Maybe learning more about Margaret and what she went through might help me understand my own mother and why she made the choices she did."

"The situations are very different."

"I agree, but there's always more to every story. All I ask is that you try not to be so harsh where Margaret's concerned. Give her a chance."

Still frowning, Mr. Hinze nodded. "I won't interject my thoughts when you tell Annie. I'll let her make up her own mind."

"Thank you."

Vern stirred the bowl of creamy glaze, then dipped his fingers into it and drizzled it over the cooled sweetbread, as Mrs. Hinze had taught him to do. The sugary mixture fell from his fingertips and formed perfect lines on the bread.

Once again, the kitchen fell silent.

Surely, Mr. Hinze was contemplating all Vern had said, which was a good thing. Vern had been mulling it over in *his* mind ever since Margaret had blurted out her secret. After he'd gotten over the hurt and anger, he'd tried to put himself in her shoes.

His mind would rest once he learned all of the truth. Considering it might not come for a long while—if ever—he needed to accept what he knew about her now, or let her go, just as Mr. Hinze wanted him to.

* * *

Margaret stood in the parlor with her hands folded in front of herself, feeling like a reprimanded child. "I'm sorry for the trouble, Mrs. Williams."

The old woman sat in an overstuffed chair, close to the flickering fire. Her cat, Hamlet, lay curled up on her lap, and she mindlessly stroked the feline's long gray fur. "You're an odd young woman. Telling me one minute you're catching a train, and the next, informing me you decided not to leave. I should charge you extra for the inconvenience."

"But I've paid what I owe for m' rent. M' indecision cost you nothing."

"Perhaps." She pushed Hamlet from her lap, and the cat raced down the hallway. "However, it's improper not to give sufficient notice when you decide to vacate your room. I need ample time to secure another boarder."

"As I said, I'm sorry. It won't happen again."

"If it does, don't expect me to be so forgiving. You'll forfeit your room." Mrs. Williams flitted her hand, silently telling Margaret to go.

She hurried up the stairs, glad to distance herself from the woman.

When the Archers had returned her to Miss Polly's, it had taken Mrs. Williams some time to answer the door. Margaret had discovered it locked and vigorously knocked, but she'd been ignored. Perhaps the old woman had been sleeping, yet Margaret believed she'd made her remain on the porch for an entire hour to punish her. Even the other tenants made no attempt to open the door. Mrs. Williams had probably warned them not to.

Margaret hastened to her room, and to her relief, found it completely unchanged. Not even the bedding had been stripped.

Soon, she'd need to ready herself for work. When she'd told Mrs. Archer she could help with the dinner parties tonight, the woman was so relieved, she'd given Margaret another hug. Maybe Vern had been right about asking for additional pay.

In time . . .

She knelt on the floor and removed the satchel from her wrist, then withdrew all the bills from within it. She bent way down, felt underneath the bed, and tucked the cash between the wood slats and the mattress.

Once she'd taken care of that business, she perched on the edge of her bed and gazed around the room. Nothing was truly *hers*. And as Mrs. Williams had so harshly reminded her, it could be taken from her use at the woman's whim. Another step out of line, and Margaret would need to find somewhere else to live.

That might be a good thing. As convenient as Miss Polly's was to Linderman's, she'd prefer living somewhere *pleasant*. Regardless of whether or not it meant a longer walk to work.

For now, she'd stay. Especially since she didn't know how long it would be. If Vern was wrong, and Mr. and Mrs. Hinze talked, nothing would keep her here.

* * *

Business had been slow for the past hour. Vern could tell Mrs. Hinze wanted to close early, but since they always abided by their posted schedule, the idea wasn't even considered. She'd started to ask him questions more than once, and whenever she did, her husband stopped her and told her to wait.

The final minutes passed, and Vern followed Mr. Hinze into the shop, expecting to gather at one of the small tables to talk.

Mr. Hinze flipped the sign in the bakery window to *closed*. "Let's go sit at the kitchen table," he said and headed in that direction. "I don't want anyone to pass by and see us, and think we're still open."

Vern silently followed him, as did Mrs. Hinze. Tension hung thick.

She quickly sat. "All right. I want to know everything. What happened to Miss Jordan that involved Vern?"

Mr. Hinze yanked out the chair beside her and sat, then pointed at the one across from him. "Vern, I'll let you tell her."

Vern lowered himself onto the seat and folded his hands on top of the table. Instantly, his stomach fluttered and tumbled. Nothing about this would be easy. "Margaret was going to leave Kansas City, and Mrs. Archer came to me to ask that I try to convince her to stay."

Mrs. Hinze folded her arms. "I don't understand. Why would Miss Jordan want to leave, and what made Mrs. Archer believe you were the one who could stop her? Simply because you accompanied her to services at St. Patrick's?"

"You know it's more than that. Margaret and I have spent time together aside from church. She and I are friends."

"Surely, she has other friends. *Females* who care whether or not she stays or goes. Why didn't Mrs. Archer go to one of them?"

Sullen and silent, Mr. Hinze leaned back in his chair. Yes, he'd promised not to intervene, but Vern wished he'd at least throw out an encouraging look or two.

"I don't think Margaret has any other friends. She hasn't been in the city that long, and—"

"Seven months isn't long enough to make friends? Something doesn't feel right about her." Her eyes narrowed. "Why was she leaving?"

Vern's throat dried and tightened. He awkwardly swallowed. "She . . ." He looked again at Mr. Hinze, who gave a slight nod.

"She was afraid to stay," Vern choked out.

"Afraid? Of what?"

"Gossip."

Mrs. Hinze's head drew back. "What sort?"

He couldn't keep skirting the issue, so he took a deep breath and plowed forward. "She told me something about herself the night of Christmas Mass, and she feared I'd tell you, then you'd tell others, until everyone in the city knew and looked down on her for it."

She glanced at her husband, then back at Vern. "Obviously, you haven't told *me*, but I assume Dietrich knows whatever this *something* is."

"He does. I was so troubled by it when I got home, I told him. Had you been awake, I'd have told you, too. And then, with Christmas and all, we didn't want to spoil the holiday by upsetting you. We agreed to keep it to ourselves till later."

She threw up her hands. "Just as before, you don't trust that I'm strong enough to cope with ill news. What was so bad you feared you'd upset me to the point of ruining my Christmas?"

Vern lowered his eyes and stared at the table. "Margaret had a baby."

Mrs. Hinze gasped. "Good heavens."

"Please, don't think badly of her. I don't know all the details, but I know there's more to it than what it seems like on the surface."

"More to having a baby? Either you do or you don't." The disgust in her voice came through plainly. "Does Mrs. Archer know?"

"No. Until now, only me and Mr. Hinze knew. Margaret didn't want anyone to know her secret, but she blurted it out that night, after getting emotional during Mass."

"Of course, she wouldn't want anyone to know. It's shameful!" She leaned across the table. "Shall I assume you convinced Miss Jordan to stay?"

He nodded.

"You should've let her go. You don't need to be involved with a woman who carries around such despicable complications. You're a good boy, Vern, and you deserve—"

"Stop." He held up a hand. "I don't want to hear it."

Frowning, she sat back, appearing utterly heartbroken.

Vern looked straight into her eyes. "When you took me in all those years ago, you pitied me and eventually loved me. The two of you have enormous hearts. I understand how you're trying to protect me, but you're not the kind of people who'd turn their backs on someone simply because they learn something about that person that doesn't set right. None of us have all the facts, so it's wrong to judge her. And I include myself in that—because I thought the worst of her when she first told me.

"Yes, she had a baby. I don't know how long ago, where the child is, whether it was a boy or a girl, or who fathered it. But I know enough about Margaret to realize there's a lot more to her story. However the baby came to be, it's caused her a whole lot of pain. Aside from the shame she's felt from giving birth while being unmarried, something greater has hurt her."

After spewing out everything so fast, he stopped to catch his breath.

Mrs. Hinze seemed so uncertain of everything he'd said, she just sat there, brows weaving. Mr. Hinze remained as stoic as ever, as if waiting for him to say more.

"It was easy to love you," she whispered. "You were a faultless boy, who didn't choose his circumstances. Miss Jordan is a grown woman. It's not as simple to forgive her situation. She could be pulling you into a horrible ordeal." She grasped her husband's hand, but kept her eyes on Vern. "We don't want to see you caught up in a scandal." Her head snapped to the side. "Isn't that right, Dietrich?"

He cleared his throat. "Yes." His eyes cut toward Vern, then he turned fully sideways and faced his wife. "I've had all day to stew over this. Vern's right. It's wrong of us to judge her without knowing the facts. We don't want our boy hurt, but in many ways, we're adding to his troubles by not allowing him to make his own decisions. We want him to become a man, and he should be allowed to choose his friends. I admire his compassion."

Every word he said warmed Vern to his very core. He never should've doubted how understanding the man would be.

Mrs. Hinze pulled his hand close and cradled it against her. "But, Dietrich, you know his feelings go beyond friendship. If he pursues her—"

"I'm still sitting here," Vern interjected.

They both faced him.

"I don't know what'll happen," Vern went on. "I'll likely not see Margaret for a while. I think she needs some room to breathe and figure things out. But if she needs someone to talk to, I want to be there for her. Can I trust you both to keep her secret? I promised her you would."

Mrs. Hinze rapidly blinked. "I certainly don't *want* to say a word about it to *anyone*. Do you, Dietrich?"

"No. Not a peep. It would only lead to further complications."

"Good." Vern finally relaxed. A sense of relief eased the tension in the air, and his stomach stopped roiling. "I could use a smoke."

"Me, too," Mr. Hinze said with a light chuckle. "I think I'll try Annie's pipe." He stood and placed his hands on her shoulders. "Do you mind if we leave you for a time?"

"You've earned it." She looked up and *tentatively* smiled, but at least it was a vast improvement from her frightened concern. "Today was one of our busiest ever."

Her husband bent down and kissed the top of her head, then motioned for Vern to follow him out.

Vern slowly got up. Before leaving, he went around the table and knelt beside Mrs. Hinze. "You're the finest woman I've ever known, and I never want to disappoint you. Can you trust me to do what I feel is best?"

She smoothed her hand over his cheek. "Yes. As hard as it is for me, I know I need to let you make your own choices. You *are* becoming a man, but no matter your age, I'll always try to protect you."

"I know." He grinned and stood, then headed out the door with Mr. Hinze.

The cold night air greeted them like a painful slap to the face, but they welcomed it and lit up their respective smokes. They sat on the bench and said nothing, yet conversation wasn't necessary.

Plenty had been said, and Vern believed wholeheartedly that somehow, everything would be all right.

CHAPTER 14

"Let me help you with that." Mr. Hinze readjusted Vern's tie, then stepped back and studied his work. "Much better."

Vern frowned. "I should stay home and let you two go without me."

"Nonsense." Mr. Hinze made another slight alteration to the tie, then grinned. "The invitation included you. Besides, doing something enjoyable will be good for you. What could be better than celebrating the New Year? I know we can expect exceptional food—especially the pastries, since we supplied them."

The man heartily chuckled, but Vern couldn't bring himself to even slightly smile. "Your wife has ulterior motives. Isn't it true Mrs. Pennington's niece will be there?"

"Yes." He shook a finger. "That shouldn't keep you from wanting to go. Are you afraid to meet the girl?"

"No, but . . ." He crossed to his bedroom window and peered outside. The snow had let up and was no longer falling, yet a thin layer of white blanketed the ground. "I feel bad that I've not gone to see Margaret." He spun to face Mr. Hinze. "Shouldn't I be with *her* tonight?"

"I'm sure Miss Jordan is working. Mrs. Archer purchased more rolls than usual for this evening and said they were hosting several large New Year's dinner parties. Besides, you saw Miss Jordan only five days ago. I doubt she's expecting to see you anytime soon."

"Or she's wondering why I haven't come by since our discussion at the train depot. I convinced her to stay, so it seems odd that I've not checked on her to make certain she's all right."

"Are you ready to go?" Mrs. Hinze hollered from the base of the stairs.

"In a minute, Annie!" Mr. Hinze bellowed over his shoulder, then crossed to Vern. "If you're worried about Miss Jordan, why not go by the boarding house and see her tomorrow? Businesses will be closed for the holiday, so I'm sure you'll find her there. For tonight, will you try to enjoy yourself?"

"You'll let me use the buggy tomorrow?"

He laughed. "I don't want you out walking in this weather. You'd probably freeze, and Annie would never forgive me."

"Thank you." At the thought of seeing Margaret, a smile easily emerged.

"Now that's what I like to see," Mr. Hinze said, then jerked his head toward the hallway. "I'll go get the buggy, and you can wait with Annie on the porch."

He followed the man downstairs.

"Wow . . ." Vern stopped cold on the bottom step and gaped at Mrs. Hinze. "You look beautiful."

She coyly tilted her head and fanned her skirt. "Thank you. I decided this party was as good a place as any to wear my new dress." She crossed to the kitchen counter, lifted the matching hat, and placed it on her head. "I've never been inside the Pennington's residence, but we've ridden past it, and if the interior is as fine as the exterior, it'll be spectacular." Broadly smiling, she tied the turquoise hat ribbon into a large bow under her chin.

"Yes," Mr. Hinze said. "Mr. Pennington is in shipping. I believe he does quite well for himself." He kissed his wife's cheek. "You truly are beautiful. I'm a blessed man."

She tittered. "You both look exceptionally fine yourselves. Quite sophisticated in those suits."

Mr. Hinze grabbed his overcoat and put it on. "I'll be back as fast as I can." He headed for the door, then stopped and spun around. "I almost forgot Mr. Simpson's pastries." He nabbed a large box, then rushed out the door.

"We'd be in a world of trouble if Mr. Simpson wasn't so fond of baked goods," Vern said, grabbing his own coat. "Another liveryman might not be so accommodating." He motioned toward the shop. "Do you want to sit on the front porch while we wait?"

"I'd like that." Mrs. Hinze beamed.

He loved seeing her so happy. Far better than the glum frowns she'd cast when he'd told her about Margaret. From that day on, he'd decided to say as little as possible about her to Mrs. Hinze.

He helped her with her coat, and they walked through the shop, out the front door, and onto the porch.

The sun had started to set.

Mrs. Hinze carefully perched on the bench, making a point to pull the fabric of her dress smooth before sitting on it. "Isn't it lovely how the colors mix together this time of day?"

"Yes, it is." He sat beside her. Whenever he was in this particular spot, he craved a cigarette, but he never smoked around her, so he dismissed the desire. "Hard to believe tomorrow will start a new year. And in twelve short days, I'll be eighteen."

"Don't remind me." She lightly patted his leg. "Not when I know your plans. Once the weather warms . . ."

He shrugged. "Plans can change. Nothing's set in stone."

She turned and studied him. "Are you saying you might not leave?"

"I've decided to take one day at a time. Sure, I'd love to go west, but right now, I don't know. And I've been so busy, I haven't seen Oscar in weeks. Although he intends to go with me—if I go—he's probably disowned me by now." He laughed. "I've not been punched lately, so maybe it's good I'm not spending as much time with him."

She shut her eyes and shook her head, grinning all the while, then sat tall and gazed out. "Well . . . business will be slower for a while. Everything will return to normal." She eased back against the wall, then jerked rigidly straight. "I don't want to muss my dress."

He pointed at the lapel of her coat and grinned. "You're wearing my broach. It looks good on you."

Staring downward, she fingered it. "I love it, as well as the giver." She pursed her lips and once again looked toward the horizon as if mesmerized by it. "You're a fine young man, Vern . . ." He knew this tone, and he held his breath, waiting for what might come next. ". . . and I hope you won't mind, but I intend to introduce you to Mrs. Pennington's niece." Her eyes cut toward him, then rapidly returned to the skyline.

He chuckled. "Does the girl have a name? As often as you've mentioned her, you've never given her one."

She shifted sideways and stared at him. "You don't object to meeting her?"

"Her, *who*?"

This time, Mrs. Hinze laughed. "Her name is June. June Baker."

"Baker?" He found himself gaping. After snapping his mouth shut, he folded his arms. "Is that her real last name, or are you trying to be funny?"

"It's real. Honestly, when Mrs. Pennington first told me about her, she thought it fitting that a Baker would be interested in a baker. Mrs. Pennington most definitely saw the humor in it."

"How much do you know about this *Baker* girl?"

"Only that she's seventeen, like you, and her aunt claims she's lovely and sweet."

"Of course, she does." Vern shook his head. "A sweet Baker," he muttered. "It'll be interesting to meet her."

Mrs. Hinze grabbed his hand and squeezed.

He understood the implication. The dear woman hoped this sweet, lovely, young girl would take his mind off the *woman* who'd already captured his heart.

* * *

"Welcome to Linderman's." Margaret had lost count of how many times those words had left her mouth. Guests kept pouring in, and Mrs. Archer had indicated they expected to fill the restaurant to capacity.

One hundred bodies pressed between the four walls.

Mrs. Archer hastened across the floor to where Margaret stood at the front station. "Everything appears to be in order. I only hope our guests go easy on the champagne." She glanced around her, then pulled Margaret to the side. "If you notice anyone over-indulging, please let my father know. He intends to spend the evening in the office, in the event we need him."

"With Matthew?"

"No." Mrs. Archer looked at her strangely and tipped her head to the side. "Eustace is keeping Matthew at home tonight. Since we'll be here till midnight with our guests, and even longer, cleaning up after them, I didn't want our baby out so late. Why did you ask?"

"I know how much your father enjoys the lad." She peered beyond her to where more guests were coming in. "Welcome to Linderman's."

Mrs. Archer turned around, then smiled and nodded at the four people who'd entered. "Yes, welcome." Once she learned which party they were with, she sent them in the proper direction.

The woman acted more nervous than usual, darting her eyes every which way.

"Are you unwell, Mrs. Archer?"

"I'm fine. I just . . ." She leaned close. "My uncle is out of sorts," she intently whispered. "He found the champagne meant for our guests." Her eyes widened, driving her meaning. "He's currently upstairs, and I doubt we'll see him. But if he should happen to appear . . ."

"I should go to your father and let him know."

"Yes." Mrs. Archer fidgeted with the sleeve of her dress. "I thank God every day that you didn't get on that train. Oh, and before I forget . . ." She went behind the front station, lifted the money box, and pulled out an envelope from beneath it. "This is for you. Happy New Year, Miss Jordan." Smiling, she passed it over.

"Thank you." She held it against her heart, not even knowing what was in it, but assuming it was a bonus in pay.

"I should've given it to you at Christmas, but it slipped my mind. Just promise you won't leave us."

Margaret stood tall. "I can't guarantee I'll stay *forever*, yet I don't plan on leaving anytime soon."

"Good." Once again, her eyes darted around the room. "Now, if you'll excuse me, I need to see how Mr. Green is coming along in the kitchen and make certain our wait staff is ready to serve."

"Everything will be fine, Mrs. Archer." Margaret gave her best smile, and the woman hastened away.

As Margaret took her place behind the station, a heavy thud resounded overhead. Not a good thing, considering who occupied the upstairs quarters.

"Miss Cynthia," Margaret called out to the young waitress who stood beside a table nearby filling water glasses.

She stopped what she was doing and crossed to her. "Yes'm?"

"Can you mind the front door for a few minutes? I need to tend something."

The young girl's eyes popped wide. "What do I do?"

"Welcome people as they come in and direct them where to go."

Cynthia's head bobbed, yet she still looked frightened and utterly unsure of herself. However, Margaret didn't want to trouble Mrs. Archer with more concerns—not when this could be nothing at all and the woman already seemed ready to crumble. Margaret chose to take this little task upon herself, but she needed to do it quickly.

She went out the front door and around to the staircase that led to the upstairs apartment. Without a coat, the brisk air stung, but since she wouldn't be in it long, she could bear it.

Maybe she should've gone directly to Mr. Linderman in the office and told him what she'd heard. However, just as she'd felt about Mrs. Archer, she hated to bother *anyone* if nothing was wrong.

She rapped on the apartment door. It had been left slightly ajar, and the action pushed it farther open.

"Mr. Linderman?" she called out and took a step inside. "Are you all right?"

"Who is that?" The slurred words of the man calmed her. She'd assumed he'd passed out and fell, and she was relieved to know he was conscious.

"'Tis Margaret Jordan. I heard a thump and feared for you."

Edwin Linderman stumbled across the room and stood within inches of her. In one hand, he held a half-empty bottle of champagne. "I know you." He cast a sideways grin, then poked a limp finger into her arm. "You're that Irish *lassie*."

Of course, he knew her. They'd interacted on several occasions, but his drunkenness had made him senseless.

His alcohol scented breath drifted across her face, and she stepped back. "You should sit down, Mr. Linderman."

"Don't want to." He teetered, then righted himself. "Oops." He tipped the bottle high and drank several long swallows. "Ah . . ." He swiped across his mouth with the back of his hand. "Seen that Vern Harpole lately?"

"What?" How would he know about him, and why would he care?

"Vern. *Harpole*." He took another drink, then belched. "I knew his mother." He licked his lips. "*Really* knew her, if you understand my meaning. She was sumthin'."

Margaret's heart raced. Though the man was drunk and most definitely untrustworthy in this state, he could have important information about things Vern needed to know.

He swayed and stepped toward her. "Ain't been no one like her, since she left." He reached out, but before he could touch her, she backed up and leered at him.

Smirking as if they were playing a game, he advanced and grabbed her arm. "You're pretty. Same as her."

She jerked away. "*Never* touch me!"

"C'mon. Stay here with me. It's New Years and I wanna celebrate." He reached for her a second time.

Quick as a whip, she firmly swatted his hand.

"You hit me!" he sneered and stumbled backward. "I'll tell my brother, an' you'll be on the street. Right where you belong."

"I'm the only one who will tell your brother anything, you filthy old man!" She hurried out the door and slammed it shut.

As she descended, she nearly landed on her rump, but she kept going. Right to Mr. Linderman's office.

She marched in and shut the door. "Your brother is a foul disgusting man! He just made advances, then threatened me when I smacked his hand to keep him from touching me."

Frank Linderman was two years younger than Edwin, but Edwin's heavy drinking had aged him in a terrible way, making him appear *much* older. Frank had always acted professional and respectful, and it hurt to see the disgust on his face now.

"I'm so sorry, Miss Jordan. I just don't understand why you approached him at all. Didn't Clara tell you he'd been drinking?"

"Yes, but I heard a thud overhead and I feared for him, so I went to affirm his wellbeing." She gazed upward, then returned her attention to Mr. Linderman. "You would do well to lock him in that room. If he were to interrupt the dinner party, it would be disastrous. Not to mention, he could stumble down the stairs and harm himself."

"I'll check on him." The crease in his brows deepened. "But please, never again go up there alone. When he drinks, he's not himself. You're an attractive woman, and—"

"I understand. I'll have better sense from here on."

He nodded and smiled, yet his face retained the same amount of concern. "Did Clara give you our gift?"

"Yes, sir. I haven't opened it, but thank you for whatever it might be."

"You're welcome. And I truly am sorry about Edwin. I'll do everything I can to make certain it doesn't happen again."

"Thank you, sir." She opened the door. "I'd best see to our guests. Happy New Year, Mr. Linderman."

"Happy New Year."

As she left, she glanced over her shoulder, only to see the man shake his head in frustration. It couldn't be easy having a brother with such problems. Her mum used to say that spirits were the devil's drink, and Margaret believed it.

At least she didn't have to worry about Vern partaking.

Poor Vern . . .

If Edwin Linderman had spoken truthfully, he'd been involved with Vern's mum. What if the man knew where she'd gone?

The possibility didn't seem feasible. Not when she'd left so many years ago. Regardless, as painful as it would be to tell him, Vern needed to know exactly what Mr. Linderman had said.

* * *

"Amazing . . ." Vern whispered in awe of what lay before him.

Mrs. Hinze giggled. "I told you the house was exceptional."

"And *I* told you Mr. Pennington has money," Mr. Hinze added. "This is what a decent fortune can buy."

As he steered Betsy around the circular dooryard that led to the front entrance, men wearing black frock coats and derby hats approached. They helped Mrs. Hinze to the ground, and once he and Mr. Hinze had exited, one of the men hopped in and drove the buggy away.

Another of the men waved his hand toward the front door, and the three of them headed up a stone pathway to the grand entrance. It had been swept clean of snow, and since none was currently falling, it remained clear.

Vern took in the three-story, red-brick house. Every window had been topped with fancy white wood carvings that framed them like artwork. The front of the house rose higher than the rest with a structure resembling a castle turret. Tall spires jutted upward from the peeks of the roof, which was also lined with black wrought iron in a crisscross pattern—similar to a small fence that bordered the rooftop.

"I want a house like this," Vern whispered to Mr. Hinze as they approached the front door.

"It's something to wish for, Son, but difficult to attain." He smiled, then lifted a hand to knock. Before it touched the wood, the door swung open.

"Welcome," a tall man in a sharp suit said and waved them inside.

Music surrounded them. It sounded as if an entire orchestra was playing somewhere within the walls of the house.

As they stepped from the small entrance rug and onto a spectacular marble patterned floor, Mrs. Pennington hastened toward them. Vern recognized her from her many visits to the bakery, but he'd never seen her so well-dressed. Her red gown had even more layers and lace than the one Mrs. Hinze was wearing.

"Happy New Year!" Mrs. Pennington chirped and extended her hands to Mrs. Hinze.

Mrs. Hinze took hold. "Happy New Year."

The woman pulled her into a brief hug. "I'm so happy you could come," she said in a much calmer tone and nodded to Mr. Hinze and Vern in turn.

"Thank you for inviting us," Vern said.

As hard as he tried to keep his attention on her, his eyes kept wandering to everything around him. Not only was the stairway before them quite spectacular and enormous, the house had incredible wood archways that led from the foyer to three separate hallways. Stained glass windows had been embedded in the sides of each arch. Not only did it seem strange to have windows that didn't face outside, but every one of them had a wreath design made up of entwined green boughs with red ribbons tied to them. They were fitting for the recent Christmas holiday, yet a little odd for year-round. Even the brown varnished woodworking above the windows had a similar Christmassy pattern.

"I see you're admiring the stained glass," Mrs. Pennington said.

His cheeks warmed. He'd not meant to be so obvious. "It's incredible. But the design is unexpected."

She walked closer to the archway and pointed upward. "This house was my father's final gift to me. He had it specially built. We had many fond memories of our Christmases together. It was our favorite holiday, and he wanted me to carry on the spirit of the season throughout the year. This was his way of accomplishing it." She gestured to one of the side walls. "You'll see the same crown molding throughout the house on every floor." Beaming, she hugged her hands to her bosom as if embracing herself. "Doesn't the design look like the garland you'd hang on a Christmas tree?"

"It does," Mrs. Hinze said, gazing upward. "It's so lovely, and what a special reminder of your father."

"Yes. His spirit lingers in our home—in a good way."

More guests arrived behind them.

Mrs. Pennington motioned a young girl over. "Lucinda will take your coats and show you to the ballroom, and I'll join you momentarily."

"Thank you," Mr. Hinze said, bowing his head.

The formality of the affair felt unusual, but good. Vern had never been exposed to this kind of wealth, and he couldn't deny it was drawing him in. All the more reason to strive for success.

Lucinda looked younger than he. He'd thought she might be another one of Mrs. Pennington's relatives, but since she was dressed in a crisp blue uniform, he doubted it. She took their coats and disappeared briefly, then returned and led them down one of the hallways.

As they walked, the music grew louder. They passed through additional archways and the final one opened into an enormous room. Finely dressed people were gathered in small groups, talking and laughing. Some were even dancing.

Vern pointed to a table on the far side of the room. "I see our pastries."

Mrs. Hinze grabbed his arm and lowered it. "It's not polite to point." She turned to her husband. "Isn't this remarkable?"

"Yes. I'm not sure why we were invited this year. Somehow we got into their good graces."

"I think *I* know." Mrs. Hinze pushed a strand of wayward hair from Vern's brow. "We should credit our boy. I'm not certain how Miss Baker came to be interested in him, but her aunt is eager for them to meet."

Vern found it difficult to believe. "You're saying it's because of *me* that we're here enjoying *this*?"

"Yes." She eyed him up and down. "So, please, be on your best behavior and when you meet Miss Baker, be polite."

"He's always polite," Mr. Hinze said as he grabbed a drink from the tray of a server passing by. He took a sip, smacked his lips, then pointed to a man not far away. "Isn't that Mr. Pennington?"

With a reprimanding glare, Mrs. Hinze lowered *his* arm. "At least I know where Vern learned his behavior." She glanced in the man's direction. "Yes, that's Mr. Pennington."

Vern studied the man. He had excellent posture and held himself well, though he looked rather old. Aside from a little hair that hovered over both of his ears, he was bald. And what hair he did have was speckled with abundant gray. The salt and pepper appearance carried over into his mustache.

Vern put his back to him and leaned close to Mr. Hinze. "I thought you said their wealth came from his shipping business.

From what Mrs. Pennington said, it was her family money that got them this house."

"I was thinking the same thing," Mrs. Hinze whispered. "Seems to me they've reaped rewards from both sides of the family."

Mr. Hinze yanked his shoulders back. "Money isn't everything. We've been blessed in many other ways, and we certainly don't lack for anything."

"Oh, Dietrich. You sound so defensive." She linked her arm into his. "I love our home *and* the life we've made for ourselves. And you're right, we have everything we need."

Vern gestured to the glass in his hand. "What are you drinking?"

"I believe it's champagne."

"Oh. I hope there's something else."

"There is."

He spun to see who'd spoken so sweetly and found himself face to face with an attractive girl. The blue satin of her dress matched the color of her eyes. Her blonde hair had been done in ringlets, reminding Vern of how Mrs. Archer had worn her hair when she was still Miss Clara.

"There's fruit tea on the table beside the pastries," the girl said, then cast a large smile, exposing a slight gap between her front teeth. Not only did it make her more unique, she looked *cute*.

He returned her smile. "Thank you."

"You're Vern Harpole, aren't you?"

"Yes, I am." His insides fluttered, and he feared he already knew who she was. Would it betray Margaret if he felt this young woman was *cute*?

"I'm June Baker. My aunt has told me a lot about you."

When he turned to see the reactions of Mr. and Mrs. Hinze, he discovered them nowhere to be seen. Boy, did he have a bone to pick with them later . . .

As before, his face warmed and he chuckled nervously. "I hope she didn't say anything *bad*."

"Not at all. Aunt Mabel says you're a respectable, hard-working boy." She tipped her head toward the food tables. "How about some of that fruit tea?"

"I'd like that. Thank you." A stone formed in his throat, making the beverage even more appealing.

He followed the pretty girl across the floor, and it felt as if every eye in the room rested on them.

She lifted a glass from the table, gave it to him, then took one for herself and daintily sipped.

He downed his in several swallows.

She lightly laughed. "More?"

"Please." He thrust his empty cup toward her and she passed it over to one of the servers who stood behind the table. He dipped a ladle into a large bowl and refilled the glass.

This time, when Vern got hold of it, he sipped.

"Do you want to see the rest of the house?" June asked. "It's quite spectacular, and I'd be happy to show it to you."

"With our tea?" Vern took another drink.

"Once we've finished, we can go."

"By ourselves?" Surely not. It would spark all kinds of gossip.

Again, she giggled. "I live here, Vern. No one will mind." Her gleeful expression turned serious. "Is it all right to call you by your first name?"

"You can call me Harp. That's what all my friends use."

"Harp." She coyly batted her eyes. "I like that. And you can call me, June. I have no other names—though my uncle sometimes calls me June *bug*."

"I won't do that. You're too pretty to be compared to a beetle." His cheeks flushed hotter than ever. Why did those words pop from his mouth?

She modestly lowered her head. "Thank you, *Harp*."

He chugged down the rest of his fruit tea and set the empty cup on the table. She put hers down as well, though it was nowhere close to being finished. "May I take your arm?"

"Where do you plan to take it?" He let out another nervous laugh. Maybe it wasn't wise to jest, but something other than good sense had taken over his mind.

She giggled harder, then placed her hand in the bend of his elbow.

It felt strange having a female touch him—and in such a comfortable manner. She showed no hesitation and seemed eager to make the connection.

As they left the ballroom, he glanced behind him, only to catch sight of Mrs. Hinze, whose grin stretched from ear to ear. She'd want to know everything they said to one another and would be relentless until he revealed it all. Trouble was, he had no idea what to expect from June Baker, let alone what they'd talk about. Yet, whatever might happen had his stomach in knots.

They passed two sitting rooms, a kitchen larger than the one at the bakery, a library, and an office, then they circled around and went down another long hallway. Eventually, they arrived at the foyer and faced the fanned staircase.

"The bedrooms are on the upper floors. Want to see them?"

"No," he quickly said. "That is—I'm sure they're wonderful, like the rest of the house—but I don't think it's wise for us to go up. People might talk."

She tightened the hold on his arm. "Aunt Mabel was right. You *are* respectable. I admire that in you, Harp."

She urged him along to another hallway he'd not yet been down, and they came to a small room with a piano in it. The instrument was positioned in the corner beside a large domed window.

She brightened the lamp on a small table, then motioned to a sofa. "We can talk in here."

"Just the two of us? Alone?"

"You're too nervous, Harp. As I told you, I live here. I'm trusted, and since you've been deemed honorable as well, our being together shouldn't raise any issues." She sat and patted the space beside her. "How are we to become acquainted, if we can't talk privately?"

This wasn't what he'd expected from the evening, but he couldn't be rude to her, so he sat. "Can I ask you something?"

"Of course. How else are we to become familiar?"

Her behavior screamed she *wanted* familiarity. He only hoped he wouldn't offend her in any way by his line of questions. "Why do you live with your aunt and uncle? Did something happen to your parents?"

"You're very straightforward. I like that."

Margaret had said the same, and the instant he was reminded of her again, guilt washed over him. It would surely hurt her to see him sitting beside June.

Or would it?

June folded her hands on her lap. Pretty as a picture. "My mother and Aunt Mabel are sisters—or I suppose I should say they *were* sisters. Mother died when I was quite young, and Father shortly thereafter. I've lived with my aunt and uncle ever since."

"I'm sorry to hear it. At least you've grown up in a fantastic place." He kept his gaze on everything but her. "Do the Penningtons have children of their own?"

"They had a baby that lived a mere six months, and after that, Aunt Mabel lost every child she conceived. She was rarely able to carry them long." She released a sad sigh. "I feel awful for her, but she says I helped her through it. Uncle Aster said she'd been worried who would inherit this beautiful house, yet neither of them frets over it any longer. One day, all this will be mine."

Maybe Mrs. Hinze was aware of June's good fortune, giving her another reason to push him in her direction, hoping he'd marry into money.

"You're fortunate, June." He rubbed his sweaty palms up and down his pant legs to dry them.

"Harp?"

"Yes?" He managed to face her, wishing she wasn't so fine to look at.

"Is it true your mother abandoned you? And that's why you were raised by Mr. and Mrs. Hinze?"

He nodded.

"You poor dear." She flattened her palm against his cheek. "Do you know what became of your mother?" Her fingers softly moved, sending shivers throughout his body.

"Nope." He gulped. "I don't know why she left or where she went."

Fortunately, she lowered her hand, but to his dismay, she scooted closer. Her eyes roamed his face. "I love your freckles and the red in your hair. You're a handsome man, Harp."

She called him a man. Not a boy or a *lad*.

"What are you doing, June?"

She cocked her head. "What do you mean?"

"Why me? I'm sure there are lots of men who'd jump at the chance to be with you. I'm nobody."

"Oh, Harp." She touched his leg, causing him to jerk. Still, she didn't remove her hand from where she'd laid it. "You're most definitely somebody. Aunt Mabel chose you for me over all the other prospective beaus in Kansas City. She said you'd treat me well and you'd be loyal. And because you're such a hard worker, she says you have great potential. She's watched you for a very long while, and I trust her judgment."

If that was true, she'd not monitored him close enough to see he'd been spending his time with a full-fledged woman.

"So, she wants you paired with a baker?"

Another giggle. "It fits, don't you think? With my last name and all." She moistened her lips and slowly blinked. "Of course, it won't be my last name forever. Will you be my beau, Harp?"

His heart raced. "I—"

She lurched forward and kissed his cheek. Had she planted her lips on his mouth, he'd have been a goner.

He panted heavy breaths. "We just met, June. I think you're rushing this."

"Rushing? You want to keep seeing me, don't you? After tonight?" Her blue eyes locked onto his and didn't budge.

He found himself nodding, though he couldn't utter a sound.

"Good. Eventually, I *will* call you my beau. For now, you'll be my friend, Harp." She stood and reached out to him. "Can you dance?"

"Not really. But I can try." He took her hand and she linked her fingers through his, then led him back into the hallway toward the music.

He'd never been so confused. Something had taken hold of him, and he felt as if he'd had no control over his words or his body.

What kind of mess had he landed himself in?

CHAPTER 15

T hank goodness the bakery was closed for the day.

It had been nearly two a.m. when they'd arrived home from the Pennington's, and Vern would've hated to be up before dawn to bake bread. Mrs. Hinze had promised not to wake him at all, and had gone so far as to tell him he could sleep all day if he chose to.

She'd been giddy all night, and had grown even more so on the ride home, when he'd told her how well he'd gotten along with June Baker. He'd chided Mr. and Mrs. Hinze both for leaving him alone with her, but Mrs. Hinze had claimed it had all turned out for the best. It seemed that where he and June were concerned, every adult with a vested interest in them had tossed aside all sense of propriety. Even Mr. Hinze had appeared to have forgotten his lecture on the importance of a chaperone and hadn't seemed both-ered by the situation.

If only Vern could feel so pleased with how things had gone with June. True, if not for Margaret, he'd gladly pursue her. He'd be foolish not to. Not only was the girl likable and attractive, she was set to inherit a fortune. Any sane man would grab the chance to be in her favor.

He lay flat on his back—uncertain of the time—waiting for the hallway clock to chime. Regardless of how many *dongs* rang out, he didn't feel like budging.

As much as he wanted to see Margaret, surely, she'd ask what he did to bring in the new year. Since he'd vowed never to lie to her, he'd have to tell her about June.

He stared blankly upward. This shouldn't be an issue. After all, Margaret had made it clear she wanted nothing other than friendship between them, so maybe she'd be pleased to learn he'd met someone he found *interesting*.

But would it be wise to tell her how June and he had come close to actually kissing—thanks to the ridiculous New Year's tradition? The champagne had caused many of the people in the ballroom to be uninhibited, and once they'd counted down to the stroke of midnight, even Mr. Hinze had eagerly planted a bold kiss on his wife's lips.

June had been right beside Vern all the while, and if he hadn't turned his head when she raised up on her tiptoes . . .

"Ugh!" He covered his face with his hands, wishing he could wipe away the memory. People had to have seen how close he and June had become through the course of the evening, as well as the kiss she'd placed on his cheek. At least the first one she'd given him had been done in private.

Making matters worse, by the time he'd spent hours in her company, he'd *wanted* to kiss her. A real, genuine one. Still, something held him back, and he was pretty sure he knew what—or *who*—that something was.

He sat bolt upright and tossed aside his covers. He needed to see Margaret. It was the only way to know for certain how he felt about her.

The clock began to chime, and he counted ten loud dongs.

A glance out the window confirmed no snow was currently falling, so he hurriedly dressed, then went to the washroom and cleaned the sleep from his eyes.

Before heading downstairs, he dug into the back of the bureau drawer and retrieved the small package that held Margaret's Christmas gift. No matter what happened between them going forward, he'd bought this for her, and her alone. He needed to give it to her.

* * *

Still half asleep, Margaret rose from her bed and trudged to the window.

"Happy New Year," she whispered to herself.

The sun sparkled on the crystalline snow covering the yard. Icy crystals also hung from the trees branches and shimmered in the light. So beautiful and peaceful.

It had been easy to fall asleep last night. Once she'd gotten home, she was so exhausted, she could scarcely shed her clothes to get into bed.

The dinner parties had been successful, and Mrs. Archer couldn't have been more pleased. She'd been in such a good mood that Margaret chose to keep the incident between her and Edwin Linderman quiet for the time being. Since his brother was well aware, she didn't feel the urgency to tell Mrs. Archer.

The man had remained in the upstairs apartment all night. He'd likely finished off the bottle of champagne and passed into oblivion.

A heavy-handed fist beat on her door. "Are you alive in there?"

Patsy . . .

The last person Margaret cared to see today, or truthfully, *any* day.

She donned a robe, plodded to the door, and opened it. "Is something wrong?"

Patsy jutted her chin high and stared down her pointy nose. "Do you know what time it is?"

"No."

The woman eyed her from head to toe. "It's nearly eleven o'clock and you're not even dressed. It's shameful."

"Why? I worked quite late, and I was exhausted. What concern is it of yours if I choose to spend m' day sleeping?"

Patsy pursed her lips. "Didn't Mother tell you?"

"You have me at a disadvantage. I don't know what you mean."

"It's the new year, and I'm officially the landlord of this boarding house."

The wretched news spoiled the beauty of the day. "I see. Yet, I still don't understand why you're concerned over m' sleeping habits."

"You missed breakfast, and I assume you would've missed lunch as well if I hadn't come to your room. It's rude to keep everyone wondering where you are."

"I doubt they were bothered by m' absence. I was sleeping while they were dining."

"Exactly." She curtly nodded. "You were being inconsiderate. Mother prepared breakfast for every resident, including you."

"I pay for room and board. I'd think that if I choose not to partake, it would save your mother money." Margaret took a similar rigid stance. "I'm a grown woman and I should be allowed to spend m' days as I wish."

Patsy folded her arms and scowled. "You're also under *my* roof. If you can't abide by the schedule of this house, you'll need to find another place to live." She stood firm as if waiting for Margaret to object.

Maybe she *should've* gotten on that train.

All she could afford the disagreeable woman was a long sigh.

"Patsy!" Mrs. Williams bellowed from the lower floor.

"What, Mother?" Patsy yelled over her shoulder just as harshly.

"Tell Miss Jordan that boy is here to see her!"

Patsy faced her, smirking. "You're entertaining *boys*?"

"He's not a boy. If I'm not mistaken, your mum is referring to Vern Harpole, a friend of mine."

"Hmm." Patsy grunted. "You'd best get dressed so you can speak with him downstairs." She pointed a stiff finger. "If I ever hear you're *entertaining* in your bedroom, I'll put you on the street so fast your head will spin. This is a reputable house, not a brothel." With another rude glare, the woman marched away.

Margaret shut the door and dressed as quickly as she could. She didn't want to keep Vern waiting—especially in such ill company.

* * *

Vern had made certain to clean his boots before entering the boarding house, and not surprisingly, Mrs. Williams had examined them closely after he'd done so, then directed him to the parlor.

He happily warmed himself in front of the fire, but the instant Mrs. Williams yelled up the stairs, announcing his arrival, he wanted to shrivel. Surely, everyone in the house had heard her. Oddly, he'd never seen another resident, yet he knew they existed. Maybe they all kept to their rooms.

A younger version of the old woman descended the stairs. She wore the same sour expression as Mrs. Williams, and he assumed she was Patsy, her daughter.

She crossed to him. "Are you the boy waiting for Miss Jordan?"

The demeaning way she said it bothered him more than her calling him a *boy*. "I'm Vern Harpole, and yes, I'm here to see Miss Jordan."

"Why?"

Her question took him aback and he simply stared at her.

The woman tapped her foot. "I asked you a question. You've come to my home to see one of *my* residents. I'm entitled to know your purpose."

"Actually . . ." He squared his jaw. "My intentions with Miss Jordan are not your concern. This may be your home, but you have no rights over her personal affairs."

"Affairs?" She tittered. "That's an interesting term for a boy of your age to use."

"I'm not a boy. I'll soon be eighteen, and I'm plenty old enough to speak as I please."

"Hmm. Were you taught to be impolite to your elders?"

He pointed at himself. "Impolite? In my opinion, you're the one being rude. I'm a guest in your home and you've treated me with anything but kindness."

Mrs. Williams shuffled in, leaning on a cane. "I see the two of you have met."

Patsy jutted her nose high. "Yes, Mother. Our *guest* refuses to tell me his purpose."

The old woman waved a hand. "For heaven's sake, Patsy, you don't have to pry into every little detail. As long as he doesn't accompany Miss Jordan to her bedroom, it's none of our concern."

Patsy huffed, then tossed her head, spun around, and marched from the room.

Vern had always found Mrs. Williams irritable and grumpy, yet he appreciated her setting her daughter straight. The younger woman had been far more annoying and downright rude.

"You don't have to worry about me going to Miss Jordan's room," he said. "I know my place."

She lifted her cane and poked him in the chest with the tip of it. "I certainly hope so." After casting a brief leer in his direction, she pointed her cane at the sofa. "Sit and wait for Miss Jordan. I need to see about lunch."

Without another word, she walked from the room, once again using the cane for support.

He sat, glad to be rid of the frustrating women. Several silent minutes passed, then the raised voices of Mrs. Williams and her daughter filtered in from the hallway. He couldn't understand what they were fussing about, but they put an enormous damper on the mood of the house.

What a horrid place to live.

"Vern?" Margaret slowly approached.

He stood, immediately intoxicated by her. He loved how her long hair fell across her shoulders. She wasn't wearing anything special—just a simple day dress—yet her mere presence increased the rate of his heartbeat. And although June had had an effect on him, it paled in comparison to this. "Hello Margaret. Happy New Year."

"To you as well." She smiled, but something tentative lay behind it.

She moved to a chair across from the sofa and sat, so he did the same and returned to his spot, facing her. "I assume you worked last night at Linderman's?"

"Yes. Quite late." She twisted her fingers together, all the while staring at them. "I'm surprised to see you."

"Surprised? I assumed you'd be upset that I didn't come sooner. After all, I convinced you to stay." He let out a light chuckle, hoping to ease the tension coming from her.

"You did indeed." She pointed over her shoulder, to where the voices had grown louder. "I assume you met Patsy." She leaned forward, lessening the space between them. "She's taken over as landlord." Her voice lowered further. "I need to find another place to live."

"I don't blame you," he whispered back. "She's a hateful person, but it makes no sense for her to act that way. Her ugly disposition will be bad for business."

Margaret rapidly nodded. "And I thought Mrs. Williams was crotchety. She's an angel compared to her daughter." She sat a little taller, grinning. "What brings you by?"

He appreciated how talking about the disagreeable women seemed to have taken away some of her anxiety. It was good to see her smile. "Patsy asked me the same thing, but I wouldn't tell her. You, on the other hand . . ." He dug into his pocket and pulled out the package. "Happy Christmas, Margaret. Sorry it's late."

As he passed it over to her, she frowned. "I didn't get *you* a gift, Vern. Honestly, I had so much on m' mind, even the thought of it escaped me. I feel awful being so unthoughtful."

If he'd known the gift would remove her smile, he might've waited a bit longer to give it to her. "I didn't buy you a present expecting one in return." He gestured to the box. "When I was shopping for Mrs. Hinze, I saw this and it reminded me of you. I thought you'd like it."

She turned the package over, but didn't unwrap it.

He cleared his throat. "You're supposed to take the paper off to see what's inside."

Her head slightly lifted, and she rolled her eyes. "I know full well what to do with a present, Vern Harpole." She tugged at the strings.

Even the way she said his name tumbled his insides. If only she'd let him near her.

After setting the brown paper aside, she opened the small box. "Oh, my . . ." Her eyes misted over. "'Tis no wonder this reminded you of me." She withdrew the three-leaf, clover-shaped broach and held it close to her heart. "Most everyone knows the shamrock is a symbol of Ireland, but do you know why?"

He shook his head.

"Our patron saint, Patrick, used the clover to illustrate the Holy Trinity. The leaves represent the Father, Son, and Holy Ghost." She rapidly blinked and sucked in a large breath. "Thank you, Vern. I'll cherish this always."

"I'm glad you like it." Mrs. Hinze had said something similar about the broach he'd given *her*. Women definitely had a fondness for jewelry, but he was merely glad to see them happy. "What does Saint Patrick say about clovers with *four* leaves?"

"They're said to be lucky." She gazed upward. "Specifically, they represent not only luck, but faith, hope, and love as well. They're hard to find, yet if you ever do, it's wise to hold onto them."

"Are you talking about the four-leaf clover, or the four things it represents?"

Her eyes met his. "All of it, I suppose." As quickly as she'd made the connection with him, she looked away and broke it.

"Something's troubling you, Margaret." Again, he lowered his voice. "Are you still worried the Hinzes will talk?"

"No." Ever so slowly, she looked at him once more. "I'm glad you came because I need to talk to *you* about something important."

Her intensity drew him in and he scooted to the edge of the sofa. "I'm listening."

Her chest heavily rose and fell. She was obviously finding it difficult to say whatever she intended to. "Have you ever had a conversation with Mr. Linderman? Edwin, the baker, not Frank Linderman, the restaurant owner?"

What an odd question. "I don't believe so. Whenever I've made deliveries to Linderman's it's always because the baker was said to be *out of sorts* and therefore, was nowhere to be seen. I didn't know what that meant until several years ago, when Mr. Hinze felt I was old enough to be told."

She fidgeted with the shamrock broach. "He was *out of sorts* last night. He'd gotten into the guest's champagne and when I saw him, he'd already consumed half a bottle."

"What reason did you have to see him that way?"

"I'd been told he was in the upstairs apartment and I'd been warned he'd been drinking. I was at my station and heard a loud thump, so I feared he'd passed out drunk and may have hurt himself. Mrs. Archer was already overwhelmed with our large number of guests, so I took it upon m'self to look in on him."

Vern's protectiveness kicked in. "Did he hurt you?"

She shut her eyes and lowered her head. "No, but he tried to touch me. I smacked his hand as hard as I could."

"Good. If I ever see the man, I'll give him a piece of my mind."

She reached over and lightly touched his knee. "I appreciate that you care, but please, hear me out. There's more to be said."

He stared at her dainty hand, wanting to cover it with his own, yet resisted the urge and did nothing. "Go on . . ."

She pulled away, likely regretting having touched him at all. "Before he made the advances, he asked about you."

"Me? Why?"

"He claims to have known your mum."

An unusual numbness took hold, and he slumped back into the sofa cushions. "What exactly did he say?"

"He started by asking if I'd seen you lately, then he went on to say he knew your mum. He claimed to have *really* known her—as he put it—taking pleasure in the implication. He said there'd been no one like her since she left. Then, he told me I was pretty like her and he wanted me to stay with him so we could celebrate the New Year together."

Her chin quivered. "It was then that he tried to grab me, and I hit him and told him never to touch me."

Anger and defensiveness boiled up inside him. "Did you tell his brother what happened—and Mrs. Archer?"

"I told his brother, but I didn't want to trouble Mrs. Archer. Mr. Linderman assured me he would see to Edwin." She took several deep breaths. "If you can control your anger, Vern, I believe you should go and talk to him. If he truly knew your mum, he might be able to answer some of your questions about her."

He tightened his fists. "What I really want to do is bloody his nose. He had no business putting his hands on you."

"I'm fine. I doubt he'll bother me anymore. Mr. Linderman gave me his assurance, along with a bonus in pay, and neither he nor Mrs. Archer want me to leave. If she hears about Edwin's advances, she'll give him what for."

"If?" Vern leaned forward. "She needs to know."

"I'll know when the time's right to speak of it. I'd honestly prefer not to. The entire ordeal was uncomfortable, and I'd rather forget about it and move on."

He stood and wandered over to the fireplace. "You do that a lot, Margaret." He put his back to the flames and faced her. "When something bothers you, you just sweep it under a rug and pretend it never happened. Then you end up with all kinds of dirt inside you that festers and weighs you down. It's impossible for you to move on, when you can barely budge from the heaviness of it."

"I know you're not talking about Edwin Linderman any longer." Her entire body deflated. "Are you judging me over m' decision to keep m' past private?"

"No. I'm simply making an observation." He returned to the sofa, sat, and reached for her hand.

She jerked away.

"Margaret." He swallowed the lump in his throat. "You know I won't hurt you, right?"

She nodded.

"Put your hand in mine."

"Why?"

"Because I want you to know that a touch can be good."

Her breathing became more labored, and several tears trickled onto her cheeks. She trembled as she reached toward him and rested her hand on his.

It pained him to see her struggle, but he felt confident he was helping her. As slowly as he could manage, he drew his fingers in and encased her delicate hand. "I'll never hurt you, Margaret. And I'll do whatever I can to keep you safe." He rubbed his thumb back and forth.

She stared at their joined hands and a trace of tension melted from her features. The desire to kiss her emerged stronger than ever, but it would require a lot more than a gentle coaxing, and now was not the time.

At least he'd gotten the answer he'd come for. His heart belonged to Margaret Jordan, and no amount of money or *cuteness* from June Baker would ever change that.

Aside from the motion of his thumb, they sat without moving for quite a while.

"This isn't so bad," he whispered. "Is it, Margaret?"

"No." Her teary eyes penetrated his. "You're a gentle soul, but I'm undeserving of your affections."

"Because of the *baby*." He said the word as delicately as he could.

She cringed, yet didn't pull away. "I'm not pure, Vern."

"None of us are." He inched a bit closer. "I'll be eighteen in eleven days, and I'd like to court you. Will you allow it?"

"Your birthday is the twelfth of January?" Her face screwed together.

"Yes. What's so strange about that?"

"M' birthday's the eleventh." She let out a little laugh. "You and I are one day and *six years* apart." With a slight tug, she withdrew from his grasp. "I know you're becoming a man and you want a woman in your life, but it can't be me. You may have convinced me to hold your hand, however, that's where it ends. I won't allow you to court me." She stood and moved toward the hallway. "Find another woman who will appreciate you."

Before he could stop her, she raced up the stairs.

Heavy hearted, he stood and trudged to the front door. He'd not had to tell her about June, but in an unexpected way, Margaret was pushing him toward her.

Maybe he should be grateful. She'd given him permission to be with someone else, so why did he feel awful about it?

Seems he'd have plenty of time to sort it all out. But before he did that, Edwin Linderman had some explaining to do.

CHAPTER 16

"Oh, no . . ."

Margaret bent down and adjusted the torn fabric. Her foot had gotten hung in the hem of her dress and slightly ripped it. She'd gone so quickly up the stairs to her room, she'd neglected to lift her skirt. Fortunately, she hadn't tripped and fallen on her face.

It seemed whenever Vern was near, she frequently tripped over herself.

Her small room wasn't the best refuge, but she was grateful she had *somewhere* to go to distance herself from him.

She locked her door, then carefully placed her beautiful shamrock broach on the table beside her bed. The pin was the most thoughtful gift she'd ever received, and she hadn't lied when she'd told him she'd cherish it always. However, the very fact he gave her something so considerate made her feel worse and emboldened her decision.

She knelt beside her bed and reached beneath it, feeling for the money she'd placed there.

It wasn't too late to run away. Taking the train to somewhere unknown would solve more than one dilemma. She'd rid herself of Patsy Cramer and free Vern from his worries over her. If she left the city entirely, he'd be more likely to do as she'd suggested and find someone else to court.

Court.

His upcoming eighteenth birthday appeared to be pushing him into manhood. If only he weren't so eager for courtship and marriage.

Her fingertips touched the stack of bills that had grown substantially after last night's bonus, yet something froze her in place and she didn't take it.

She withdrew her hand from beneath the bed and sat back onto her bottom, landing with a hard thud. She doubted she could be more disgusted with herself.

Since she'd promised Mr. Linderman she'd stay for a while, it would be wrong to leave this soon. Not after they'd been so generous.

But it was something much greater than that keeping her here.

She shut her eyes, recalling the feel of Vern's tender touch. It had been pleasant to say the least. After her ordeal, she'd believed she would never find a man's touch agreeable or enjoyable.

She'd been dreadfully mistaken.

"And that's why you truly want to run," she mumbled to herself.

How much more of an emotional mess could she be? What person in their right mind would want to run away and stay for the very same reason?

She *wanted* to be with Vern, but didn't deserve him. As often as she'd told herself that very thing, she needed to force it firmer into her mind. It was wrong to enjoy his affections.

She pushed herself up from the floor, then reclined on her bed. At least she'd done *some* good by telling him about Edwin, and now it was up to Vern to find his own answers.

Utterly miserable, she curled into a ball and closed her eyes—this time, hoping to sleep and drift away from every thought.

Patsy would surely be knocking on her door again soon, but she didn't care. She had no intention of acknowledging her.

Stop!

She jerked upright, then swung her legs around and planted her feet on the floor.

"I'm tired of wallowing."

It had been years since she'd been victimized, and she'd allowed the horrid act to carry over far too long. Every day she chose to be miserable was another victory for her assailants. Though she might feel unworthy of a good man's affections, she deserved some form of happiness. Her life would be meaningless if she continued acting like a victim.

So, what brought her the most joy?

Having just sent Vern away, it would be wrong to tell him she'd changed her mind and wanted to be with him. Additionally, if Edwin Linderman revealed some disturbing details about his mum, Vern would need time to digest it all. She'd give him that.

Perhaps it would be wise to acquire a *female* friend. With all the people living in Kansas City, there had to be some other woman worthy of friendship. Or at the very least, she could become better acquainted with the other residents in the boarding house. If they disliked Patsy as much as she did, maybe they could have a mutiny and overthrow her.

Margaret laughed at the thought. Silly as it might be, it felt good to think it.

She crossed to her window and drank in the beauty of the winter day, just as she'd done earlier.

It was almost lunchtime, and she had acquaintances to make. Other than their names, she knew almost nothing about them.

Mrs. Fitch was a widow, Mr. Woolum had served in the war and rarely spoke, Miss Underhill taught school, and Mr. and Mrs. Pope were old and did next-to-nothing. Thankfully, they weren't sickly.

If she was fortunate, maybe one of them would be a decent conversationalist. The school teacher showed the most promise—considering they were closer in age—but Mrs. Fitch could also be a viable candidate.

Somehow, Margaret needed to dig down deep inside herself and find a remnant of her former character—the carefree, happy lass her da adored—and bring her back to life.

She plastered on her best smile, opened her door, and headed down the stairs to the dining room.

"Happy New Year," she said to Mrs. Williams. "Shall I help you set the table?"

The woman froze in the middle of the floor, clutching a plate. Her mouth dropped wide open, then she snapped it shut again. "Patsy! Miss Jordan wants to help!" It made little sense for the two women to constantly yell. Especially when they weren't that far from each other.

"Indeed I do," Margaret said when Patsy appeared from the kitchen. "Happy New Year, Patsy."

The two hateful women exchanged the most humorous glances, but Margaret kept her laughter at bay. If she had to endure them, she might as well shower them with kindness and make them believe she was up to something.

Which, of course, she was.

She'd taken the first steps to bettering her life, and with God's help, she intended to succeed.

* * *

Vern steered Betsy to the back entrance of Linderman's—the usual place for deliveries and the door he normally knocked on. But he had no intention of knocking on that particular door today. The one that beckoned him was at the top of the stairs leading to Edwin's apartment.

On the short drive from Miss Polly's, Vern had managed to dampen his anger. And as much as his thoughts were still tangled between Margaret and June, he forced himself to put his mind right and focus on what was to come. If Edwin had information about his mother, he needed to figure out a way to get the man to tell all he knew.

He paused at the base of the stairs. Maybe he should speak to Frank Linderman first and seek his permission to question his brother.

No. If Vern made his presence known, he risked Mrs. Archer being in the restaurant, and she'd likely question his reason for being there.

Besides, why would he need *permission* to talk to anyone? As many times as he'd claimed to be a man, he needed to act like one.

He ascended the stairs as quietly as he could, feeling it best not to be heard by anyone in the restaurant. Even when he rapped on the door, he did it softly.

He waited, then knocked a bit louder.

"What do you want?" a man—presumably Edwin—called out from the other side.

Vern put his mouth close to the door. "I need to talk to you."

"Frank? Is that you again?"

"No." Vern's heart pounded. "It's Vern Harpole," he loudly whispered.

Silence.

Vern pressed his ear to the door. It sounded as if someone was moving around within, but if he didn't answer, Vern might have to force his way in. That could prove to be unwise.

To his relief, the lock clicked, and the door opened a crack. A bloodshot eye peered out. "Little Vern," the man said, then chuckled. "Just had to be sure." He widened the opening and exposed himself, wearing nothing more than underwear. "Want to talk, huh?" Edwin squinted into the daylight.

"Yes." His disgust for the man grew, yet his need for answers overpowered it. "Can I come inside?"

"Better than standing there with the door open, letting all the cold in." Edwin stepped back, while holding onto the doorknob.

As Vern walked in, the nasty aroma that greeted him nearly knocked him on his tail. He placed a hand over his nose.

Edwin laughed. "I take it you smell my upchuck. Haven't had a chance to clean it up yet." The man scratched his gray-haired head. "I had a tad too much *happy New Year*." Sniggering, he pointed at an empty bottle laying sideways on the sofa.

"Yes, you did," Vern dryly said.

The man wavered a bit. "I'd better sit. I'm still sort of woozy." He stumbled to the sofa, pushed aside the empty bottle, and plopped down. He then grabbed a blanket and thankfully covered himself with it.

The small untidy apartment boasted little more than an un-made bed in one corner, the sofa where Edwin had planted him-self, and a table with four chairs. Vern grabbed one of them, set it a short distance from the man, and sat.

Edwin shivered, then let out a slight moan. "That made my head hurt."

"Maybe you shouldn't have had so much to drink." Vern didn't feel an ounce of sympathy for him.

"You sound like Frank." Edwin's lip curled. "He send you here?"

"No. I don't recall the last time I spoke to your brother." Vern sat taller and glared at him. "I came because of Margaret—that is— *Miss Jordan*."

The disgusting man cackled. "Sweet Margaret. Lassie of Ire-land." He spoke in a sing-song attempt at an Irish accent.

"Don't talk about her that way. She's a respectable woman."

He waved a hand. "You're young, but you're just as stuffy as Frank." Sighing, he wiggled the blanket higher up toward his neck, then leaned forward and licked his lips. "What did *Miss Jordan* tell you?"

"Do you remember her being here last night?"

"Yep. Tried to get her to stay. Seems she's too *respectable* for that."

The man was rudely using his own words to irritate him. "If you ever even *try* to touch her—"

"What? You think you can whip me, boy?" He laughed, and again waved in dismissal. "You should be thanking me, not chiding me."

"Why should I thank you? From what I can tell, you've not done a thing worthy of gratitude from anyone."

"Your *mama* used to thank me. She liked what I did for her— or better said—*to* her." He smirked, all the while eyeing Vern and no doubt expecting a strong reaction.

He chose not to give him the satisfaction. Because of what Margaret had told him, he'd expected this, though not so vilely said.

He firmed his jaw. "Why should I believe you actually knew my mother?"

"Lottie Jean Harpole," the man arrogantly said. "Believe me now?"

Vern slumped back in his chair. He couldn't remember the last time he'd heard her full name spoken.

"You're pale as a sheet," Edwin said. "It must be hard for you picturing your pretty mama with a man like me. But I admit, I was finer to look at ten years ago."

"Did you love her?"

Edwin smacked his own leg and laughed. "As often as I could."

Vern could scarcely keep from lunging at him. "Can you *try* to be serious? You're talking about my mother, and if you know as much as you claim, you're aware she left me without reason. And even though she did, she's still my mother, and I won't have you talking so ugly about her."

Edwin looked away, then scratched up and down his neck and sighed. "I'm sorry, boy. I can be an ass."

Vern nodded. "At least you realize it. If you're *really* sorry, tell me what you know. Obviously, you've known all these years that I'm her son. What made you say something about her to Miss Jordan after all this time?"

"I was drunk. Seeing that pretty gal at my door made me think of Lottie." His eyes narrowed. "Are you happy with your life, Vern?"

"That's an odd question from a man who's been nothing but obnoxious to me since I walked through the door. Why do you suddenly care about my happiness?"

"Because I played a part in it." He rubbed his unkempt beard. "Mr. and Mrs. Hinze have been good to you, haven't they?"

His demeanor had completely changed. No longer was he acting like a careless cad, he seemed calm and genuinely interested in knowing the answers to the questions he'd posed.

"We're a family," Vern said, stone-faced. "If not for them, I don't know where I'd be. I probably would've been sent to an orphanage, and I doubt I would've learned a trade. But how could you have played a part in my life? I don't question your relationship with my mother, yet it had to have been brief. We'd only been in Kansas City a few weeks before she left."

As soon as he said the words, a disturbing thought struck him. He rose up in his chair and bent forward, leering at the man. "Did you do something to her to make her want to leave?"

"Maybe."

Vern grabbed the edge of his seat to keep from wrapping his hands around the man's throat. "What did you do?"

"I told her how good she was and gave her the confidence she needed to go west."

West? The very place his heart kept leading him. "I don't understand."

Edwin shut his eyes, shook his head, then opened them again and stared straight at Vern. "Your mama was a whore, Son. I didn't *love* her, I paid her for her services."

Vern lunged and grabbed hold of the man's shoulders. "Don't say that!"

"It's true! Why do you think she left you behind? She couldn't go off whoring with a boy at her side!"

He gave the man a shove, then fell back into his chair.

Vern's head ached, trying to process what he'd said. When he'd gotten old enough to understand what went on between men and women, he'd suspected his mama had been entertaining men on the nights she put booze in his cider. He'd always wanted to believe they'd been beaus—men who could've become his daddy one day.

Edwin cautiously eyed him. "She'd heard about the kind of money women like her could make in San Francisco. And one night, she flat out told me she wanted to go, but didn't know what to do with you. She didn't feel right just leaving you in the hotel and cared enough to want assurance that someone would look out for you."

The more he talked, the bolder he became, as if by telling all this made him righteous. "She asked if I knew anyone who might have pity on you and take you in—someone with money who could afford another mouth to feed. I immediately thought of the baker and his wife. I knew they were childless and had a good business." His eyes searched Vern's face. "I helped her the night she put you on that porch. Showed her exactly where to go."

"I should report you," Vern hissed. "What you did was a crime. You know that, don't you?"

"A crime?" Edwin shot to his feet and hovered over him, letting the blanket drop to the floor. "If not for me, your life would be worthless. I saved you, boy, and you should be grateful."

Vern averted his gaze, not wanting to see the man. Not only was it disturbing to see him undressed, now that he knew what he'd done, he despised him further. "Aren't you ashamed of what you did?"

"What? Having your *mama*, or helping her get rid of you?"

"Every bit of it."

"First of all . . ." The man held up a single finger. ". . . prostitution is perfectly legal. I paid her decent money, and she provided a more-than-satisfactory service in return. As for you, she wanted a better life for her boy, so I helped her achieve it. So, no, I'm not ashamed." He grunted. "Maybe if you'd man up and get yourself a decent poke, you wouldn't be so irritable and pompous about it."

"I'll never be like you." Every word that spewed from Edwin's mouth sickened him more. Then something awful came to mind, making things horribly worse.

Virginia . . .

"I had a sister. Do you know what my mother did with her? Did she leave her somewhere, like she did with me?"

"Jenny." Edwin grinned. "Lottie offered her to me one night, but I refused. She was a little too young, and besides, I preferred your mother. I suppose I do have some moral guidelines. Something about the idea of having both mother and child didn't set well."

"Virginia was sixteen. Are you saying Mama had her service men, too?" His throat tightened, and with the smell already in the room, he feared he might vomit.

"You're looking green, Vern." Edwin walked away and went to the table, where a pitcher of water and several glasses sat. He poured a glassful and returned to Vern. "Drink this. It'll help."

Before sipping, Vern sniffed the contents. Deeming it water, he drank it down.

"I know I don't need to answer that last question," Edwin said. "You're smart enough to put the pieces together, now that you know the full picture. Lottie took Jenny with her to San Francisco. Well, I assume it's where they ended up. Lottie wanted to go there, and unless they got sidetracked or ambushed along the way, I presume they're still there."

He sat back down on the sofa and recovered himself. "Life as a whore can be rough. Especially if they wound up in one of them mining towns. The stories I hear . . ."

Vern bent over and clutched his stomach. Up until now he'd glamorized the idea of the mining camps. He'd pictured himself there, baking bread for the newly rich miners, and gathering a load of wealth for himself. He'd even joked with Oscar about finding a woman for him out west. But the only kind of women who'd brave going to those places were those like his mama. Women who'd sell themselves for gold.

"She cared more about money than me," Vern muttered under his breath, rocking back and forth.

"Lottie was a feisty woman, and I'm sure that hasn't changed." Edwin tapped Vern's shoulder, bringing him upright. "Now that you know, will it make a difference?"

"I don't know." He'd never said anything truer.

He'd thought he'd been confused over Margaret and June, but knowing all this about his mother and sister added a new level of frustration and pain to his mixed-up mind.

He stood on shaky legs. "I need to go, but before I do . . ." He poked his finger into Edwin's chest. "Don't go near Margaret again. She's nothing like my mother."

"Are you sure about that?"

Vern leered at him. "Margaret's an upstanding woman."

Edwin shook his head. "I can tell simply by looking at her, she's not so pure. There's more to Miss Jordan than you think."

Vern pushed harder. "Stay away from her."

The man peered downward and glared at Vern's finger.

He backed away, then headed for the door.

He'd heard more than he cared to and couldn't leave fast enough.

CHAPTER 17

On days that the bakery was closed, Vern always used the back door to go inside. While walking from the livery, he'd gone over every wretched detail Edwin had revealed.

It wasn't easy knowing his mama sold herself, but it caused deeper pain learning Virginia had followed her lead and done the same. Surely, it couldn't have been his sister's choice. Maybe their mama had forced her—told her it was the only way they could make a living and put food on the table.

After all these years, how many men had taken advantage of their services? It disgusted him to think he had family members who were no better than the tainted women who worked the docks, and whom he purposefully avoided.

He hung his coat on a peg by the door, then went to the icebox for milk. He intended to heat it and make cocoa—something that would warm him from the inside out and hopefully make him feel somewhat better.

As he set the pan of milk on the stove, Mr. and Mrs. Hinze descended the stairs.

Mrs. Hinze hastened to his side. "You're making cocoa?" Her brows drew in, and she faced her husband. "You see. He only does this when he feels poorly. I told you he shouldn't have gone to see that woman."

Mr. Hinze took a seat at the kitchen table, but didn't say a word.

Vern shook his head. "It's not what you think." He looked her in the eyes. "I can add extra milk if *you'd* like some, too."

"Am I going to need it?"

"Yep."

She let out a little whimper, then went to the icebox herself, got the milk, and added plenty more. "For Dietrich, too," she said as she poured.

Vern remained at the stove and stirred the milk, while she put in the cocoa powder and sugar. He welcomed the pleasant aroma, especially after what he'd inhaled earlier.

Not another word was said as the mixture heated. Mrs. Hinze took her place beside her husband at the table and latched onto his hand.

Vern hated to see the worry in her eyes, but since he'd vowed not to keep anything of importance from her, this had to be shared. Besides, he *needed* to tell it. He couldn't bear the burden alone.

The cocoa steamed, so he removed it from the heat before it boiled and scalded, then he poured it into three mugs and set them on the table.

Mrs. Hinze grabbed one and cradled it in her hands. "Sit down, Vern, and tell us what happened. I'm about to bust with nervousness."

He yanked out a chair and dropped onto it. Before sharing his news, he lifted his own mug and took a careful sip, finding it to be just the right temperature.

When he glanced at Mr. Hinze, the man widened his eyes, as if to say, *we're waiting*.

"As you know," Vern began, "I saw Margaret, and—"

"It seems silly," Mrs. Hinze quickly said. "After all, you had a perfectly lovely evening with June Baker. I'd hoped you'd forget about Miss Jordan."

Mr. Hinze patted her arm. "Don't interrupt the boy, Annie."

"Fine." She pinched her lips together. "I'll be quiet."

Vern took another fast sip. "I had a Christmas gift for Margaret, and that was the main reason I went to see her. Then the instant we were in the same room, the feelings I have for her reemerged with a vengeance. Before I knew it, I was asking if I could court her."

"No." Mrs. Hinze shook her head, frowning. "Tell me you didn't."

"I just said I *did*, but don't worry. She told me *no*."

Mrs. Hinze let out a long, relieved sigh. "Thank heavens." She smiled, then slapped a hand to her mouth. "Forgive me, Vern. I understand now why you're upset. Rejection is difficult to accept."

"That's not why I'm troubled. True—it bothers me that she said no and told me to find someone else—but there's a lot more to this. She told me something that led me to have a talk with Edwin Linderman."

"Edwin Linderman?" Mr. Hinze's face scrunched together. "What does he have to do with Miss Jordan? Or you, for that matter?"

Vern held his mug in front of his mouth and merely stared at it, wondering how to gently put this. Trouble being, there was nothing mild whatsoever about his news.

He returned the mug to the table and cupped his hands around it. "Edwin knew my mother."

"What?" Mrs. Hinze's eyes darted from him, to her husband, and back again. "Are you certain?"

"Yes. He told Margaret, and she told me. That's why I went and spoke to him."

Mr. Hinze leaned forward. "Does he know where she is—or why she left?"

Vern painfully nodded. "Her plan was to go to San Francisco— along with my sister. He assumes they're still there."

"And why—"

"Please." Vern held up a hand. "Stop asking questions. Just let me tell you everything. It'll be easier that way."

The both sat back and didn't make another sound.

Vern told them each detail from the moment he'd arrived at Edwin's door to the minute he'd left. Mr. and Mrs. Hinze remained quiet the entire time, but Vern would never forget their horrified expressions whenever he revealed each ugly new tidbit.

"He asked if knowing all this would change anything," Vern mumbled, then looked from Mr. to Mrs. Hinze, whose concerned gazes overwhelmed him. "I told them I didn't know. Does it change anything for *you*?"

Mrs. Hinze rubbed over her heart. "I'm sick for you, Vern, but I thank God you were brought here. Mr. Linderman did a good thing choosing us for you, and you for *us*."

"I agree with Annie," Mr. Hinze said roughly, then cleared his throat. "Your mother gave up the finest gift she'd ever been given, and we were blessed because of it."

Oddly, a small chuckle escaped Vern. "Cheap labor."

"No," Mrs. Hinze said, wide-eyed. "We *love* you."

"I know you do. I was kidding about the cheap labor. All this seriousness weighs me down, and I guess I was trying to lighten the mood." He took another drink, finding the cocoa that remained in his mug had turned cold. He'd lost track of how long they'd been talking.

"Not only was I rejected by the woman I think I'm in love with . . ." he continued, only to have Mrs. Hinze gasp.

Vern chose to keep talking. "I found out my mama's a whore."

Another gasp. "You said *prostitute* before. The other is such a vile word."

"I know, but it's what she is. My sister, too."

Mrs. Hinze drummed her fingers on the tabletop. "We can't let word of this seep out. If Mrs. Pennington knew, she might discourage her niece from seeing you. Your breeding would be questionable."

"That's ridiculous." Vern turned to Mr. Hinze for help. "Don't you agree?"

"I tend to agree with *Annie*. The Penningtons want someone reputable for their niece, and if people learn about your mother, it would sadly reflect on you."

"But I'm not like her—in any way. You taught me right from wrong. You raised me to be decent. June told me her aunt said I was hard-working and respectable, and I'm still that person. Nothing I learned about my mother has changed who I am."

"We know that," Mr. Hinze said. "Unfortunately, people often make judgments from what they hear. And you can't deny your blood."

"Just don't talk about it to anyone else," Mrs. Hinze interjected, then reached for Vern's hand. "Does Miss Jordan know?"

"All she knows is that Mr. Linderman had a relationship with my mother. He didn't give her any other details I'm aware of."

"Good." She gave his hand a slight squeeze. "But you should see her again and make certain she keeps this to herself. We vowed not to share *her* secret, so she should keep yours out of courtesy."

Vern sat back and folded his arms. "I know Margaret isn't a gossip. It won't take me going to her and asking her not to talk about it, she'll do that on her own. Besides, she doesn't want to see me, and I didn't think you wanted me anywhere near her."

"That's true." Mrs. Hinze frowned. "I want what's best for you, Vern." She stood and picked up the empty mugs from the table. "I need to start dinner. It's New Year's Day and we should be celebrating, instead of sitting here being glum." She wandered away and proceeded to bustle around the kitchen.

Unlike her festive actions at Christmas, she didn't hum or smile. She simply went through every motion as if necessity was the only thing that drove her to do her chores. She'd lost her joy.

Vern leaned across the table, in order to whisper to Mr. Hinze. "Will she be all right?"

"In time. It's a lot to digest, Son." Just like his wife, he looked anything but happy.

This wasn't the way Vern wanted to start the new year. He hated seeing them this way. "You know what's hardest about all this?" he said in the same hushed tone. "None of it was my fault. Not what my mama did, or my sister, or whatever it was that happened to Margaret to make her distance herself from me. But all of it affects me and therefore affects *you*. It's not fair."

"I know. Life pulls punches."

"And I want to hit back, but I don't know how." He rested his elbows on the table, then put his head in his hands. It throbbed something fierce.

"Take it as it comes and know we'll be here to help you through it." Mr. Hinze rubbed across Vern's head. "Annie told me you're reconsidering going west. Now that you know your mother went that direction, you'll surely stay here."

Vern sat up straight. "I don't know. Something keeps tugging at me to go. Maybe deep down inside, I always knew she'd gone west, and my heart wants to follow her. How senseless is that? What sane man would want to go after a mother who tossed him aside for a chance to get rich?"

"Sons never stop loving their mothers, and we're never quite sane where they're concerned. I miss mine every day."

"But yours has been dead for a long time. I understand why you miss her. She was good to you and you loved her. But mine—"

"Is alive as far as you know. And that could be the very reason you can't let go of her. Maybe you *need* to see her, to put your ill feelings to rest. You could address them head-on."

He thought about it, yet had no idea what to say. Mr. Hinze had consistently given good advice, but did he really mean for him to go all the way to San Francisco just to confront his feelings for his mama? It seemed a bit drastic.

"Mr. Hinze, I'm really tired. I'd like to go lie down for a while."

"I think that's wise. Tomorrow's work will come early, and you should take advantage of the day off. I'll wake you when dinner's ready."

"Thank you." Vern stood and trudged toward the stairs, then pivoted around and went to Mrs. Hinze. He kissed her cheek. "Happy New Year."

Looking as concerned as ever, she framed his face with her hands. "Happy New Year, Vern." The dear woman closed her eyes, then gently pulled his head toward her and kissed his brow.

He knew no one else had ever loved him so deeply, and that was why she hurt. She wanted the best for him, and she feared this new revelation would ruin everything. He wanted to tell her it would all be okay, but he wasn't so sure, and he didn't want to lie.

He headed to his room.

Maybe sleep would help.

* * *

The day had progressed beautifully, and Margaret couldn't recall the last time her spirit had felt so light.

She sat on the sofa in the parlor, resting a teacup on its saucer that perched perfectly on her lap. Mrs. Fitch sat in the chair beside the fireplace, and she sipped her own cup of tea.

"You, my dear, are a mystery," Mrs. Fitch said. She tipped her slim glasses to the edge of her nose and winked, then pushed them back into place. "I'd always assumed you were uppity and unsociable, yet all along, you've merely been *shy*."

The widow was the epitome of a sweet old lady—unlike Mrs. Williams—complete with a tight gray bun at the crown of her head. The more Margaret got to know her, the more she admired her.

"Yes, it takes me a while to feel comfortable conversing. But, being a new year, I thought it was high time to get acquainted."

"I could listen to you talk all day. Your accent is charming." As the woman sipped her tea, she extended her pinkie on the hand holding the cup. "Where in Ireland did you say you came from?"

"Castlebar. A lovely little town."

"You must miss it. Whatever brought you to America?"

Margaret knew this question would eventually be asked, and she'd prepared herself for it. "Opportunity." She wiggled slightly and sat tall. "And adventure."

"Well, you're a brave young woman, and from what I can tell, a devout Catholic."

Margaret stared at her. "How did you know I'm Catholic?"

"I've seen you at St. Patrick's." Mrs. Fitch laughed. "From the way you're looking at me, I assume you never noticed me there, though I attend every Sunday."

"Oh, my." Margaret shamefully turned her head. Surely, her cheeks gleamed red. "All these months, and I didn't know we attended the same church."

"I saw *you*."

Margaret forced herself to face her again.

"At *midnight* Mass as well," Mrs. Fitch went on, "with a young man." She grinned and took another drink, all the while gazing over the top of her cup.

"My friend, Vern Harpole," Margaret confidently said. "He'd never attended a service before and seems to be hungering for a relationship with God. It felt good to introduce him to Mass at such a special time of year."

"But you left in the middle of it." Mrs. Fitch set her cup down. "Were you ill?"

Lying would be wrong, yet for now, it was easier than telling the truth. She'd be sure to ask forgiveness at her next confession. "Yes. M' stomach was giving me grief. Honestly, it pained me deeper taking Vern away from his first Mass."

"You can always bring him again." The woman craned her neck and peered down the hallway. "Here, kitty!" She set aside her teacup and patted her lap. Within moments, Hamlet jumped onto it. He rubbed his furry face up and down her arm.

"I can hear him purring from here," Margaret said, laughing, glad to have the interruption.

"He's a good kitty." Her eyes darted around her, then she bent forward. "I'm happy he hasn't taken on his master's demeanor." She tittered. "Have you ever thought about that word? De*mean*or? Where Mrs. Williams and her daughter are concerned," she whispered, "I've never known anyone *meaner*."

Margaret scooted to the edge of her seat, then peered around as Mrs. Fitch had done, to affirm no one was within hearing. "So, it's not just me? They're rude to you as well?"

"Yes. That's why I keep to my room. I like this house, and I've been here for years, so I don't want to leave. Moving is such a headache. However, I wish there was some way to make them see the light and at least try to act gracious." She widened her eyes. "Maybe we should invite *them* to St. Patrick's."

"I suppose it couldn't hurt to try. But poor Father Tierney. I hate to unleash them on him. And if he had to take their confessions . . . oh, my."

"It would do their souls well to confess their sins, but they might not realize they're acting sinful." Mrs. Fitch lifted her head high. "I'll pray for them." She nodded a single time.

"You're a good woman. I should've thought of that long ago. I've spent too many days cursing them, when I should've been lifting them up to the Lord." She'd been so caught up in her own troubles, she'd neglected to see beyond them.

"Mrs. Fitch?" Margaret inched closer to her. "Do you suppose I can sit beside you at Mass on Sunday?"

"I'd be honored. But will you be happy sitting toward the back on the right side? It's been my place for a long while, and I noticed you usually sit closer to the front."

"It's good to have a place you feel is your own, and if you're willing to share your pew, 'tis I who am honored. Thank you." She smiled and received a beautiful one in return.

Margaret sipped her tea to the sound of Hamlet's purr. The fire crackled and put out the warmth needed to fill the room with comfort. It was as if she was seeing and feeling her surroundings for the very first time. Self-pity had darkened her world, and adjusting her outlook had altered everything.

She wasn't foolish enough to believe she'd not encounter troublesome things going forward, but she'd made a valiant start, as well as a new friend.

When Margaret had tried to engage the other boarders at lunch, everyone except Mrs. Fitch had acted disinterested. Yet, it didn't bother her. Before today, she hadn't been able to call anyone in the boarding house a *friend*, and she was thankful that had changed.

As good as she felt, she prayed for Vern. Eventually, she'd reach out to him again and perhaps they could build on something she believed was there—something deep-seated that she'd been unable to deny. And she knew Vern felt it, too. Otherwise, he wouldn't have asked to court her.

She shook her head to dismiss the thought. Thinking about how she'd told him *no* would only make her miserable again.

CHAPTER 18

Vern carefully placed the small cake into a box and closed it, taking care not to damage the swirls of icing in any way.

Mrs. Hinze followed him to the door. "You're coming right back, aren't you?"

"Yes. I'm sure she's working, so she'll probably not have time for me."

"Do you *have* to go?"

"Today's Margaret's birthday. I need to do *something* to show I care."

"Why?" Mrs. Hinze chewed her lower lip. "You said she told you to leave her be. Maybe it would be better to cut all ties."

"She told me to find someone else to court, but she didn't say I couldn't see her at all. She's still my friend." He grabbed the door handle. "Besides, don't you want me to tell her to be quiet about Mr. Linderman's relationship with my mama?"

"Shh . . ." She pressed a finger to her lips and shot nervous glances around the bakery.

He grinned and shook his head. "There's no one here besides us, Mrs. Hinze. You worry too much."

He adored the woman, but he wished she'd have a little more faith in his judgment. Especially considering the fact he was about to turn eighteen and no longer needed to be coddled.

He walked out and cautiously descended the ice-covered steps to the road, where he'd parked the buggy. With the weather being so cold, he preferred to stay in and go nowhere. Yet for Margaret alone, he chose to brave the frigid air.

He pulled his scarf up over his face and got the buggy moving. The nearer he got to Linderman's, the harder his heart beat.

For the past ten days he'd focused all his efforts on work and did what he could to stop mulling over Edwin's revelations. After all, he couldn't change the past, so he had no need to stew over it. Or at least, he'd tried to convince himself it was ridiculous to fret about it.

In all truthfulness, he hadn't stopped stewing since the first of January. Spring needed to come quickly, so he could enlist Oscar to hop trains with him again. A few good games of pool could get his mind where it needed to be.

"Or," he muttered, "I won't be able to play at all because I can't think straight."

He laughed. What could be more pitiful than a man who talked to himself *aloud*? He'd told Mr. Hinze he was still the same man he'd been before Mr. Linderman spilled his ugly news, so he needed to start acting as if it hadn't affected him.

He pulled up to Linderman's restaurant and parked the buggy near the front entrance. At four o'clock they'd be preparing for their dinner guests.

While consciously building up his courage, he stepped to the ground and grabbed the cake box, then headed for the main door. He had no idea what sort of mood Margaret would be in today.

The pleasant scent of cooking food welcomed him and rumbled his stomach. He couldn't help but smile, thinking about the similarities to the first time he'd met Margaret, and how he'd sat at the table by the window and watched her work. His life would be a lot simpler if he hadn't felt something for her that day.

"Vern?" Margaret approached from the kitchen, wearing a dark blue dress. Her hair had been twisted up onto her head and pinned, giving her an air of professionalism. No matter how she wore it, she looked stunning, and as usual, she took his breath.

"Happy birthday, Margaret." He extended the box. "It's a cake."

She practically glowed, radiating an enormous smile. "You're too kind." She took the box, opened the lid, and inhaled. "It smells delicious. Thank you."

Although he'd been uncertain what mood he'd be greeted with, he'd expected her to be a lot more distant, so her cheerful disposition seemed out of place. Maybe she'd given some thought to how negatively she'd sent him away and had been wanting to make amends. He certainly hoped so.

"You're welcome. I guarantee it'll *taste* even better." A sparkle drew his gaze to her collar, and when he realized what was there, it made *him* smile. "I see you're wearing my broach."

"I am indeed. I wear it every day for good luck." She stepped closer. "And I believe 'tis working. Ever since you gave it to me, m' days have been brighter."

"I'm glad to hear it." It most definitely worked, because she herself appeared sunnier and most unquestionably happier. "You look wonderful. Everything must be going well for you—with your job and all." He pointed upward. "Any more trouble with Mr. Linderman?" he whispered.

"None at all. He's laid off the spirits and has been spending his days baking as he's supposed to. I've seen him a time or two, and he's acted polite." She hugged the box to her bosom. "I blame the champagne for his actions that night. Did *you* manage to speak with him?"

The middle of the restaurant didn't feel like the appropriate place to tell her what he'd learned, but she deserved to know *something*. "Yes, I did. I talked to him right after I left you at the boarding house."

"Did he say anything helpful about your mum?"

A few other workers had filtered into the dining room from the kitchen, and Vern didn't want to risk being heard. "Let's go over there and talk." He gestured to the far side of the room, and she followed.

"First," he went on, "I'd appreciate you not say anything to anyone about Mr. Linderman having a relationship with my mother."

"Of course, I won't speak of it. You should know me well enough to realize that." She leaned in. "I don't gossip."

"I know. I'm sorry—I shouldn't have said it. It's just such a sensitive issue, and—"

"You don't have to explain, or feel badly. I, more than most anyone, understand about delicate matters and the need for secrecy." She offered another sweet smile. "So, did he tell you something beneficial?"

"He said my mama took my sister to San Francisco, hoping to find the means there to make a living."

"Oh." Her brows drew together. "Why did she leave *you* behind?"

"He claimed she'd worried I would be underfoot and wanted to know I'd be well cared for." It might not be the entire story, but at least he'd been truthful. "It was actually Edwin Linderman who suggested she leave me on the Hinze's porch."

"Truly?" Her concerned expression softened. "I may have misjudged him. He did a fine thing guiding her to them, though it still seems wrong in many ways. Although, I do understand how a mother wants the best for her child." She frowned and looked away.

"Margaret?" He gingerly touched her arm. "Don't think about that."

She turned and covered his hand with her own—an action completely unexpected. "You're a good man, Vern Harpole." Her eyes locked with his. "You understand me better than I do m'self. You're so worried about hurting m' feelings, yet I'm the one who should feel badly. Tomorrow, you'll be eighteen, and just as I did at Christmas, I neglected to get you a gift."

He stared at their touching hands. "You're wrong. Seeing you happy is the finest present I could hope for." Not to mention her gentle touch, but he chose not to verbalize that particular thing, fearing she'd withdraw again.

"I *am* happy. Oh, and I have a new friend."

His heart sunk. "Who is he?"

"'Tis not a *he*." She laughed. "I befriended a widow at the boarding house. Mrs. Fitch is her name, and I learned she attends St. Patrick's. We sat beside each other at Mass last Sunday."

"That's wonderful." And an enormous relief.

"You're welcome to join us anytime you'd like. I know Father Tierney would be pleased to see you."

"I'll consider it." He had a lot more to say, but other people would be arriving soon, and he didn't want to be in the way. "I hope you enjoy the cake, Margaret."

She patted the top of the box. "I know I will."

"Good." Heart still thumping, he moved toward the door, feeling as if something heavy hung between them.

"Thank you again, Vern. 'Twas fine to see you."

"You, too." Their gaze reconnected, but he whipped around and went out the door.

More than anything, he'd always wanted her to be happy. Now that she was, it troubled him. He'd been miserable since she'd refused his request to court her, yet she'd moved on as if unbothered by his absence and had even made a new *friend*.

Aside from the fact she'd touched him, he doubted she'd ever cared about him as much as he had for her.

"Women are so confusing," he grumbled and climbed up into the buggy.

* * *

Vern returned Betsy and the buggy to the livery, then headed home on foot. Darkness came early on these wintry days, so by the time he got to the bakery, the sun barely peeked above the horizon.

He hurried inside and went straight into the kitchen to stand close to one of the stoves. His ice-cold hands needed to be warmed.

Mrs. Hinze came down the stairs. "Did she like the cake?"

"She said it smelled good."

"What else did she say?"

Vern put his back to the stove. "She won't talk about my mother and Mr. Linderman—if that's what you're worried about."

"That's good." She crossed the floor and stood beside him. "My concern is for your reputation. From the day you came to us, we've taught you to be good. I don't want anyone thinking badly of you."

"Anyone? Or specifically Mrs. Pennington?"

Mrs. Hinze lowered her head, then lifted it high again and looked him in the eyes. "June Baker is a lovely young woman with exceptional prospects. She's the type of woman any mother would want for her son. Is it so terrible that I want to see you properly wed?"

"No. I know you care. But you need to trust me to make up my own mind about who I want to spend my life with. It could be June Baker, or maybe it's someone I've not even met yet. But I don't intend to change who I am to fit into someone's plan. When June told me her aunt chose me to be her beau, I found that a bit . . . I don't know . . . preconceived."

He crossed his arms. "The Penningtons have enough money to buy whatever they want, and I'm sure they're used to getting their way. They need to know I'm not a *thing* to be bought, just because they think I'm suitable for their niece."

Mrs. Hinze frowned. "But you *do* like her, don't you?"

"Yes."

"I'm glad, because Mrs. Pennington came by while you were out, and she asked us to join them for dinner tomorrow to celebrate your birthday."

He gaped at her. "How did she know it's my birthday?"

"I sort of let it slip."

"Slip?" He narrowed his eyes. "And I suppose you *sort of* already told her we'd be there?"

She sheepishly nodded.

Vern huffed a breath and grunted. "Next time, please ask me before you agree to something like this. As I said before, I'm not a little boy anymore, and I want to make my own decisions."

"All right." She turned away, pouting.

"Please, don't do that." He rested a hand on her forearm. "I hate to see you upset, but it's important you know how I feel." He tapped her arm until she looked at him. "Dinner at the Penningtons will be wonderful. And yes, I do like June."

Her frown slowly faded. "I'm happy you reaffirmed that, because I want this birthday celebration to be the best you've ever had." She cupped his cheek. "My boy will be eighteen." A slight whimper escaped her and her eyes misted over. "Eighteen . . ." she repeated and sighed.

Mr. Hinze walked in, chuckling. "Are you getting all torn up again, Annie?"

She sniffled. "I'm afraid so."

The man kissed her brow, then faced Vern. "Did she tell you about dinner at the Penningtons?"

"Yes, sir."

"And you don't mind?"

"No." Plenty had already been said on the issue, so he decided not to go into any details regarding his true feelings. "It'll be nice to see June." He eyed Mrs. Hinze, who pushed out a smile.

"Well, then . . ." Mr. Hinze clapped a single time, then rubbed his palms together. "You can stop worrying, Annie. Tomorrow, while you and Vern close up shop, I'll fetch the buggy so we won't be late for dinner."

"There's no need," Mrs. Hinze said. "I thought I told you, Mrs. Pennington is sending a carriage for us. She said it's so cold, she knew we'd be more comfortable in something enclosed."

Mr. Hinze puffed out his chest and grinned. "We'll be riding in style. I like that."

Vern forced himself to smile at the man. Although he enjoyed seeing both him and his wife enthralled with everything about the Pennington's, their niece, and most likely their money, *he* couldn't so easily embrace all of it.

Whenever he tried to picture himself as a permanent fixture in their mansion with June by his side, his thoughts always turned to Margaret. Even if things progressed with June, he feared he couldn't fully dismiss Margaret from his mind, and that would be terribly unfair to Miss Baker.

I'm a doomed man.

* * *

January twelfth.

The day had progressed like any other. Mr. Hinze had woken Vern before the sun came up, they'd shared a smoke on the front porch, then they'd worked all morning baking items to be sold.

By the afternoon, things had slowed down substantially, and Mrs. Hinze had insisted he haul water for a bath, so he'd be clean for their dinner party.

Now eighteen, Vern honestly didn't feel any different than he had the day before.

The ride in the carriage had been pleasant and luxurious. The fabric of the seats alone screamed wealth, as did the formality of the carriage driver. Once they'd arrived at the Pennington's, the man had hopped down from his perch and opened the door for them. He'd even bowed, treating them like royalty rather than common folk. At least he'd let them walk to the front door without an escort.

"Oh, dear," Mrs. Hinze mumbled as her husband reached up to knock.

"What's wrong, Annie?"

"I should've worn something else. What was I thinking wearing the same dress I wore on New Year's?"

"You're fine." He lovingly smiled, patted her hand, then lifted it to his lips and kissed it. "Beautiful as ever."

"But Mrs. Pennington might think we're poor, if she believes I have only one good dress."

"It doesn't matter what she thinks," Vern boldly said. "You *are* beautiful in that dress and I'm glad you wore it. It's special."

Mr. Hinze stood taller and firmly knocked. Nothing further was said about the dress.

As the door opened, Vern found himself facing June.

She giggled, took hold of his arm, and brought him inside. Mr. and Mrs. Hinze followed.

"You look surprised to see me." June's laughter still warmed her voice. "We only use a doorman on special occasions. I told Aunt Mabel I wanted to greet you when you arrived." Her eyes searched his face. "Happy birthday, Harp." Right there in front of the Hinzes, she lurched forward and kissed his cheek.

He wanted to hide in a hole. "Thank you, June."

She cuddled into him. "You're as red as my favorite Christmas scarf." Giggling, she faced the others. "Your boy is so shy."

"Yes, he can be," Mrs. Hinze said. "But the longer you're around him," she quickly added, "the more at ease he'll be."

"Well, then." June tossed her head, making her ringlets bobble. "We'll need to spend a lot of time together." The girl beamed. "I hope you're all hungry. Mrs. Dingbaum made a feast."

"*I'm* hungry," Mr. Hinze said.

June smiled at him, then squeezed Vern's arm. "Are you?"

All he could do was nod, yet he had a stronger urge to run out the door and continue sprinting until he reached the comfort of the bakery. Nothing about this felt right.

Mrs. Pennington walked briskly toward them. "Happy birthday, Vern." She reached for his hands and gave them a squeeze, then turned and eyed Mrs. Hinze up and down.

Instantly, the poor woman looked as if she wanted to hide, and Vern could only imagine what thoughts must be going through the heads of both women. Mrs. Hinze's worries over her dress may have been valid, but it was wrong for Mrs. Pennington to judge her.

She gave Mrs. Hinze a half-hug—barely a pat—and finally, she dipped her head at Mr. Hinze. "Please, follow me to the dining room. Our dinner is ready."

Thankfully, they could get down to the business of eating and maybe they wouldn't have to stay long.

June remained plastered to his side as they walked along one of the hallways to the archway that led into the immaculate dining room. Vern had never seen so much shining silverware and crystal stemware in one place. Every table setting had more than one fork, spoon, and knife, and in addition to the china dinner plates, there was a small bowl atop each one and two smaller plates positioned above them.

"You get the place of honor," June said and led him to the captain's chair at the head of the table.

Mr. Pennington walked in, chewing on the end of an unlit pipe. "I usually sit there, but June insisted you take it for this affair."

"Are you sure?" Vern pointed at the chair. "I don't want to put you out."

The man chuckled. "My girl is at the helm of this ship tonight." He mock-saluted her, wandered to another chair and sat, then gestured to the empty seats across from them. "Please sit, Dietrich. Annie." He nodded to them in turn.

The casual way he addressed them made Vern believe they'd become quite familiar on their previous visit. He'd been so caught up in June that night, he'd paid little attention to what had been going on around him.

June took the place beside him, and as soon as Vern sat, she grabbed his hand. It didn't feel right to pull away, so he entwined his fingers with hers, yet he struggled with her forwardness. The instant their digits locked, she coyly smiled.

"Ah . . ." Mrs. Pennington clutched her bosom. "Isn't that sweet?" She motioned to the two of them.

Not even a bucketful of ice could cool the warmth in Vern's cheeks.

Lucinda entered the room, dressed in a similar uniform to the one she'd worn on New Year's Eve. A white cap covered her braided hair, and a long white apron shielded a good portion of her dress. "Shall I serve the soup?"

"Please," Mrs. Pennington answered.

Good.

Once they started eating, June would have to keep her hands to herself.

A sharply dressed footman appeared with linen napkins draped across his arm. He circled the table and positioned one on every lap.

Lucinda exited, but soon returned, holding a tureen. She passed it over to the footman and they went around the table together— starting with Vern—and ladled a portion of soup into the bowls at each place.

Vern waited to taste it until everyone had been served. Besides, he wasn't sure which spoon to use, so he watched the Penningtons and followed their lead.

The production that followed overwhelmed him. Once they finished the chicken soup—which turned out to be quite tasty— the footman removed their bowls and Lucinda brought out a series of vegetables and breads. After she'd put portions on every plate, she left and soon came back with the footman who held a platter of roast beef. She portioned it out as well.

Vern continued to take notice of which utensils to use, and eas- ily came to the conclusion that dinner shouldn't be so compli- cated.

Conversation was limited—mostly involving talk about snow and how cold it had been. The majority of the time, everyone simply enjoyed their food. Vern especially liked the roast beef and wanted to ask for more, but feared it would be impolite.

He preferred the simplicity of the meals they had at the kitchen table in the bakery.

June leaned toward him. "Mrs. Dingbaum made a special cake, so please save room."

"There's always room for cake." He grinned and speared the last bit of beef on his plate. "What kind is it?"

"It's a simple vanilla cake, but the filling makes it special. She uses strawberry preserves."

"We sometimes use preserves in our cakes, too."

She rapidly blinked. "I feel so silly. Cakes are an everyday thing for you. I imagine they aren't special in the least."

He looked her in the eyes. "Don't say that. This entire night has been special, and I appreciate everything you've done for me." He peered around the table, realizing he had everyone's attention. "*All* of you. This is a birthday I'll never forget."

"Nor will we," Mrs. Pennington said. "We'll have to do this again for June's eighteenth birthday, which happens to be in *June*." She laughed and gazed upward. "My dear sister gave her a fitting name."

June shyly lowered her head. "If names were truly representative, I'd fare better in the kitchen. I'm no baker."

Her aunt reached across the table and tapped the spot in front of her. "You won't need to be. Not only will your name change, no girl of mine will perform menial labor."

Vern glanced at Mrs. Hinze, who had her eyes on her near-empty plate. He certainly didn't want her to feel demeaned in any way, not when he admired how hard she worked every day.

He decided to be bold. "What are your plans for the future, June? If you don't work, what will you do?"

She sat primly straight. "I want only one thing—well actually, *two*." After moistening her lips, she cut her eyes toward him, then jutted her chin high. "I want to be a wife and mother, and I intend to devote all my time to my husband and children. This house has room for plenty."

Mrs. Pennington curtly nodded. "That's exactly what a woman *should* do. As the good Lord intended."

Now, not only was Mrs. Hinze staring downward, her shoulders slumped.

"Sometimes," Vern defensively said, "women *need* to work. There's no shame in that. I think it's wonderful when a woman can stand beside her husband and help him make a living for them."

Mr. Hinze jutted *his* chin. "Yes, I agree. I couldn't manage the bakery without Annie." He cast a smile in her direction, but since her eyes were focused downward, she didn't see it.

"Please don't misunderstand me," Mrs. Pennington said. "I'm sympathetic to those less fortunate, and I do admire your dedication. However, where my June is concerned, there's no need for her to toil away and blister her delicate hands. She'll better serve this community by becoming heir to this estate and carrying out charitable acts whenever she sees fit. And, she'll be an exceptional mother."

The woman tipped her head to one side and put her attention on Vern. "My June will never abandon her children. What happened to you was a dreadful injustice." She intensified her gaze. "How many children would you like to have, Vern?"

His throat tightened, so he took a quick drink of water. "*Four*?"

June beamed. "That's the same number I've imagined for myself." She reached over and nabbed his hand. "Isn't that an incredible coincidence?"

Her aunt tittered.

"Actually," Mrs. Hinze whispered, "we don't always get what we want." She lifted her head and sat tall. "And when it seems our lives are nowhere near what we anticipated, we're blessed with something utterly unexpected." She smiled at her husband, then at Vern, and finally, she set her sights on June. "You and Vern are both very young, Miss Baker, and I can tell you from experience, you should appreciate every day of your life and not rush any part of it."

"That's excellent advice, Mrs. Hinze. I assure you, I *do* appreciate every day. Even more now than I did last year." She caressed Vern's hand.

Unlike before, he felt nothing except her fingers.

Somehow, he had to find a way to end this *friendship* before he got in much deeper. He might not be a mind-reader, but June's actions said a great deal. She already considered him her beau and future husband.

CHAPTER 19

After the dinner party at the Pennington's, Vern made no effort to see June again. He'd put every ounce of his energy into work, and on more than one occasion when business had slowed in the afternoon, he'd walked to Fields' Tavern and lost himself in several games of pool. He'd enjoyed seeing Oscar, but had intentionally avoided conversations about women.

He and Oscar made tentative plans to train hop once the weather improved, and Vern was eager to start bringing in some gambling money. Whenever the subject arose with the Hinzes, he still referred to it as a match of skill, yet he knew full well that the way they orchestrated the games couldn't be called anything but gambling. The possibility of someone else besting him always existed, so he took a risk every time he and Oscar laid money down.

At least Mrs. Hinze had stopped pestering him about June. He'd hated that she'd gotten her feelings hurt that night at dinner, but having Mrs. Pennington speak as she had—bordering on snobbishness—helped *him* in the long run.

"Mr. Hinze?" Vern swirled some icing around a layered cake. "I've been thinking about what Mrs. Pennington said at dinner on my birthday."

"I've tried to forget most of it." He punched his fist into a mound of dough.

"I know . . . but something's been bothering me about it. Not only the way she hurt Mrs. Hinze, but I can't understand why they chose me for June. I told June from the start I'm a nobody. You'd think they'd want some hoity toity, uppity rich guy for their niece."

Mr. Hinze laughed. "I understand your confusion, however . . ." He stopped what he was doing and looked directly at him. "I think I know why they selected you. Want to hear my theory?"

"I wouldn't have brought it up if I didn't."

He crossed the floor to where Vern was working and leaned against the wall. "You're non-threatening. If June took interest in someone of stature, they'd have to cope with his parents, who would also be of importance and would likely have strong opinions. With you, I believe they see a young man who can be controlled. Yes, June will one day inherit their house and their fortune, but they're in good health and I don't anticipate they'll be departing this earth anytime soon. If you were to marry the girl, they'd have a lot to say in regard to the way you two live your lives. They'd pull every string, and if for some reason you didn't budge, June would be their go-between to sweet talk you into doing what they want."

He gaped at the man. "Have you been mulling this over long, or did you just come up with all that from the top of your head? Because if you did, it's impressive."

"I confess, the way they acted that night has bothered me and I've lost sleep over it." Mr. Hinze returned to his dough. "I doubt they'd want you to keep baking. Mr. Pennington would probably teach you *his* trade."

"I don't want to be in shipping." He dipped his knife into the icing and glided more of it onto the cake. "I like what I do here."

"I'm glad. Sales that involve shipping aren't as stable as what we do. There's security in providing food, because people will always want to eat, regardless of the state of the economy."

"You've told me that before." He stopped with the knife in midair. "So, what should I do about June? I don't want to hurt her feelings."

The man's mouth shifted from side to side—his mustache along with it. "I imagine if you keep your distance long enough, things will take care of themselves."

The kitchen door burst open.

Mrs. Hinze rushed in, then secured the door behind her and moved to Vern. "Mrs. Pennington is here," she intensely whispered. "She wants to talk to you."

So much for allowing things to take care of themselves . . .

Vern shook his head. "Please, tell her I'm busy." He flashed a tentative smile and dipped the knife for additional icing.

Mrs. Hinze grabbed his wrist. "You need to talk her. It's impolite not to."

He looked to Mr. Hinze for help, but he shrugged. "Annie's right."

"Is she alone?" Vern asked.

"Yes. And fortunately, there's currently no one else in the shop."

"All right." He set aside the knife, then removed his apron and headed for the door. He would've rather run out the back, but he needed to face her, no matter the consequences.

As he entered the shop, he plastered on his best smile. "Hello, Mrs. Pennington."

"Vern." She brusquely nodded.

"How can I help you?"

She repetitively tapped her foot. "Do you know how many days have passed since our dinner party?"

He gazed upward and rapidly calculated. "Twenty-three?"

"Yes. Twenty-three *long* days." She pursed her lips and folded her arms across her large bosom. "My poor June is wondering why you've not made an effort to see her. I know you don't constantly work every day of the week, so I presume you're purposefully try- ing to avoid her. We went above and beyond to make certain you had a special birthday, and if this is how you show gratitude, then you're not the man I proclaimed you to be."

"I'm extremely grateful. The last thing I ever wanted was to upset her or you. I've just been . . . busy."

"Well. It's high time you make it up to her." She stared down her nose at him. "Valentine's Day is less than two weeks away, and it will afford you the perfect opportunity to show her you care."

"You want me to come for dinner again?"

"No. I want you to take her to a restaurant. Just the two of you. It will give you an ample opportunity to become better acquainted without the interference of others." She peered beyond him to the kitchen door.

When Vern turned to look that way, the door shut. Surely, Mrs. Hinze had been poking her head out, trying to listen.

"I suppose I can manage that."

"Good. I'll have my driver bring her here in the carriage that evening at five o'clock. She wants to go to Linderman's, and following dinner, you can take a drive along the river."

"Linderman's?" The simple thought of it constricted his chest.

"Yes. I know you're aware of it. Mrs. Hinze told me how you sometimes deliver baked goods there. Their food is exceptional, and that's where my June chose. She's been so distraught over your absence, I asked what would cheer her."

His mind spun. "So . . . she told you she wants me to take her to dinner for Valentine's Day at Linderman's specifically?"

"Yes."

"Isn't there somewhere *finer*? Their food doesn't compare to what you served the other night, and their dinnerware is lacking. Each table setting has only one knife, fork, and spoon." He threw out a nervous grin, praying she didn't read into his sarcasm.

Her head drew back. "I doubt Mr. Linderman would appreciate you saying something so negative about his business." She eyed him cautiously. "I have my concerns about you, Vern Harpole, but

June has grown fond of you, and since her happiness means more to me than anything else, I'll have to put my worries to rest."

She dropped her arms to her sides and crossed to the door. "February fourteenth. Five o'clock. Wear something suitable and don't disappoint my girl."

With a huff, she left.

Vern yanked out a chair and slumped down into it. He hadn't been there long, when Mr. and Mrs. Hinze emerged and joined him at the table.

"Did she say Linderman's?" Mrs. Hinze whimpered.

Vern nodded, unable to verbally reply.

Something told him this wasn't going to go well.

Not. One. Bit.

* * *

Margaret rubbed across her shamrock broach. More than most days, she needed some luck tonight. The restaurant would be busy for the lover's holiday, and although she'd been successfully keeping her spirits up, she couldn't deny feelings of jealousy for those who shared something she'd never allow herself to have.

Mrs. Archer had suggested she wear red for the evening, but Margaret didn't own a dress that color, so she donned herself in black. It seemed fitting.

She went to the front station to confirm everything was in order, then headed for the fireplace to add more logs.

"Black?" Mrs. Archer quickly crossed to her and fingered Margaret's lacy sleeve. "It's rather glum, Miss Jordan."

"I don't have anything red—or pink. Besides, I doubt any couples eating here tonight will notice me at all. Their eyes will be on each other."

"I suppose you're right." Mrs. Archer peered around the restaurant. "The paper roses were a lovely idea. The tables look beautiful."

"Thank you. Real flowers are impossible to come by this time of year, so I thought 'twould be a nice touch, and once the candles are lit, they'll project a romantic mood."

Mrs. Archer took her hand. "I've noticed a change in you, Miss Jordan. Ever since you made the decision to stay in Kansas City, you've acted happier." She leaned close. "Is there a gentleman in your life you've neglected to tell me about?"

"No, ma'am. I simply made the decision to improve m' disposition. I'd been pining over Ireland, and I knew 'twas time to embrace m' life here." She stood tall and smiled. "I'm glad you noticed a change."

"We all have." Mrs. Archer's brows rose knowingly high, and she released her. "Even Uncle Edwin remarked about it. He admires you, Miss Jordan. If you were older, you could prove to be the answer to his loneliness." She waved a hand. "Forgive me. It was silly to say."

If Margaret had told her what he'd done while being drunk, she doubted Mrs. Archer would *think* it, let alone say the words.

She pushed out another smile. "I'd best get busy. I imagine our guests will arrive soon." Without waiting for a response, she bent down and grabbed a log from the wood pile beside the fireplace and carefully set it in the flames.

"I'll check on Mr. Green to make certain all the food is coming along well," Mrs. Archer said and flitted away.

The dear woman probably felt embarrassed saying what she had about Edwin, and rightfully so. Her uncle was surely in his fifties—old enough to be Margaret's da and then some.

Vern was the only *man* who remained on her mind.

Her smile grew as she thought of him and how she'd so hatefully called him a lad. Thank goodness they'd gotten beyond all that and could be friends. If only her heart didn't want more.

She checked every table setting, then went to speak to the waitresses to make them aware of the menu for the special occasion.

As soon as she finished telling them every detail, Cynthia sniffled and wiped her eyes.

Margaret moved closer to her. "Are you ill?"

The girl's chin quivered. "No'm."

"Are you crying?"

Cynthia bobbed her head.

Gracie, one of the three other girls tapped Margaret's shoulder. "She's sad because she doesn't have a beau."

"I see." Margaret crossed her arms and sympathetically faced Cynthia. "I normally frown on things unbiblical, but I heard long ago that in the middle ages 'twas believed that February fourteenth held mystical powers. And on that night, if someone truly desired love, their heart's mate would be revealed to them—with another unmarried soul, of course. Sadly, most of our arrivals will be paired, yet you never know what fate has in store for ye."

Cynthia sucked in a staggered breath. "I *do* desire true love."

"I know how painful loneliness can be, but you're young and pretty. If your intended isn't revealed to you tonight, eventually, I'm certain you'll acquire a beau."

Again, she sniffled. "You're old and *you* don't have one, and you're one of the prettiest women I know. If you can't get a beau, there's no hope for me."

"There's always hope." She took hold of Cynthia's shoulders and peered into her eyes. "Now, go dry your tears. You need to look your best for our guests."

"Yes'm." With a final sniff, she wandered away.

Margaret watched her go, then faced the others. "'Tis time to light the candles, so please do so at each of your tables. And because of the special holiday, after all our patrons leave, Mr. Linderman has invited all employees to dine. So, work hard, keep our customers happy, and once we close the doors for the night, we'll enjoy eating together."

"Thank you, Miss Jordan," they said in almost perfect unison, then wandered away to their assigned tables.

Miss Cynthia also took her own place, and she hoped the girl's tears wouldn't reemerge. A weepy server wouldn't be appreciated.

Margaret returned to the front station, and within minutes the door opened and the guests began to arrive. Couple after couple entered, and their eyes reflected a romantic dreaminess. Considering they were all paired, it may have been wrong to lift Cynthia's hopes in finding a beau tonight, but Margaret had always loved that story, and she wanted to tell the girl something to stop her from crying and give her hope. Even if she had none for herself.

With every arrival, she managed to retain her professionalism. She cheerfully greeted them, then directed them to a table.

The clock had scarcely ticked past five o'clock and already the restaurant buzzed with conversation and laughter. Surely, a handful of young women would receive proposals of marriage over dinner.

She scanned those present, feeling the warmth and love that radiated around the room. A waft of cold air dusted the back of her neck as the front door reopened.

A pretty blonde walked in, bearing the same love-filled eyes as those of the other guests.

Margaret smiled at her. "Welcome to Linderman's."

"Thank you." The girl reached for the man behind her.

Margaret shifted her attention to him. "Welcome to Lind—" She froze mid-word and simply stared.

Vern inched forward, with the girl's hand tucked into the crook of his arm. "Good evening, Miss Jordan," he solemnly said.

"You know each other?" The girl looked from him to her, then giggled. "Oh, yes. Of course, you do. Aunt Mabel told me my Harp oftentimes delivers baked goods here." She cuddled into his arm, all the while eyeing Margaret. "We'd like your finest table."

Her *Harp*?

It felt as if every bit of air had been drawn from the room. Margaret's chest hurt so badly, she had to grip the edge of the counter to keep from buckling. "All our tables are fine," she finally said.

"Vern?" Mrs. Archer appeared out of nowhere and hastened toward them.

"Hello, Mrs. Archer," he said.

She eyed him strangely, then smiled at the blonde. "Welcome to Linderman's. I'm happy to show you to a table."

"Thank you," the girl chirped, all the while attached to Vern.

As they followed Mrs. Archer and passed Margaret, he turned and looked straight at her. His eyes didn't reflect the same kind of joy she'd seen from everyone else, or anywhere near the elation in those of the young woman with him. Honestly, he acted almost apologetic.

She whipped around the other direction so she wouldn't have to see them any longer.

She'd told him to court someone else, so it appeared he'd done as she'd requested. So why did it feel as if he'd just plunged a knife into her heart? And why did he bring her *here*? Was he purpose-fully flaunting his new love?

But the expression he'd had didn't seem anywhere close to gloating.

Still . . .

She startled at the touch of someone's hand on her back.

"Are you all right, Miss Jordan?"

She slowly faced Mrs. Archer. "I'm fine."

"I don't believe you," she whispered. "You didn't know Vern was seeing someone, did you?"

"No, ma'am. But it's not m' concern. Granted, he's m' friend, yet it's obvious he doesn't tell me everything." She forced herself to stand fully upright. "She's a lovely lass."

"Not as pretty as you." Mrs. Archer's eyes searched Margaret's face. "You care about him more than you realized, don't you?"

"I . . ." She couldn't say what she honestly felt and turned her head.

"It's all right. I understand. If you need a moment to catch your breath, I can cover the front."

"No. 'Tis my job." She deeply inhaled and lifted her head high.

"If you change your mind or need to talk, I'm here for you."

Margaret gave a brief nod, then moved behind the front station and put her attention on the door, preparing herself for new arrivals.

Mrs. Archer cast a pitiful look her way, then walked off.

More questions than she could count drifted through Margaret's mind, but she wondered most prevalently how long Vern had been seeing the young girl. The way she'd clung to him and so easily called him *her Harp* made her believe they'd been familiar for some time. Maybe she'd be one of the handful who received a proposal tonight.

Margaret's eyes burned as she fought back tears. A weepy hostess would be even worse than a tearful server. Long ago, she'd learned how to stop herself from crying, so she drew on her past experience and stifled her feelings.

* * *

"Isn't this romantic?" June fluttered her lashes at Vern and reached across the table. "Thank you for bringing me here."

He hesitated and glanced around the room before setting his hand on hers. He gave the back of it a light tap, then pulled away completely. "I'm glad you're happy."

She tipped her head to one side. "You're acting strange. Are you ashamed to be seen with me?"

"*No.*" He leaned forward. "Why would I be? You're pretty and sweet, and . . ."

"Yes?" As before, she batted her eyes.

"What man wouldn't be proud to have you at his side?" He kept his voice as low as he possibly could.

"If you're proud of me, then why are you whispering? And why wouldn't you hold my hand?"

He swallowed hard. "This setting is so . . . public. I'm not comfortable saying and doing things openly that are meant to be private."

She pursed her lips. "We'll be in an enclosed carriage after dinner. I realize we already were, but we spent the entire time coming here talking about why you hadn't been by to see me. Once we're alone again, we'll have already said everything of importance. Words won't be necessary any longer, if you understand my meaning."

He unfastened his top button, feeling suddenly constrained. He had no doubt what she expected of him, and it went beyond a simple kiss on the cheek. The very reason Mr. Hinze had once explained the necessity of a chaperone. Vern had thought the idea was primitive, now he wished the Penningtons had insisted on it.

June had her back to the front station, but Vern faced it, and his eyes kept being drawn there as if Margaret's magnetism pulled them in. He'd seen the hurt in her stunned expression, and it cut deep within himself. He didn't belong here with June—or anywhere at all with the girl.

She pivoted in her chair, looked behind her, then at him again. "What are you watching? Your attention is on everything except me."

"Sorry. I've just been curious as to who's coming through the door. There are a lot of couples here tonight."

"Yes, and we're one of them." She pushed out her lower lip. "Did Aunt Mabel force you to do this? Because I'm beginning to think you don't care for me."

"Force?" He lightly chuckled. "I'm my own man, June."

"And Aunt Mabel can be quite persuasive." She re-extended her hand, then wiggled her fingers. "Prove you want to be with me."

He cut his eyes once more toward the front, then obliged her and took hold.

"Will you kiss it?"

"Huh?"

"My hand. Show me you care by kissing it."

His heart thumped out of his chest. "Here? *Now*?"

Her eyes widened. "Yes."

He bent down quickly, gave it a peck, then shot straight back in his chair.

"I believe that was the most unromantic kiss ever given since time began. My *uncle* has kissed me more sweetly." She stuck out her lower lip farther than before. An *ugly* pout to say the least. "Can't you do better?"

As her pleading eyes searched his, he breathed harder and faster. If he wanted this, the rapid beat of his heart would indicate a good thing, but he knew it was telling him to flee.

The longer he sat without taking action, the worse things became. Her chin quivered, and her face scrunched tight. "Harp, *please*?"

All he needed was for June to start crying in public. Mrs. Pennington's wrath would surely ignite the bakery on fire after tonight, unless he could figure out a way to keep her niece happy.

Her small hand still rested in his, so he slowly lifted it and leaned in. With his eyes locked on hers, he brushed his lips over her knuckles.

Her entire body trembled. "Oh, my, Harp . . ."

To his relief, every indication of an inevitable bawl disappeared and with each passing second, her newly formed smile broadened.

He gave her hand a final kiss, then cradled it inside both of his and caressed her fingers.

She let out a soft whimper.

"Forgive me for interrupting, but have you made your selection?"

He jerked his head up and stared at the waitress. "I . . . um . . ."

June giggled. "We'll have the roasted chicken."

"Very well." The server looked as if *she'd* been crying. She sniffled and wandered off.

"That was odd," June said. "Maybe she's jealous." She reached over and stroked his cheek. "My handsome Harp."

By wanting to keep Mrs. Pennington at bay, he'd further ignited June's fire.

I'm a bumbling idiot.

* * *

"It's hopeless," Miss Cynthia mumbled and trudged up beside Margaret. "There are no *unmarried souls* here tonight. And I've seen more affection than I care to have witnessed."

"Don't be disheartened. Just do your job, and we'll soon enjoy a meal together."

"But you don't have to watch what I'm forced to." Cynthia stood in front of her and lifted her chin toward the back of the room. "That baker, Vern, was slobbering all over the hand of the girl he's dining with. I heard she's the niece of those rich people who live near the river. The Penningtons. Do you know them?"

Margaret could've gone all night without hearing this. "No. I don't."

"Well, I doubt they'd be pleased knowing their niece was being fondled in public." She leaned close. "I always thought he was somewhat shy and respectable."

"As did I. Maybe you misinterpreted his actions."

Cynthia shook her head. "His lips were practically *inhaling* her knuckles. He'd better marry the girl." She let out a staggered breath. "I feel better now that I've talked about it. If I have to wait to find a man who'll respect me, I'd rather have that than someone who behaves so brashly."

The girl wandered away, much to Margaret's relief. She'd heard enough and it only made her more miserable. She certainly wouldn't feel like eating once everyone left, but she'd stay regardless, out of gratitude to Mr. Linderman for his kind offer.

The next hour passed in a blurry emotional fog. Margaret greeted new guests and also thanked those who had finished their dinner and made their way out again.

"That was such a wonderful meal, Harp."

Margaret stood stone-still the instant she heard the lilting voice come up behind her. And when she felt Vern's presence, she stiffened further.

Within moments, the pair came so near she could've easily touched them.

"Excuse me, ma'am," the girl said. "Do you know if it's snowing?"

Margaret turned toward her. "I don't believe so. I've seen no flakes on the shoulders of anyone who's come in."

"You have such a beautiful accent." She grabbed hold of Vern. "Doesn't she, Harp?" With her arm firmly linked with his, she returned her attention to Margaret. "Are you Scottish?"

Margaret mindlessly fingered her broach. "No. 'Tis a common error. I'm Irish."

"What a pretty pin." The girl peered closer. "From your husband?"

"No." She cut her eyes toward Vern, who looked ready to bolt.

"We should go, June," he said. "I promised your aunt I wouldn't have you home too late."

June. A pretty name for a lovely lass.

"He's eager," June said, grinning. "We're taking a ride along the river in my carriage. Isn't that romantic?"

Margaret painfully nodded.

Vern gestured to June's coat. "You should button it up all the way. It's quite cold outside."

The girl coyly tipped her head. "I have you to keep me warm." She grinned at Margaret again, then urged Vern out the door.

As he exited, he glanced over his shoulder.

Margaret put her back to him. It was the only way to cope with her pain.

CHAPTER 20

Vern trudged behind June to the waiting carriage. When he opened the door to let her in, he found the driver huddled inside, wrapped in a blanket.

The man quickly rose. "Is it time to go?"

"Yes, Nicholas," June said. "And I promise I won't tell Aunt Mabel you were resting."

He gave her an enormous smile, then pointed upward. "It's freezing out there." As he stepped from the carriage to the ground, his eyes lingered on June. "I hope you had a pleasant meal."

"We did." She cuddled into Vern. "And now, we'd like to ride for a while."

The man nodded, and his smile disappeared. Vern sensed from his immediate change in demeanor that he wished she hadn't said it —and not because he didn't want to be out driving in the cold.

He cares for her.

Vern helped June inside, then leaned toward Nicholas. "Just a *brief* ride along the river," he said low enough so only he could hear. "Then, please return me to the bakery."

"Yes, sir." Nicholas perked right up and hopped with new enthusiasm onto the driver's seat.

Since he looked several years older than Vern, it felt odd being called *sir* by him. No doubt, the man had been well-trained to respect anyone he was asked to serve. Yet, Nicholas was the least of his worries.

Vern stared at the open doorway of the carriage, feeling as if he were about to enter a den of iniquity. Somehow, he had to dissuade June.

He stepped up and shut the door behind him. The second it clicked into place, June grabbed his arm and yanked him onto the seat beside her, then burrowed into him. Before he could raise any sort of objection, she hugged him and laid her head on his chest. "You see, Harp. I'm plenty warm like this."

He kept his own arms hovering in midair, unsure what to do with them. Eventually, they tired, so he let them drop to his sides.

The carriage jerked and moved forward.

"Why don't you hold me, Harp?" June wriggled a bit and held him tighter, then tilted her head back and looked up at him. Being blanketed in near darkness, it was difficult to fully see her features, but he saw enough to know what she wanted. She'd puckered her lips.

No.

When he didn't oblige her, she let out a whimper. "Hold me, Harp." Her tone had changed from syrupy sweet to demanding.

He breathed harder. "I can't."

"What did you say?" She huffed and thankfully, sat up.

"I can't hold you, June. Actually, I don't *want* to hold you *or* kiss you."

Even in the darkness, he knew she was leering at him. "So, the sensual one you placed on my hand meant nothing? Were you playing with me? Leading me on in a cruel way?"

"I was trying to keep you happy, but if I continue this farce, *I'll* be miserable."

"*Farce?*" She yanked her coat together and fastened every button. "I despise you, Vern Harpole. I deserve to be treated better than this. You've been lying to me all night. Just wait till I tell Aunt Mabel."

As harsh as she sounded, it didn't faze him. "You're right. I haven't been upfront with you. I don't like to hurt anyone's feelings, but it's wrong of me to make you believe I care more than I do." The clip-clop of the horse's hooves wasn't moving nearly fast enough. He wished Nicholas would speed them along.

Nicholas . . .

Being a carriage driver, Vern doubted he had greater prospects or relatives to interfere in a relationship with June. He could be the perfect solution to this mess.

"And you're also correct that you deserve to be treated well," he said with greater conviction.

"I'm glad you have enough sense to realize it. Do you understand how wealthy I'll be one day? As you said earlier, I'm pretty and sweet, and with my inevitable fortune, I should be able to have anyone I want."

She had a lot of her aunt in her. "Anyone but *me*."

"Hmph." She jerked around and put her back to him.

"I have a confession. Before I was introduced to you, I met someone else, who I care for deeply. Sadly, she rejected me, yet I can't seem to forget her and move on. I tried with you, but . . ."

"It didn't work." June snapped her head around, finishing his sentence, then lifted her chin high. "I'm glad you told me. It shows *some* character and maturity."

Simply by telling her how he actually felt, an enormous weight lifted from his shoulders. He decided to press forward. "How long have you known your driver?"

"Nicholas?"

"Yes."

"About a year. He was a footman, then advanced to the position as carriage driver. Why do you ask?"

The air in the small enclosure had already warmed from their heated discussion. With the more comfortable temperature and the baring of his soul, he'd actually started to enjoy himself. If this worked, maybe *everyone* would be happy.

Except Margaret. But he intended to work on that issue as well. From her behavior tonight, he knew without a doubt she cared more for him than she was willing to admit.

"Haven't you ever noticed the way Nicholas looks at you?" Vern confidently continued his mission. "I thought I'd recognized a sparkle in his eyes when he'd helped you from the carriage at Linderman's, but I definitely noticed something there only minutes ago, by the way he smiled at you when you told him you wouldn't report him to your aunt. He cares for you, June."

"You're certain?" She sounded stunned, yet intrigued.

"A man is always aware when another man is attracted to the woman on his arm." He chuckled. "Primal instinct, I suppose. He's older than you, but not by much. I think you should pay closer attention the next time you interact."

The curtains on the side windows had been left open, so whenever they passed one of the street lamps, light filtered in and he could see her expressions. No longer did she seem angry. Her eyes held curiosity, and she fidgeted as if eager to end the ride.

She crossed to the other seat, put her face to the window, and peered upward. "Nicholas is probably cold out there." She fingered the blanket he'd dropped when he'd exited.

"I'm sure he's all right. From what I could tell, he's used to the weather, and his heavy coat and driving gloves looked plenty warm."

"I shouldn't have asked him to take us along the river. With the cold that drifts off the water, it's the chilliest place in the city. I was being selfish and should've asked him to take us straight home." She touched the window as if trying to reach out to Nicholas.

The girl was fickle, but Vern didn't care. He wanted her to shift her affections, and she'd merely needed a gentle nudge. At least he felt confident Nicholas cared about her, so he wasn't casting her frivolously aside.

They remained quiet for some time, accompanied by the gentle rhythm of the horses' hoof beats.

"Will you tell me who the girl is whom you care for so deeply?" June asked, breaking the silence.

"I'd rather not. She's a private person, and since she refused me, I don't feel comfortable revealing her name. I wouldn't want to cause her any embarrassment."

"Hmm..." June looked out once more, then faced him. "When you talk that way, it shows you *do* have a heart. I'm sorry I was angry, but you hurt my feelings."

"I didn't mean to, and I hope you'll accept my apology."

She turned and swirled her finger down the partially fogged-over window, making lines in it. "I understand. You were put under a lot of pressure by my aunt. I can be demanding when I want something or some*one,* and she tries to keep me happy." She roughly cleared her throat. "I'm sorry *you* were hurt—by that woman you mentioned. Maybe she'll change her mind."

"I hope so."

The carriage stopped, and the door opened. Nicholas stood in the doorway with his shoulders pulled back. "We've arrived at the bakery."

"Thank you," Vern said and got up to leave.

"Yes, thank you, Nicholas," June rapidly added in the sweetest voice ever.

Nicholas dipped his head to her, then widened the opening for Vern.

He carefully stepped to the ground. "Goodnight, Miss Baker."

"Goodnight, Mr. Harpole."

Their formality said a great deal, and he hoped Nicholas noticed.

As Vern walked around the building to the back door, he could've sworn he heard June giggling. Apparently, she'd already begun to pay closer attention to her driver, and soon, Vern felt certain it would be reciprocated.

He also assumed her aunt would be gifted with new demands, and the freshly promoted carriage driver would advance to an even higher position.

* * *

"Miss Jordan?" Mrs. Fitch lightly rapped on Margaret's door. "You missed breakfast, dear. Are you ill?"

"I'm fine, Mrs. Fitch," she called out, yet stayed lying down. "I worked late, and I'm tired."

"I understand. I hope I didn't wake you."

"You didn't, but I'd like to rest a while longer."

Mrs. Fitch made no response, and Margaret assumed she'd left. So, she let her head sink deeper into the pillow and shut her eyes.

"We can have tea later," Mrs. Fitch chimed.

Margaret's lids popped open. Much later . . . "That sounds lovely, Mrs. Fitch."

"Sleep well!" The woman's delicate retreating footsteps affirmed she'd finally left Margaret's door.

She appreciated their friendship, yet the sweet lady had become a constant fixture and hovered close to Margaret whenever she was home. She'd even come by Linderman's a time or two, simply to say *hello*.

Perhaps she viewed her as the daughter she'd never had, and Margaret couldn't fault her for it. Still, at times such as this, she wanted to be left alone.

Until she'd seen Vern with the young blonde, she'd done well, keeping her attitude positive and cheerful, and she'd had every intention of seeing Vern and telling him . . .

What?

She sighed.

That was the problem. She'd not seen him because she had no idea what to say to him. If she'd listened to her heart and expressed *those* particular feelings, she'd have misled him into believing they had a future together. Her mind told her it was impossible. She refused to tear down the defensive walls she'd erected, and because of them she couldn't let him near her.

Now, none of it mattered. He'd found someone else, and it hurt worse than the pain she'd endured when she'd left Ireland. Vern had wound his way around her heart *and* soul, but it made no sense. On most occasions, he irritated her.

She sat up and hugged her knees to her chest. She'd been foolish to think she could sleep again—not with her thoughts so viciously tumbling.

She'd heard the expression, *opposites attract*, and maybe it fit in regard to her and Vern. Aside from both of them enduring painful trauma when they were young, they were nothing alike. Maybe love worked that way.

The very fact she contemplated actually being in love with him bothered her the most. It didn't trouble her to *like* him, but love was another issue entirely.

She'd already mulled over much of this in her mind. The only thing she knew without question was that she couldn't bear seeing him with that girl again.

Leaving Kansas City was the only solution.

* * *

Even in the crisp, cold air, Vern managed to whistle. He'd not felt like doing it for months, but the off-key melody erupted from him with vigor.

Betsy let out a whinny, and he laughed. Surely, the horse wasn't showing her disapproval of his inability to carry a tune, was she?

He steered her toward St. Patrick's.

It had been hard not to go straight to Margaret after Nicholas had returned him to the bakery the other night, but Vern knew she'd have to work late, and he didn't want to trouble her further. Besides, once he'd gone inside, he'd spent a full hour telling Mr. and Mrs. Hinze everything that had happened, and they'd advised him to let things rest for a few days.

They'd all come to the conclusion that they'd have a visit from Mrs. Pennington in the near future, but even Mrs. Hinze acted unbothered by the possibility. She'd seemed just as relieved as Vern, to be done with that family.

However, she wasn't thrilled with the idea of him pursuing Margaret once more, mainly because she feared he'd be hurt again. He'd assured her his heart wouldn't lie, and he knew he was doing its bidding by going to her.

He drove along with his head high, his spirit light, and his horse apparently annoyed by his whistling. When he reached the church, he parked near the front entrance and waited.

As the service ended, people emerged and either walked away, or got into buggies and carriages. He craned his neck and searched for Margaret. Woman after woman came out, yet not the one he wanted to see.

When it appeared the church had emptied, he set the brake, then got down and headed for the entrance, careful to wipe his feet before going inside.

He spotted Father Tierney speaking to an old man. Vern patiently waited for them to finish their conversation, then casually walked up to the priest. He'd not met him the night he'd come for Mass, but he presumed the man would be caring and helpful.

"Hello, sir. I mean . . . Father." His blunder brought heat to his face, yet he figured it was already red from the cold and wouldn't be noticed.

"May I help you, Son?"

"I was looking for a friend of mine who attends here. Miss Margaret Jordan. Do you have a back door she may have slipped out of?"

He kindly smiled. "We do have a rear exit, however, I'm afraid I didn't see her at Mass. Is there something *I* can do for you?"

"Not today. But, thank you." He turned to leave, then spun back around. "Father?"

"Yes?"

"I just wanted you to know I was here for Midnight Mass on Christmas Eve. I enjoyed it."

"I'm glad." His smile widened. "You're welcome to come again. We worship the Lord throughout the year, not only in celebration of His birth."

"I knew that." He nervously chuckled, feeling slightly in awe of the man. "Being that churches are open every Sunday."

The priest let out his own laugh. "That they are. I hope I'll see you *here* on one of them soon."

"Thank you." He bowed to the man, then hastened away, all the while scolding himself for acting so foolish. He had no idea what had compelled him to bow.

As he climbed into his buggy, he put his mind back on Margaret. It wasn't like her not to be at Mass. From his understanding, she never missed a Sunday.

He hurried Betsy along to the boarding house, wishing he'd not listened to the Hinzes and had followed his instincts to go immediately to Margaret after the Valentine's Day dinner debacle.

Once he arrived at Miss Polly's, he nearly sprinted up the pathway to the porch, then rapidly knocked on the door.

"Good gracious." Patsy opened the door, already fussing. "Are you trying to dent the wood?"

"No, ma'am. I didn't realize I'd hit it so hard. Is Miss Jordan here?"

"Not for long." She scowled, then rolled her eyes. "She's leaving tomorrow."

"What?" The mere thought of it sickened him. "*Why?*"

"If I remember correctly, you're the boy who wouldn't answer *my* questions, so I'm not inclined to answer yours."

"Can I see her, please?"

"I doubt she wants to see *you*." She tapped her foot and smirked. "I assume you're at the top of her vast list of problems."

"Excuse me." An elderly woman appeared over Pasty's shoulder, then nudged her to the side. "Aren't you Miss Jordan's friend?"

Patsy leered at her, then tossed her head and walked off.

Good riddance.

Vern smiled at the old woman. "Yes, I'm Vern Harpole, Miss Jordan's friend. You must be Mrs. Fitch."

She nodded. "How do you know me?" Her smile brightened, and she seemed pleasantly surprised by his recognition.

"Margaret told me about you and how kind you are. She also said she sits by you at Mass, but I went to St. Patrick's and she wasn't there, so I came here." Words spewed out of his mouth as if somehow talking quickly would get him faster to Margaret.

"You poor young man. Come inside before you freeze."

He looked beyond her, fearing Patsy might reemerge, then carefully stepped onto the floor mat and wiped his feet.

Mrs. Fitch lifted his hand and gave it a pat. "Go sit by the fire in the parlor, and I'll fetch Miss Jordan. I pray *you* can change her mind, because I've had no luck. If she leaves as she plans, I'll miss her horribly."

"I will, too." The pit in his stomach weighed him down, but he trudged to the parlor and waited. He *had* to change her mind.

* * *

"Miss Jordan?" Mrs. Fitch knocked, interrupting Margaret's packing. Fortunately, she wouldn't have to endure the disruptions much longer. "You have a guest, dear."

She crossed the room and opened her bedroom door. "Is it Mrs. Archer again? I can't bear the thought of listening to her plea for me to stay. It was hard enough telling her goodbye the first *and* second time."

"No. It's no one from the restaurant. It's that young man I saw you with at Midnight Mass. Vern Harpole."

Margaret shook her head and backed away. "Tell him to go home. There's nothing he can say that I want to hear."

Mrs. Fitch stepped into the room. "I can tell you're afraid, but I also noticed how eager *he* is to see you." She moved closer. "I care about you, *Margaret*, and I know you're running from something."

She'd never called her by her given name before. "You don't understand."

"You're right. I know very little about you, but I *do* know you have a good heart. One that's been broken. If that man downstairs is the one who damaged it, I believe he's come to make amends. You should give him the opportunity."

"I can't." She sat on the edge of her bed. "'Twould be best if I get on that train tomorrow and put him and everything here behind me."

Mrs. Fitch sat beside her. "My husband was the love of my life, and when he died, part of me died with him. It took a great deal of faith and plenty of time for me to find joy again. Claude was such a good soul and irreplaceable."

The sweet woman shut her eyes as if caught up in a blissful memory. "He would've given me the moon if I'd asked for it, if only he'd had the capability of roping it from the sky." She let out a soft laugh. "Men like that aren't easy to come by. Sadly, many of them want a woman simply for their own pleasure and they don't take *her* feelings into consideration. They certainly don't give any credence to her desires."

Mrs. Fitch shifted sideways and faced her directly. "I may have just met Mr. Harpole, but I don't believe he's one of those kinds of men. He's heartsick. He went to the church to find you, then came here. With all that effort, you should at least speak to him—tell him *goodbye*, if that's what you want to do."

"He's probably come to tell me he's getting married." Again, Margaret shook her head. "I don't want to hear it."

"You won't know, unless you go down there and see him." Mrs. Fitch tipped her head ever so slightly. "You're a strong woman, Margaret, now do what's right and talk to the man." She stood and walked to the door, then stopped, facing the hallway. "Shall I tell him you're coming down?"

Margaret wrung her hands. "In a few minutes."

Without looking back, the woman left, and Margaret prepared herself for greater heartbreak. Mrs. Fitch may have called her strong, yet she hadn't felt this weak since she'd fled St. Patrick's the night of Christmas Eve Mass.

CHAPTER 21

Margaret ran a brush through her hair, smoothed her skirt, bolstered her courage, and marched out her bedroom door.

She stomped down the stairs, then abruptly stopped, realizing how much anger she'd been forcing through every step. Strength was commendable, but uncontrolled rage never did anyone any good.

When she reached the bottom, Mrs. Fitch met her with a tentative smile. "Take a breath, Margaret," she whispered, "then go into the parlor. Allow the man to speak before you do."

"All right." Margaret deeply inhaled, then passed by her.

As soon as she crossed the threshold into the parlor, Mrs. Fitch pulled the double doors shut, sealing her and Vern within.

Margaret believed the parlor doors had always remained open, and Pasty would certainly object. However, it was likely Mrs. Fitch would stand on the other side as a dutiful guard and wait for her to reemerge.

She'd definitely been thrust into conversation, whether she wanted it or not. Her twisting insides suggested the latter.

Vern stood from the sofa. "Margaret . . ." He whispered her name like a prayer.

"Hello, Vern," she curtly said, wanting to say substantially more. Yet, if Mrs. Fitch happened to be listening, she wanted to do the woman a courtesy and abide by her request to let him talk first.

He took a few steps closer. "I don't know what I would've done if I'd gotten here and you were gone." His face was so ashen, he looked ill.

Frowning, he rubbed across his chest. "Why are you leaving? I thought we'd worked through all that."

"Everything has changed." She firmed her jaw and jutted it high, but thought better of it and lowered it back down. "Then again, nothing has."

"What? That makes no sense."

"It makes perfect sense. I agreed to stay because you assured me your parents wouldn't tell m' secret, and you agreed to be m' friend and not push me to discuss things I didn't care to."

His lip curled. "And the Hinzes *haven't* told your secret, I'm *still* your friend, and as far as I can recall, I've never made you talk about anything you didn't want to. So, like I said, you're not making sense."

She stomped her foot. "*Are* you m' friend?"

"Well . . . yes."

She eased forward and took another breath, hoping to control her rising anger. "What *friend* would flaunt his new love in front of the woman he'd asked to court a short time prior?"

He firmly folded his arms and grunted. "You rejected me. Or did you forget that? You told me to find someone else, so if anyone's at fault here, it's you."

"Me?" She glared at him. "I thought you had a heart. Not only did you bring her to my place of employment, you fondled her in front of my wait staff. 'Twas a shameful thing to do!"

"Fondled?" His head drew back.

Margaret dramatically lifted her hand to her lips and repetitively kissed her own knuckles. "Remind you of anything?"

"That's what you call fondling?" He grunted again. "You may not believe me, but I was only trying to appease the girl. She'd been whining that I didn't care."

"And how else did you *appease* her on the carriage ride home?" Anger had morphed into pain, and tears threatened. She quickly stifled them.

"In no way at all," he whispered, then dropped down onto the sofa and covered his face.

She hovered above him, unsure what to say.

After several long, uncomfortable moments of silence, he slowly lowered his hands and looked up. "This isn't how I wanted this conversation to go. Can we start over?"

With her feet soundly planted, she crossed her arms in front of herself and stood fully erect. "I don't see the need. 'Tis obvious your feelings for me have changed, and besides, your young woman wouldn't appreciate you being alone with me like this. You should go, Vern."

"I don't want to."

"Perhaps. Though I doubt Miss June would approve."

"She wouldn't care. I told her on the ride home that I had deep feelings for someone else. Feelings I couldn't overcome. And, I'm pretty sure I guided her into the arms of her carriage driver. Since Mrs. Archer found happiness with hers, I figured it might work with June." He nervously picked at the sofa. "June's not an issue."

Margaret cautiously lowered herself onto the chair beside him. "One day, I might want you to tell me how she came into your life, but for now, I need to know more about these deep feelings. Do they still exist, and are they the reason you're here?"

He looked straight at her. "Of course, they are. I think you love me, Margaret, and I *know* I love you." His eyes glistened with tears, and her own returned.

This time, she couldn't push them aside. "How can you say you love me, when I'm nothing but trouble?"

He reached out and carefully set his hand atop her knee. The simple action sent pleasant shivers across her skin, and she wasn't repulsed in *any* way. She *wanted* his touch.

He looked from his hand to her face. "You've troubled me from the moment I met you, but you somehow ingrained yourself into my heart, and no matter what you do or say, I can't let go of you. I don't want you to leave."

She leaned forward to whisper. "What about m' baby?"

"If you want, we can bring it here. I know you've pined for your child, and I'd gladly raise it as my own." Fortunately, he, too, kept his voice low, yet every part of this discussion brought on deeper pain.

She clasped onto his hand with both of hers. "We can't bring it here, because I don't know where it is. I don't even know if I had a boy or a girl."

"How could you not know?"

The agony of every memory relating to her child rushed in. As much as she wanted to dismiss it as she always had, she'd finally found someone she trusted enough to speak of it, and maybe she *needed* to.

After a glance behind her to make certain the doors were still secure, she tightened her grip. "After the babe was born, m' da took it away. I wasn't allowed to hold it. I remember m' mum saying it was best to know as little as possible about the wee one."

Vern stared at her, and a tear seeped from his eye.

She had to look away, or she couldn't go on. "I know how cruel it seems. At the time, they believed they were doing what was right. Because they wouldn't allow me to keep the child, they didn't want to risk m' bonding with it." She sniffled. "They promised the babe would go to a good home."

"What about the baby's father? Didn't he have a say?"

She shut her eyes and lowered her head. "I don't know who he is." Her heart pounded as the image of that night emerged in her mind's eye. "There were *two* men." She choked down the bile that had risen in her throat. "I was walking home alone one night, and they grabbed me from behind and covered m' head with a bag made of sackcloth." Even the sound of their tormenting laughter vividly returned to her memory.

"I—I struggled to breathe." She panted harder and faster, experiencing once more, the panic she'd felt then. "They took turns with me, then left me trembling and bleeding in the dirt on the ground. 'Twas seven years ago, yet I can still feel it all."

Her entire body shook, and her tears streamed.

"Oh, Margaret . . ." Vern wrapped his arms around her and drew her close to him on the sofa. He swayed with her, just as her mum had done, when she'd told her what happened. "I'll make sure you're never hurt again." He tenderly stroked her hair. "*Never* again."

She clung to him and sobbed.

* * *

Vern ran his fingers through Margaret's long hair, then placed a soft kiss on her damp cheek. "I love you, Margaret."

She trembled, and he strengthened his hold.

"It's all right," he whispered. "You're safe with me."

"Open these doors at once!" Patsy shrieked from the hallway.

Aside from her shuddering troubled breaths, Margaret froze in his grasp.

"You can't go in there!" Mrs. Fitch forcefully said.

"Oh, yes, I can!"

The commotion worsened as heavy thumps shook the doors.

"Ooh!" Mrs. Fitch squealed, then the door swung wide.

Patsy stomped through the parlor, shaking her nasty finger at them. "Stop that at once!"

Mrs. Fitch hastened in and grabbed her arm. "Shame on you! They needed privacy, and I afforded them that."

"Privacy to frolic on my sofa?" Pasty hissed. "I think not!"

Margaret buried her face against Vern's shoulder.

He scowled at the hateful woman. "We weren't *frolicking*. Can't you see how upset Miss Jordan is? I was merely offering comfort."

Mrs. Williams appeared from the hallway. "What's all the ruckus? It's impossible to take a Sunday afternoon nap with all this commotion." She pointed the tip of her cane at him. "You again?"

"Look at them, Mother." Patsy flitted her hand in their direction. "It's disgraceful what they were doing in our parlor. They're *touching*!" Air wheezed from the woman's nostrils. "It's a good thing that woman is leaving. She could tarnish our reputation and make people believe this is a house of prostitution."

Margaret jerked away from him and hastened to the stairway. Before Vern could stop her, she vanished from view.

He shot to his feet. "How could you be so hateful? You don't know what she's been through." He pushed past the others and headed for the stairs.

"You can't go up there!" Pasty screeched. "If need be, I'll get the authorities!"

Vern spun toward her. "Go on then. I won't stop you. I doubt they'd arrest me for speaking with my fiancée."

"Oh?" Mrs. Fitch clapped her hands and beamed. "What wonderful news."

"Fiancée?" Mrs. Williams plodded toward him. "Why would she tell us she's going away, if she intends to marry you?"

"Because she didn't know *my* intentions until today. Miss Jordan isn't going anywhere." He grinned confidently at Mrs. Fitch, then hastened up the stairs.

When he reached the top, he peered over the rails. "Which room?"

"Second door on the left!" Mrs. Fitch called out.

He hurriedly knocked on Margaret's door, doing all he could to ignore the argument that carried on between the three women below. Even if Patsy managed to bring the law, by the time they arrived, he'd have said his piece.

"Margaret?" He rapped a bit harder.

"You can't come in, Vern."

He tested the knob and found it unlocked, so he carefully pushed the door open.

She gasped and clutched her bosom. "I said, you can't enter."

"Because you don't want me here, or because of what the others will think?"

Her eyes pinched shut and she lowered her head. Her body lurched with silent sobs.

This wouldn't do . . .

He clicked the door shut, then moved closer to her. "I don't want to court you any longer, Margaret."

Her body stilled completely, and her sad eyes lifted. "You don't want me anymore," she said as if she believed it as fact.

"That's not what I said. I honestly don't *need* to court you. I want to marry you as soon as possible." He dropped onto one knee and stretched out his hand. "Will you be my wife?"

She stared at him, utterly expressionless. Almost *dazed*. "Even after I told you m' entire secret, you still want me?"

"Yes." She'd been damaged worse than he'd imagined, and he ached for her. Her pain cut deep inside him, and he wanted to strip it from her and cast it so far away it couldn't touch her again. "I want you with me forever, and if you plan to get on another train, I'd better have the ticket to the seat beside you."

Her face puckered, and her chin vibrated. "I can't marry you, Vern."

The words slapped hard, but he knew she didn't mean them. He'd tired of her always putting up ridiculous obstacles. "Why?" He crossed his arms over his chest and sighed. "Because you lost your virtue?"

She looked away and said nothing.

He shook his head back and forth. "Don't you understand, I don't care about that? What happened wasn't your choice. Those men . . ." Just imagining what they'd done to her infuriated him, and he tightened his fists. "They should've hung for what they did. And if I ever find out who they are—"

"No, Vern." With tears trickling down her cheeks, she held up a hand. "It's impossible to know. I couldn't see them, and aside from their laughter—and some other horrid sounds that haunt m' sleep—they didn't speak. I could've easily passed them on the streets of Castlebar many times and didn't even know them. You have to let it go, as I have. One day, they'll face the Lord's reckoning, and He'll punish them for what they did. I don't want you to carry around the same anger I've worked so hard to set free. It would only fester in your soul and make you bitter."

"It's not right. They need to pay for assaulting you."

"They will." She gazed vacantly beyond him as if she'd grown numb.

"Do you love me, Margaret?"

Her head lethargically turned, and she blinked out more tears. "I do."

"Then, why won't you marry me?"

"You're not Catholic."

He gaped at her. After all her terrible revelations, it had come down to something so simple? "That's it? The only reason?"

She nodded. "There were others, but now that you know everything about me, 'tis all that remains. M' faith means more to me than the air I breathe. If you don't share it, I can't be your wife."

"Well, I went to Midnight Mass, and I liked it. Doesn't it help that I'm interested in learning more about it?"

"Being interested isn't the same as dedicating yourself to the Lord." She wiped across her face and sniffled. "I love you, Vern, but that doesn't matter. My love for the Lord exceeds it."

She'd said the words he'd wanted to hear, yet hadn't expected stipulations. How could he compete with Jesus?

"So . . ." He scratched his head. "How do I become a Catholic?"

"No." She waved her hands like dueling white flags. "I won't have you embrace the faith simply to marry me. You must want to commit your life to God."

"Then, tell me how."

"You need to feel it inside." She tapped her fist over her heart.

"I felt *something* that night at Mass, but we left so suddenly . . ." He moistened his dry lips, then wiped across them. "I saw Father Tierney earlier, when I went looking for you at St. Patrick's. Maybe I should go and talk to him about all this."

Finally, a slight smile lifted the corners of her mouth. "That's exactly where you need to start. He'll explain everything."

Vern glanced behind him at the closed door, then eased across the room and gingerly sat on the edge of the bed, near her.

Her eyes widened. "'Tis a bad place for you to be."

"One day, I hope it won't be. I never want you to think that having me close is *bad* in any way." He carefully took her hand, and as before, she didn't pull away. "I told the Hinzes I wanted to follow where my heart was leading me. I feel as if you and I are already a part of each other."

He peered deeper into her eyes. "Do you remember when I told you I thought maybe God brought us together so you could teach me about Him, and we could help each other?"

"I do."

"Well, I still believe that. We can give each other the strength to heal from everything that's happened to hurt us. If nothing else, I need to go to St. Patrick's to give God some thanks for bringing you into my life. You've already helped me feel more alive than I ever have since my mama left. And when I go to see Father Tierney, if I feel I belong at St. Patrick's, I'll do whatever he tells me to become a part of the congregation."

"Only because you want me?"

"No. Well—I *do* want you—but it's not only that. If I become a Catholic, I don't want you to think it's done falsely as a means to get you. I'm not like that. If I embrace something, I hold it close and never let go."

She slowly placed her free hand over the top of their joined ones, then lightly moved it and brushed across his skin. "You embraced *me*, and I felt safe in your arms."

"That makes me so happy, because with you, I finally feel whole." He stared at her puffy red lips that were swollen from crying. As much as he wanted to kiss them, he knew it was too soon.

He put his hands to the sides of her face, then brought her head toward him and kissed her brow. She voiced no objection.

He'd have to take every step forward with a great deal of thought and patience. She'd been brutalized, but eventually he wanted to prove that however he touched her, it would be done with love and gentleness, and she'd never have cause to fear him.

CHAPTER 22

Vern cradled a cup of hot cocoa and positioned it close to his face, allowing the steam to warm his cheeks. His skin had grown extremely cold while he sat on the front porch enjoying a well-earned cigarette. His emotions were spent.

It hadn't been easy listening to the details Margaret had shared, and the minute he'd left her, they'd trolled through his mind like a moving picture. He envisioned the brutal men pinning her down and hurting her—taking something sacred from her that couldn't be regained.

She'd told him not to hold onto anger, but how could he let something this horrible go?

Mrs. Hinze lightly cleared her throat. "I thought the cocoa would help you. If you don't drink it, it won't do much good."

He lowered the mug to the table, then looked from her to Mr. Hinze. They'd been more than patient since he'd returned home and given him plenty of time to gather his thoughts, but he knew they were eager to hear every detail. Of course, they had no idea what he'd reveal, and he wished he could keep it to himself. Once heard, like him, they wouldn't be able to erase the ugly images from their minds.

If he *didn't* tell them, they'd never understand Margaret, and they might always look down on her for having a baby out of wedlock. They *had* to know the truth.

He ran a finger around the rim of his cup. "I asked Margaret to marry me."

"What?" they said simultaneously.

"You heard right. But she said *no*, just as she did when I asked to court her."

"Oh, Vern." Mrs. Hinze stretched out her hand and patted his. "I worried while you were gone, fearing she'd hurt you. I hate being right."

"Actually, you're wrong." He sat taller and took a careful sip of the hot drink. "I'm not hurt."

"Not hurt?" Mr. Hinze cocked his head. "You don't care that she rejected you?"

"She didn't completely. At least, not exactly."

Their faces screwed together and they cast perplexing gazes at each other, then turned back to Vern.

"I don't mean to confuse you," he went on, "but it's hard to simply jump in and tell you all the facts."

Mr. Hinze spun his hand in the air, telling him without words to do just that.

"*Margaret* has been *horribly* hurt." His throat felt as if it was completely closing, so he eased another swallow of cocoa down it. "When I learned she'd had a baby, I told you I knew there was more to it. More than a mistake she'd made in the heat of passion, which I think you both assumed was what had happened. Right?"

Again, they glanced at each other, then they both sluggishly bobbed their heads.

"I wish *I* hadn't been right about *this*, but Margaret was molested."

Mrs. Hinze covered her mouth, and the sadness in her eyes revealed genuine pity.

"Oh, Son . . ." Mr. Hinze looked just as pained.

"I know. It was horrible." As difficult as it was to repeat the details Margaret had shared, Vern told them everything he knew about her experience.

"Dear Lord . . ." Mrs. Hinze latched onto her husband's arm and cuddled against him.

Tears stung Vern's eyes. They'd emerged the minute he'd voiced the wretched details. "It's impossible for me to comprehend what she must've gone through. The pain, and shame, and fear, and anger . . ."

"She's been through utter torture," Mrs. Hinze whispered.

"And what about the baby?" Mr. Hinze asked, while stroking his wife's hair.

Vern explained the confusing situation and actually found some relief in telling them. It helped him rehash it in his own thoughts and gain a better understanding of Margaret's state of mind.

"Unlike my mother," he concluded, "I think Margaret *wanted* her child. If it lived, it's six or seven years old by now."

Mr. Hinze's brows drew in. "Did you propose to her before or after you learned all this?"

He thought briefly. "*After*. I don't see why it matters."

"Since you did it after hearing her story, I fear you were trying to take on more than you realize. You have a big heart, Son, and I'm sure you merely wanted Miss Jordan to feel better and believe she was still worthy of being loved. It's best she rejected you. I don't think you're ready to cope with someone so damaged."

"*Cope* with her?" He leaned back, shaking his head. "I *love* her. And isn't that what love's all about? Caring for and helping each other? Like the two of you have always done?"

"What Dietrich is trying to say," Mrs. Hinze interjected, "is that you're young and not fully mature. Aside from the issues with Miss Jordan, I suppose it's good you're not pursuing Miss Baker—considering her aunt's manipulation—but when all this settles down, you should find someone your own age, who's undamaged."

He shut his eyes and turned his head. "I'm not a little boy anymore."

"We know that, Vern." She released an exasperated sigh. "But—"

"You only want what's best for me, right?" He shot to his feet, then bent over and braced his hands on the table. "I love Margaret, and that's not going to change. So, if you really care about me and want me to be happy, I'd appreciate your support."

He stalked across the floor, grabbed his coat from the peg on the wall, and walked out the door.

His heart pounded. Part of him wanted to run, but since he didn't know where to go, he returned to the front porch and lit up another cigarette.

He savored every puff and did all he could to let his thoughts rest. He'd nearly finished his smoke when both Mr. and Mrs. Hinze came out the front door of the bakery.

They inched toward him.

Mr. Hinze gestured to the bench. "May we join you?"

Vern silently nodded.

The man sat beside him and lit up his pipe. He'd been smoking it more than cigarettes lately.

It felt strange puffing away with Mrs. Hinze standing so close. Vern knew she didn't care for the smell of tobacco, and he'd never smoked around her before. Even so, he didn't extinguish his cigarette, wanting to enjoy it to the very end.

"Dietrich and I have been talking," she said. "And we realize we let you down. It couldn't have been easy sharing such an awful story with us, and the fact you care about Miss Jordan as much as you do must've made it terribly painful to listen to *her* tell it." She fingered the collar of her coat. "We're confused about one important thing."

Vern hated seeing her discomfort, so he snuffed out his cigarette. "What is it?"

"If she told you *no* more than once, why are you still pursuing her?"

"Because she also said she loves me. And she told me the only reason she won't marry me is because I'm not Catholic. I intend to change that."

Mr. Hinze shifted sideways and faced him straight on. "A person's religious beliefs are important and shouldn't be minimized. It's not right to embrace a particular faith simply to please a woman."

"Dietrich's right," Mrs. Hinze added. "Even if you love her, acting that way would be wrong."

Vern gazed beyond her to the city street. There was almost no activity whatsoever, typical of a late Sunday afternoon. "There's no *if* about it. I *do* love her." He put his full attention on the woman he'd always seen as his mother. "As much as I love you. It's the kind of love that lasts forever, because it feels like *family*. And one day, I hope you can find a way to love her, too, because she's going to be a part of everything I do."

It felt good to say it, and he sat a lot taller. "As for becoming Catholic, we'll see how that goes. I may not be any good at it, but I experienced something special that night at Midnight Mass, and I need to know if it was real. The only way I'll find out is by going back. And tomorrow afternoon, when things slow down, if it's okay with you, I'd like to use the buggy and go to St. Patrick's to have a talk with Father Tierney."

Mr. Hinze blew out a ring of smoke. "You may have to permanently alter your afternoon activities. As Annie pointed out to you, when we first discussed the issue of Miss Jordan's Catholicism, we don't believe they approve of gambling."

He hoped the man was wrong. Even if he wasn't, surely, there had to be a way around the issue. "I don't gamble," he said with his chin high. "I play games of skill." The very thing he'd tell the priest if the subject arose.

Mrs. Hinze firmly tapped him on the shoulder. "Now is not the time to jest with terminologies to suit your needs. Your passion for playing pool could be an issue."

He grinned at her. "You *do* care."

"Of course, I do. If you're so determined to marry Miss Jordan, then I want you to succeed. Otherwise, you'll be impossible to live with."

The idea that one day he might actually be able to call Margaret his wife sped his heartbeat in a good way.

He got to his feet and stood beside Mrs. Hinze. "If I marry Margaret, you won't have to live with me at all anymore. She and I will have a home together."

The dear woman rubbed across her heart. "In Kansas City?"

He shrugged. "First things first."

She cast the saddest smile and stroked his cheek. "Dietrich and I will try our best to be supportive. I knew I couldn't keep you little forever, but letting you go is harder than I imagined. It's truly difficult for me to admit you're a man now."

"Yep. A surprisingly *hungry* man. Can I help you fix supper?"

She smiled and jerked her head toward the door. "I'll let you make the biscuits."

"I always do."

Laughing, she went inside.

Mr. Hinze stood and stretched, then let out a moan. "I wish you *would* stay in Kansas City. I'm feeling older every day, and I'd like you to take over my business."

"Now?"

"Well . . . in a few years." He walked to the door and reopened it.

Vern followed him inside and let the subject drop. He couldn't bring himself to agree to stay. A lot depended on Margaret, but the urge to go west remained.

* * *

"So, once again, you're *not* leaving." Patsy thrummed her fingers on the dining room table.

Margaret wished she'd said all of this privately, yet the minute she'd joined the other residents at the table, the hateful woman had started in on her.

"That's right," Margaret confidently said. "I'm staying."

"She's getting married," Mrs. Fitch chimed in, much to Margaret's dismay.

Mr. Woolum grunted, but as usual, voiced no further opinion. The others just kept eating, which was a good thing.

"I'm not getting married anytime soon," Margaret said. "However, Mr. Harpole convinced me leaving wasn't wise. I have a good job and—"

"That young man isn't welcome here any longer," Mrs. Williams grumbled and heaped a mound of mashed potatoes on her plate. "He's a trouble-maker."

"No." Margaret leaned toward her. "He's a good man. He—"

"Had his hands all over you," Patsy said, "and closed himself up in the bedroom with you. We can only imagine what the two of you were doing."

Margaret glanced around the table at all the judgmental faces. "If you're imagining ugly things, then shame on you all." She pushed her chair back and stood. "I may not be leaving Kansas City, but I'll find another place to live." She eyed Mrs. Fitch. "It troubles me to leave *you*, yet I'm not welcome here, and I won't tolerate such hatefulness any longer."

The sweet old woman frowned, but the sympathy in her eyes proved her understanding. It wasn't difficult leaving the others behind. Margaret didn't even care about forgoing dinner. After she'd bared her soul to Vern, it had been silly to come to the dining table at all with a nonexistent appetite.

The worst part of their conversation had been how she'd so flippantly refused his proposal of marriage because of her faith. Although it was true she'd only marry a Catholic, she feared she'd thrown it up in his face as another means to stall. The hopefulness in his eyes hovered at the forefront of her mind and heaped additional guilt onto her shoulders, making her load heavier to bear.

She grabbed her coat and headed out the door.

Hopefully, Mrs. Archer would be understanding—as well as forgiving—and perhaps even *happy* to see her.

A coat of ice had formed on the ground, and Margaret's rapid strides kept her moving so quickly, she slipped more than once.

When she walked into Linderman's, she discovered Miss Cynthia at the front station.

"Welcome to Linderman's," the girl said, then her head drew back as she realized who she'd greeted.

"Thank you," Margaret said. "Is Mrs. Archer in the office?"

"You're not supposed to be here. Mrs. Archer said you're moving away."

"I changed m' mind."

The girl pouted. "I like your station. If you don't go, I'll surely be put on tables again."

"A task you're exceptional at performing." Margaret smiled at her, but it did no good. Cynthia's glower remained.

"Miss Jordan?" Mrs. Archer hastened toward her. The elation in her eyes prompted a whimper from Cynthia.

Margaret chose to ignore her and focused on Mrs. Archer. "May we speak privately?"

"Of course." The woman turned to Cynthia. "Mind the front."

"I *am*," the girl adamantly replied.

Mrs. Archer gave her a wary gaze, then motioned for Margaret to follow her to the back. She then led her to the office and closed the door.

As soon as it was shut, Mrs. Archer hugged her. "I doubted I'd see you again." She released her and stepped back, then cast a look similar to the one she'd given Cynthia. "Why do you keep doing this to me? Have you altered your plans again?"

"Yes." She shamefully lowered her head, hating to have troubled her.

"Thank the good Lord!"

Mrs. Archer pulled her into a more vigorous hug—so forceful, Margaret gasped.

"Forgive me." As Mrs. Archer released her, she apologetically patted her shoulder. "I appreciate Miss Cynthia's ability as a waitress, but she doesn't have the social graces necessary for welcoming our patrons, nor is she able to proficiently manage the cash box. Her math skills are lacking. I've found it necessary to hover close to her, and it keeps me from tending to other areas in the restaurant."

She hadn't seen Mrs. Archer this overwhelmed since New Year's. "I'd like to start working right away, but I have a bit of a problem."

"Sit and tell me." Mrs. Archer motioned to a nearby chair.

Margaret sat. "I need to find another place to live."

"Did they already rent your room?" The dear woman took her own seat.

"No, ma'am. But Mrs. Cramer is intolerable. Mrs. Williams was bad enough, then, when her daughter took control, life at the boarding house became utterly miserable."

"Mrs. Cramer? You mean, *Patsy*?"

"Yes'm. It's odd. I don't think I've ever referred to her as Mrs. Cramer before now, because everyone calls her Patsy. Likely because she's constantly ill-mannered and no one truly respects her. I don't know why she hates *me* so much, or why she treats everyone with disdain, but I suppose she's simply an unhappy person. She made it clear she doesn't want me as a boarder, and even if I stayed, her mum said Vern isn't welcome to visit me at the boarding house any longer. I'm a grown woman, and it upsets me that they believe they have such control over m' life." Every word erupted from her, releasing her bottled-up frustration.

"I see . . ." She gazed upward, then back at Margaret. "One issue at a time . . ."

"What do you mean?"

"Well, I've known Patsy for a long while. I've *never* called her Mrs. Cramer. Most people used to refer to her as Patsy, Miss Polly's girl, then eventually she was just *Patsy*. She wasn't always bitter, but about five years ago, her husband left her. He ran off with a young woman, and Patsy never saw him again."

"I assumed she was widowed like her mum."

"No. As far as everyone knows, he's still alive. Sadly, what he did changed her. She doesn't trust anyone anymore."

Margaret hadn't bothered to uncover the reason why she'd acted so cruelly. Though it was inexcusable for Patsy to take out her frustrations on others, her distrust made sense. No wonder she'd assumed the worst between Margaret and Vern, when she'd seen them together on the sofa. And when she'd known they were alone in her bedroom . . .

No. Margaret already carried around enough guilt. She refused to add Patsy's misconceptions to her burdens. "I feel badly for her, but I can't tolerate her rage. She and her mum screech at each other endlessly."

"I understand. That wouldn't be pleasant to listen to." As before, her eyes lifted upward, then rested on Margaret.

"Is something troubling you? You keep looking up."

Mrs. Archer laughed. "I suppose my eyes followed my thoughts." She scooted her chair a bit closer. "I'm sure you noticed the absence of my uncle the past few days."

"Actually, I didn't. I'm afraid since Valentine's Day, I've had m' mind on other things."

"Valentine's Day," Mrs. Archer whispered. "It was that night, after all our customers left, that Uncle Edwin went on a horrible binge. You may not be fully aware, but my uncle has an issue with excessive drinking."

"I suspected it." Knowing it to be *fact*, her remark wasn't fully true, yet she'd never told Mrs. Archer what he'd done on New Year's, and she chose to keep it that way.

"I hate to hear that. We try so hard to hide his behavior from our employees, and everyone for that matter. Something awful happened this last time that prompted us to take stronger measures." Mrs. Archer twisted her fingers together. "He made advances to Miss Gracie as she was leaving." She leaned closer. "He inappropriately touched her."

"Oh, my." Margaret's heart drummed hard. Gracie was the youngest of the wait staff. A pretty young girl, scarcely sixteen. "Is she all right?"

"Thankfully, yes. She ran from him straight to my father, and when he discussed the issue with me, we decided to send Uncle Edwin away. The reason I kept looking upward, is because his apartment is newly empty. You're welcome to it, if you feel it will suit your needs."

"Truly?" All the pain and frustration she'd been feeling melted away into unbelievable relief.

"Yes. I confess it needs a great deal of cleaning, but otherwise—"

"Thank you!" Margaret lurched from her chair and flung her arms around the woman's neck. "I'm not afraid of working hard to tidy it up." A bit embarrassed by her outburst, she returned to her seat. "Whatever rent you need can be taken from m' pay."

"If you tend the apartment, there will be no rent. Once again, you've saved us. We weren't sure what to do with Uncle Edwin gone, because we've always felt comforted knowing someone is near the restaurant on days we're closed. Now, you can be our new overseer." Mrs. Archer smiled broadly. "As for Vern Harpole . . . Since you mentioned your frustration over being told he was no longer permitted at Miss Polly's, I'm assuming he's become a more important part of your life. Is he the reason you decided to stay?"

"He asked me to marry him."

"*Oh.*" Her eyes widened. "Then we'll have *two* overseers."

"No. Only one. I refused him."

Mrs. Archer shook a finger. "Where are your good senses? If you're staying because of him, why not marry him?"

The reasons were too complicated to share, so she decided to offer the easiest answer. "He's not Catholic."

"Neither am I."

Margaret let out a little laugh. "You're m' employer, and although we spend many hours together, 'tis not the same. I know full well you're toying with me, but please understand that m' faith is important, and I can't bind m'self to a husband who doesn't share it."

"But you love him, don't you?"

"Yes'm, I do." She said it with confidence, and it felt unexpectedly good to do so.

"Then, somehow, it will all work out." Mrs. Archer got to her feet. "I'd best make certain Miss Cynthia hasn't frightened away our guests. As for you, Miss Jordan, go to Miss Polly's and pack your things. You're welcome to stay here tonight, and you have ample time to begin cleaning. Being that tomorrow is Monday, and it's always been your *free* day, I imagine you'll be comfortably settled in before you're needed on Tuesday morning."

"I'll get started right away." She rose on trembling legs. After all that had happened, a ray of hopeful promise had finally shined through, yet she still felt emotionally weak. "Before I go, I need to know about your uncle. When do you expect his return?"

"Likely never." She rested her hand on the doorknob. "Miss Gracie's father threatened to press charges, but when we assured him Uncle Edwin was sent to another state, he let the issue drop, to Gracie's relief. She didn't want to become the center of gossip."

No one understood that better than Margaret. "I won't say a word."

"I know. That's something else I appreciate about you. You're trustworthy." Mrs. Archer cast a dimmer smile, then walked out.

As much elation as Margaret felt with her new prospects, overcoming guilt in regard to Edwin Linderman kept her from truly embracing it. If she'd told Mrs. Archer what he'd done to *her*, perhaps Miss Gracie would've been spared. Then again, part of that burden rested on the shoulders of Mrs. Archer's father. Had Frank Linderman taken action, Edwin would've already been long gone.

"What's done is done," she whispered, then headed out.

Soon, she'd leave Miss Polly's behind for good.

CHAPTER 23

Once again, Vern felt compelled to whistle. The instant he started, Betsy's ears twitched, but her action only tickled him and increased his enthusiasm, as well as his volume.

His meeting with Father Tierney had gone better than expected, and once he told Margaret the good news, surely, she'd want to start making wedding plans. From his understanding, most women thrived on that sort of thing.

Then again, Margaret was nothing like most women, still . . .

He shook his head and kept whistling, pushing away all ill thoughts.

When he arrived at Miss Polly's, he rushed up the pathway and as politely as possible, knocked on the door, giving Patsy no reason to fuss.

However, when she opened it, she leered down her nose at him. "Why are *you* here?"

Not even her hatefulness could ruin today, and just for her, he plastered on his best smile. "Good afternoon, Miss Patsy."

"I'll have you know, I'm *Mrs. Cramer*."

"Forgive me. I was unaware. From here on out, I'll address you properly."

Her scowl remained. "From here on out, I don't expect you to speak to me at all. You're not welcome here."

He shook his head, saddened by her unending negativity. Regardless, the inward joy he felt remained. "I recall my parents telling me that if you carry around a lot of anger, it can literally make you sick. And if you want to live a long, healthy life, you should be cheerful."

"Poppycock."

He laughed. "I've heard Mrs. Hinze use that expression before, but—"

"Why are you here?" She repetitively tapped her foot.

He'd seen the same action from Mrs. Pennington and assumed it to be a trait of all cranky women. "I've come to see Miss Jordan, of course."

"She's gone." Patsy jutted her chin, gloating.

"Gone? Today's Monday. She doesn't work on Mondays."

"I didn't say she went to work, I said, she's *gone*. Left for good and won't be back." In the most hateful manner, she squinted her eyes nearly shut. "Do you understand *now*?"

He wouldn't put it past Patsy to play a cruel joke, so he peered beyond her, hoping to hear or see Margaret. Yet, with the rude woman blocking his view, he could scarcely see into the house at all.

"She's gone, Mr. Harpole," Patsy repeated in a harsher tone than before.

He stared blankly, suddenly numb. After all he and Margaret had been through, he was certain he'd finally reached her heart and kept her from running away.

"No, she's not!" Mrs. Fitch scurried up behind the hateful woman, then wormed herself into the doorway. "Shame, Patsy, for being so unfeeling." She nudged the woman with her shoulder, then faced Vern. "Miss Jordan moved out, but she's not *gone*." As she said the word, she cut her leering eyes toward Patsy, then softened her gaze and put it back on him. "You'll find her at Linderman's."

"But she doesn't work on Mondays."

Mrs. Fitch grinned. "And because of it, she'll have plenty of time to talk with you." She flitted her fingers toward the road. "What's keeping you here?"

"Nothing, ma'am." He easily returned her grin. "Thank you."

As he hastened down the pathway to his buggy, the boarding house door slammed shut. Even so, he could hear the heated argument that continued on within.

Poor Mrs. Fitch.

At least he believed her to be strong in character, like Margaret, and from what he could tell, she could stand on her own against Patsy's ranting. It appeared Margaret had found another place to live, and if Mrs. Fitch was wise, she'd find one, too.

* * *

Margaret doubted Edwin Linderman had ever dusted his apartment. She'd scrubbed away so much grime, her hands had chafed. Yet, that didn't bother her. For the first time since she'd arrived in Kansas City, she felt as if she'd been given a place to call her own, and it made her happy to put all of herself into it.

To add to her pleasure, Mrs. Archer had told her she could help herself to whatever she cared to eat from the kitchen. Even Mr. Green seemed pleased to have her residing above him. He'd said he planned to call on her whenever he needed someone to sample his new creations.

It seemed as though God was finally smiling on her. She'd been taught the importance of lifting up thanks to Him even in hardship, but her human heart had an easier time offering praise when good things happened.

She'd removed the filthy curtains from the front window that overlooked the street below and had them soaking in a washtub. The water had turned completely brown. As she contemplated whether or not to dump it for fresh, a knock at the door startled her from her thoughts.

She ran her fingers through her unruly hair and hurried across the floor to answer it. "Vern?"

He puffed out his chest and grinned. "Hello, Margaret." His head tipped from side to side, and his eyes searched past her. "Mrs. Archer said I'd find you up here."

She glanced behind her, then faced him. "If you're worried I'm not alone, lay it to rest. Mr. Linderman is gone."

"I know. Mrs. Archer told me that, too. I just wanted to be certain no one else was here." He folded his hands in front of himself. "Do you think it would be improper for me to come in? There's some things I'd like to talk to you about."

She craned her neck outside and couldn't see a soul. "I suppose you may."

"The way you said that doesn't convince me. However, since it's a little cold and uncomfortable out here . . ." He motioned inside, and she stepped back to let him in.

The room felt suddenly warmer, simply by having him in it. She crossed to the sofa, fluffed up one of the decorative pillows she'd added, then gestured for him to sit.

He stared at the place, frowning, as if he'd seen something undesirable.

"I promise it's clean," she quickly said and smiled.

"I'm sure it is. I just . . ." He huffed. "I was remembering when I was here before. Edwin was sitting in that very spot, half-naked."

Half-naked? Vern had neglected to mention that detail when they'd previously spoken about the incident. No wonder he acted reluctant to put himself there. "Well, then. Why don't we sit at the table?"

He nodded and moved into one of the chairs.

She sat across from him. "'Tis probably best this way. The last time you and I were on a sofa, we caused quite a stir."

Finally, he smiled again. "And it was perfectly innocent." He rested his hands on top of the table. "I'm glad you're able to talk about that without being upset. Yesterday was so hard. Especially for you."

"'Twas indeed, but it all ended well. Mrs. Archer said I can stay here indefinitely." She studied the concern in his eyes and could tell he had a lot on his mind. "You said you had things to talk about. Something bad?"

"No. Not at all." He straightened his posture, looking more like he had when she'd answered the door. "I just finished meeting with Father Tierney."

Oh, my. He'd wasted no time going to the man. "I see . . ."

"He wants me to start attending Mass every Sunday, and for the next few months, he'll be teaching me after services. Something about catechism, and baptism, and confession . . ." He scratched his head. "Honestly, it's all sort of confusing right now. I do know *one* thing for sure."

"Yes?"

"I belong there." He leaned forward. "This may sound strange, but as soon as I walked in the building, I felt at peace. Almost *embraced* by invisible arms. Is that how you feel when you go?"

The sincerity in his words touched her heart *and* magnified her guilt.

I'm a horrid soul.

She'd pushed him to go, yet because of her fear of his ultimate intentions, she wished he hadn't. There was nothing righteous in feeling that way.

"I suppose I do," she managed to say. "Honestly, I'm a bit ashamed. I've attended Mass all m' life, and because of it, I suppose I take much of it for granted. You've reminded me of the preciousness of God's grace."

"I'm glad." He slowly reached across the table and set his hand on hers. "Do you mind?"

Tingles cascaded over her skin the instant he touched her. "I . . ." Her heart pattered harder. "'Tis unwise, being we're alone."

"I understand." He pulled away, then peered around the room. "I can tell you've been working hard. When I came up here before, it was awful. It wasn't only dirty, it stunk."

"I found a dead rat under the sofa." She shuddered, recalling the discovery. "'Twas the worst of it. Otherwise, it's been mostly dirt."

He wiped the tip of his finger across the table surface, then looked at it and cast a quirky grin. "Clean as can be." After wiggling his finger, he released a long, drawn-out breath.

"I doubt you came to discuss m' ability to clean. Is there something more you want to say about your discussion with Father Tierney?" As anxious as she felt returning to that particular subject, she hated hearing the unease in the mere breaths he took.

"Yes." He sat perfectly straight. "I still want to marry you, Margaret. And I was thinking we could plan a summer wedding. I'm sure Father Tierney will be happy to perform the rite, once I learn all I can from him and officially become a Catholic, and maybe you can ask Mrs. Archer about having a reception here."

"Vern, I—"

"Before you say anything, there's something I have to tell you. Because, you told me everything that happened to you—which I know wasn't easy—and I feel I should do the same. I respect you so much for trusting me enough to reveal your past, and I don't want us to have any secrets, so . . ." He gulped, then readjusted in his chair. "I didn't tell you everything Mr. Linderman said about my mama."

This wasn't at all what she'd expected him to say, but she was thankful the subject had drifted from marriage. "You don't have to tell me, unless you truly want to."

"As I said, I don't want secrets between us. If you're going to be my wife, you should know my past, too."

Why did he have to go back to that? "*Vern.*"

He held up a hand. "Let me finish, all right?"

She painfully nodded.

"My mother wasn't a good person. Of course, you probably already came to that conclusion since she gave me booze and left me," he said matter-of-factly, then turned his head away. "Mr. Linderman *paid* my mama to . . ." Again, he swallowed hard. "Well, you know, to *be* with him. He'd bragged to you about having her, but I thought you needed to know the extent of it. It was how she made a living and still is for all I know. Worse yet, she got my sister involved in it, too. They're both prostitutes." He faced her again, and his eyes met hers. "That's why Mama didn't want me underfoot. I was an unnecessary distraction."

"Oh, Vern. I'm so sorry."

"Don't feel bad for *me*, Margaret. My life got better when I was given over to the Hinzes. I worry for Virginia. Mama should've never made her do those things." He blew out another lengthy breath. "Now you know. I hope it won't change your mind about *me*. If folks around here find out, they might be hateful about it."

"How would they know? *I'm* certainly not going to tell, and now that Mr. Linderman is somewhere far away, he won't reveal it, either." She stared into his eyes. "You're a good man. Nothing your mum did reflects on you. You were an innocent child when she left you and none-the-wiser to her activities."

A great deal of tension melted from his features. "I'm glad to hear you say that. I was worried if you knew, you might change your mind about marrying me."

She stood and absent-mindedly paced, more confused than ever before.

"Margaret?" Vern rose from his chair and moved nearer. "I know something's wrong. Are you upset about my mama? Or was it hearing about Virginia? Because she was so young when all that happened, maybe you thought about what you went through, and—"

"Shh." Heart thumping, she pressed her fingertips to his mouth. Sometimes, honesty was brutally painful, but he merited it. "I didn't think you'd go so quickly to St. Patrick's. I thought I'd have more time."

He grabbed hold of her hand and tightly held it. "Why do you need it? You said the only thing keeping you from accepting my proposal was that I'm not Catholic. Otherwise, I assumed you were eager to marry me. You said you love me." His panicked eyes searched her face. "Was that a lie?"

"No. I *do* love you, but after I lost m' virtue, I made a vow never to marry. I was so damaged, even the *idea* of being intimately touched by a man sickens me. And since Catholics believe God created the covenant of marriage in order to bind a man and woman together so they can procreate, I knew from that horrid day forward, I had to remain single. If I'm unable to give myself to you, I can't uphold God's commands." The words flew from her mouth as if someone else had said them, yet they confirmed the realization that it was the very thing keeping her from allowing his affection in any form.

His features hardened, but his grip eased. "Intimacy aside, are you sickened by *my* touch?" He rubbed his thumb gently back and forth across her knuckles.

"No, but—"

"The first time I tried to touch you at all, you pulled away. Step by step, you've grown more comfortable with me. Don't you remember saying how safe you felt in my arms?" He inched even closer. "If you'll stop trying to run away, maybe you'll see that I'm the one who was made for you."

She shut her eyes as he lifted his hand and softly stroked her cheek.

"We were both broken, Margaret, but we survived and found each other. Marry me." His lips brushed over the very spot he'd just caressed.

She shivered. "I—"

His mouth covered hers in the gentlest kiss. His lips moved as if drawing breath with her.

She'd never believed in the possibility of loving a man, not after so much had been stripped from her, but *this* blessed man had changed everything.

Without thought, she stretched out her trembling arms and drew him closer. Their kiss deepened and the walls she'd built around her heart crumbled like those decimated by the blast of trumpets long ago in Jericho.

As their mouths separated, Vern smiled brighter than ever before, and he thread his fingers into her hair. "Can I assume that's a *yes*?" His heavy breaths dusted her skin, and his beautiful blue eyes radiated with love.

She couldn't deny the obstinate, wonderful man any longer. "'Tis a yes if you're willing to put up with m' indecisiveness."

"Will you keep trying to run away from me?"

His fingers continued their soothing gesture. "I may."

"If you do, I'll follow wherever you go."

She took his hand and cradled it to her face. "I don't deserve you."

"You're wrong. I think you deserve someone who can offer you a lot more, but if you give me the chance, I know I can make a decent life for us. I'm not afraid of hard work." He grinned and gazed around the room once again. "And I know you aren't either."

"What about going west? Will you give up that notion and stay here with me in Kansas City?"

Like before, his eyes filled with confusion. He let go of her, wandered toward the window, and peered out. With the curtains down, the view was fully open. "If I asked you to go with me, would you?"

For some unexplained reason, a laugh escaped her.

He spun on his heels toward her. "Why'd you laugh?"

"I don't know. But since you just said you'd follow me wherever *I* go, I suppose t'would be unloving if I didn't afford you the same courtesy." She moved beside him, feeling drawn to him with such intensity it made her slightly lightheaded. Until Vern, she'd thought soulmates weren't real. "Do you think it's your mum pulling you toward the west?"

"No. Those ties were severed years ago."

"Are you certain? Part of *my* heart remains in Ireland with my mum and da. I don't think we can ever fully cut connections with our parents. 'Tis born into us."

"And what about the one you have with *your* child?"

Talking about this had always been difficult, but Vern had changed even that obstacle. "I've resigned m'self to let it go. I spent years searching to no avail, and all my action did was upset m' parents. So, I pray every day for the child's good health, and I put it in God's hands. 'Tis no better place to be."

"I love you, Margaret." He took her into his arms. "One day, I hope I can give you another child to love. Maybe that should be *my* daily prayer."

She comfortably nestled against his shoulder, yet her insides nervously fluttered at the mere thought of bearing another baby. "I love you, too." She tipped her head up and looked into his eyes. "Just please, be patient with me."

"Always." He kissed her brow, then released a pleasant sigh of contentment.

They stood side by side at the window for a long while, simply breathing and nothing more.

* * *

After months of pursuing the woman he loved, Vern finally relaxed. He'd overcome all of her objections—including those she may not have realized existed until her feathers had been ruffled. He'd hated pushing her, but his vast love for her had forced his persistence.

He'd never cared for the way Mr. and Mrs. Hinze had referred to her as damaged and complicated, because when he looked at Margaret, he saw only *perfection*.

As for going west . . .

He'd seen notices in the newspaper about more and more men striking it rich in places such as Deadwood, South Dakota, though that particular town had been mined for a number of years and surely had businesses like bakeries already established.

More recently, there'd been men flocking to northern Idaho, high up in the Rocky Mountains. As far as terrain, it would be easier to reach a place like Deadwood, but the idea of going into the mountains intrigued him more. It could be rough-going, simply *getting* to the mining camp, yet, as he'd told Mr. Hinze, hungry mountain men would probably appreciate fine baked goods. They'd pay whatever he asked.

He gazed down at the top of Margaret's pretty head. They'd been standing at her apartment window for quite a while, just looking out. Each lost in their own thoughts.

The love he felt for her overwhelmed him, and as he'd told her, he wanted the chance to show her he could make a successful life for them. With the money he'd make in those mining camps, they could afford the life he'd dreamed of and Margaret deserved.

"One thing at a time," he whispered.

She looked up at him. "What did you say?"

He held her a bit firmer. "Our future. We'll take it day by day, all right?"

"As God intended." She lowered her head and stared outward once more.

It was slightly awkward, merely standing there. But until they were properly wed, he couldn't stay in her apartment forever, and this particular spot felt *safe*.

At least, he could remain for a little longer, then he'd have to go back to the bakery and get a good night's sleep, so he'd be ready for another day, while Margaret did the same.

Eventually, he'd tell Oscar his news, and maybe his friend would still want to go with him—or actually, with *them*. That in itself could pose a problem—especially since having him along would involve pool playing, or at a minimum, a game or two of poker.

Maybe in his Catholic training, he'd learn it wasn't allowed. Then again, the priest mentioned something about confession *and* forgiveness. That could mean if he *did* gamble, he could say he was sorry.

Hmm . . .

He returned his gaze to his beautiful *fiancée*. Yes, he had a lot to learn, but for her, he'd do anything.

One thing at a time . . .

ACKNOWLEDGMENTS

One day, while having lunch with my friend, Ann Wood, we were discussing some of my historical fiction books and the frequency of characters who are prostitutes. I told her that I feared my readers would think I had an obsession with them, but they've played a large part in culture throughout history, and they always seem to creep into my stories. She grinned, then shared a little tidbit about her great-grandmother. The more she talked, the more I wanted to hear, and by the end of our meal, I asked her if I could write her family's story. Fortunately, she happily agreed to the idea.

Of course, I told her I'd have to embellish a few things here and there, but she was more than willing to allow it. She gave me notes her father had written about his dad's life, and we also had further conversations about her own remembrances. Although this book is a work of fiction, Vern and Margaret Harpole were two very real people, and yes, those are their actual names. Vern *was* left in Kansas City by his mother for the reason stated in the book, and he was taken in by the Hinzes. Much of what you read truly did happen, but as I told Ann, this isn't by any means a biography. I took many liberties.

That being said, it was so much fun getting to know Vern, Margaret, and the Hinzes, realizing that they actually walked this earth. They were amazing people and successful bakers. And speaking of baking, adding to my enjoyment, I decided to try my hand at schnecken. I found a great recipe online, and it's delicious! You can look up schnecken on food.com.

So, thank you, Ann, for sharing your family history and allowing me to bring it to life. Originally, I had intended this to be a single title book, but once I started writing, Vern and Margaret had so much to share with the world, I knew I couldn't accomplish it in a single book. You can look forward to reading their further adventures.

Thank you to my editor, Cindy Brannam, my cover designer, Rae Monet, my formatter, Jesse Gordon, and my back-cover designer, Karen Duvall. Thank you also to my incredible beta readers: Charli Heyer, Diane Gardner, Jennifer Gatlin, and Joy Dent. As busy as this time of year can be, they graciously took the time to help me, and I appreciate it so much!

To all of you wonderful readers, thank you for sharing this adventure with me (and Ann!). I hope it touched your hearts as deeply as it touched mine.

God bless,

Jeanne

COMING SOON!

Embraced by Love
His Heart's Long Journey, Book 2

Vern Harpole can no longer put aside his aching need to go west. Not only does the idea appeal to his sense of adventure, something greater is pulling him in that direction. More than one person has suggested it's somehow tied to his mother, but he refuses to believe it. After all, once he'd learned the truth about her, he'd decided to forget her. He views her simply as the woman who'd birthed him, yet otherwise wants no connection to her.

Margaret Jordan has finally allowed her protective walls to come down and agrees to marry Vern. She's content in Kansas City until their lives are turned on edge, and she's once again overcome with the need to flee. When Vern suggests they get on a train and go west, she eagerly agrees.

Though they're overjoyed to be newly married, the stars in their eyes will soon be dimmed by the rugged road before them. Life in the west seemed exciting and glamorous by all accounts in the newspapers. However, they surely must've misread every word. They cross paths with some of the vilest, money-hungry people in existence; testing their courage, strength, and commitment at every turn.

Vern and Margaret embrace their faith in God and love for each other, which keeps them moving forward with hope for a promising future.

BOOKS BY JEANNE HARDT

HISTORICAL FICTION

MEDIEVAL FANTASY

The Shrouded Thrones Series:
Island in the Forest
Mountain of Masks
Bane of Black Wood
Sins of Basilia
Queen of Prophecy

CONTEMPORARY FICTION

A Golden Life
He's in My Dreams
Regenerates

For more information about Jeanne's books,
check out the links below:

www.facebook.com/JEANNEHARDTAUTHOR
www.jeannehardt.com
www.amazon.com/author/jeannehardt
www.goodreads.com/jeannehardt

Made in the USA
Columbia, SC
31 December 2019

86034994R00176